PUFFIN BOOKS

# SECRETS
### of the
# STARS

*Other books by Maria Kuzniar*

THE SHIP OF SHADOWS

# SECRETS
## of the
# STARS

## MARIA KUZNIAR

PUFFIN

PUFFIN BOOKS

UK|USA|Canada|Ireland|Australia
India|New Zealand|South Africa

Puffin Books is part of the Penguin Random House group of companies
whose addresses can be found at global.penguinrandomhouse.com.

www.penguin.co.uk    www.puffin.co.uk    www.ladybird.co.uk

Penguin
Random House
UK

First published 2021
001

Text copyright © Maria Kuzniar, 2021
Cover, map and interior illustrations copyright © Karl James Mountford, 2021

The moral right of the author and illustrator has been asserted

Set in 11/16.5 pt Sabon LT Std
Typeset by Jouve (UK), Milton Keynes
Printed and bound in Great Britain by Clays Ltd, Elcograf S.p.A.

The authorized representative in the EEA is Penguin Random House Ireland,
Morrison Chambers, 32 Nassau Street, Dublin D02 YH68

A CIP catalogue record for this book is available from the British Library

ISBN: 978-0-241-37293-7

All correspondence to:
Puffin Books, Penguin Random House Children's
One Embassy Gardens, 8 Viaduct Gardens, London SW11 7BW

*For my mum, who reads every single one of my stories.*
*And for my babcia, whose reading genes I inherited.*
*This one's for you both.*

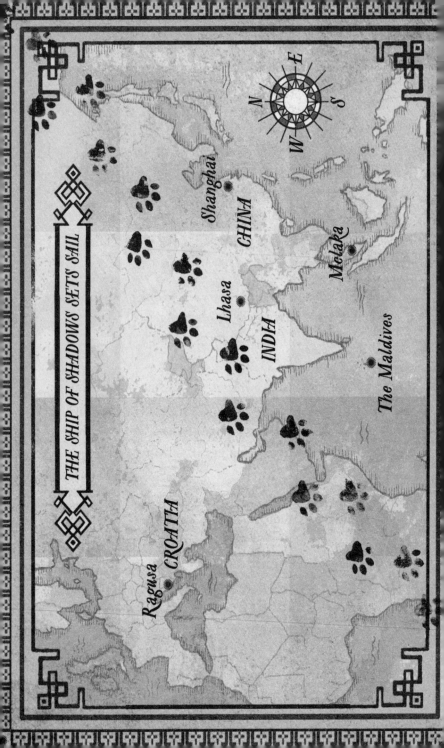

THE SHIP OF SHADOWS SETS SAIL

N    E
W    S

Shanghai
CHINA

Melaka

Lhasa

INDIA

The Maldives

CROATIA

Ragusa

## CHAPTER ONE

### *The Carnival*

Aleja cursed in Croatian. Her face was already itching under the paint that had scrawled whiskers across her cheeks and turned her lips and nose black. A mask that gleamed in red and gold wound round her dark-green eyes.

Tonight Aleja was a fox.

'How are we meant to find anyone in this?' Next to her, Frances was fidgeting with her own glossy onyx mask. Black feathers rippled down her raven costume and protruded into wings that flapped each time she moved her arms.

In front of the two best friends the ancient walled city of Ragusa sparkled with life and music and glittering costumes. The carnival was in full swing.

It was the perfect place for a spot of stealing.

Although they were dressed for the festivities, Aleja and Frances weren't here to have fun. For they were no ordinary girls; they were *pirates*. And together they made the perfect team: Frances with her slippery fingers could steal the jewels from your neck before you blinked and Aleja was a multilinguist whose sneaky ways caused secrets to tumble into her hands.

They were here to steal a key from a cartographer. It would open the cartographer's safe, hidden in his sprawling house perched on top of a nearby hill. The contents of that safe were their true target tonight – but the cartographer kept the key on his person at all times.

'Let's go,' Aleja said, and she and Frances entered the heaving crowd.

The task had seemed so simple on the ship: find the cartographer, snag the key, copy it with a device created by their brilliant shipmate Griete, then pop it back into the cartographer's pocket. Now it felt impossible.

Aleja squinted through her mask. There were too many people and she couldn't see a thing. She stood up on her tiptoes. '*There!*' Aleja grabbed Frances's feathered arm and pointed through the crowd at a bald man in a Venetian-styled turquoise peacock mask.

'Mind my wing!' Frances hissed.

'Sorry!'

# The Carnival

They slipped through the gate that led on to the Stadun, a wide walkway cutting through the city centre. It was alive with people – musicians and poets and merchants. A parade of drummers and dancers snaked towards them. Aleja and Frances stole through them, inching closer – closer – closer –

The cartographer looked over his shoulder.

Aleja whisked Frances out of sight behind an old fountain.

'What's happening?' Frances whispered.

Aleja peeked out and saw the cartographer's Venetian mask glinting under a street lantern. 'He nearly saw us.'

The drummers reached a crescendo and the crowd shattered into applause. Aleja and Frances sneaked closer, towards Sponza Palace with its sand-coloured arches cast in a buttery glow by the sunset. They stepped round a cart of hot sugar-roasted almonds, sticking like glue to the cartographer's tail.

'Now,' Aleja whispered into Frances's ear. 'The timing's perfect. You grab the key and I'll stand by in case he needs distracting.' She made to weave into the thickest part of the crowd. But Frances pulled her back.

'Oh. Oh *no*.'

'What is it?' Aleja asked, eyes still pinned to the cartographer's bald head.

'Look!' Frances said desperately.

Aleja glanced over, her heart racing –

Frances was staring at a bunch of kittens. They were wandering around the arches of the palace, leaping playfully at each other and guzzling the bowls of milk left out for them.

Aleja let out a frustrated sigh and turned back. But the cartographer had moved faster than she'd expected. 'Frances, we need to go!'

'But they're picking on it!'

To Aleja's dismay Frances stubbornly started off in the opposite direction towards one particular kitten. It was a tiny, scrawny thing with a bitten ear.

Aleja stared as the cartographer vanished into the crowd like mist. Panic rose in her chest – the captain would be furious if they failed in their mission, but without Frances to do the pickpocketing there was nothing Aleja could do. She looked helplessly at her friend approaching the scared kitten. Frances had once been homeless on the streets of London, fighting for her own scraps. No wonder she couldn't ignore it. She murmured soothing words and stroked its fuzzy little head. It was ink-black with curious green eyes. Frances scooped up the kitten and beamed at Aleja. Her bright amber eyes shone. 'Isn't she adorable?'

'Yes, very cute,' Aleja said, forcing herself to stay calm. 'Erm, Frances?'

'Hmm?' Frances was busy watching the kitten bat at her feathered costume.

'What are you going to do with it?'

'I'm taking her back on board with us.'

It didn't seem the right time to remind Frances that cats hated water. They had a more pressing issue at hand – one that Frances suddenly remembered with a gasp. 'The cartographer! Where did he go?' She looked around as if he'd be standing nearby.

Aleja shook her head. 'We lost him.'

Frances paled. '*I* lost him, you mean.'

Aleja shuffled awkwardly. She didn't want to think of what the captain might say if they returned empty-handed.

'I'm sure we'll find him again!' Frances said brightly, pocketing the kitten.

They delved back into the city. Aleja threw an anxious look in the direction of the harbour, where she could see the mast of the *Ship of Shadows* puncturing the strawberry-sweet red of the sky. From this distance the only sign that it wasn't like the other ships in the harbour was the large owl that occasionally circled in the air above.

They raced back up the Stadun, scanning the shops, churches and palaces. They knew the city by heart after spending the autumn exploring it, from the port to the huge old city gate at its opposite end. Aleja could hear snippets of Croatian and Venetian and Turkish. But no cartographer.

They searched in vain until the last streaks of sunset had melted away and the sea was night-dark. This time Frances cursed in Croatian.

Aleja stared at her bleakly. 'You know what this means?'

Frances swallowed. 'We have to go and tell the captain that we failed.'

When Aleja had first stepped on board the *Ship of Shadows*, what felt like a lifetime ago, she had mistaken the battle-scarred first mate, Malika, for the captain. Now Aleja didn't know how she'd ever made that mistake. Captain Quint stood in front of them, stance wide, arms crossed, cutlass strapped to her hip, tri-cornered hat perched on her head. Penumbra, her massive eagle owl that had been circling in the air earlier, now sat on her shoulder with the same fixed stare as the captain. Neither of them blinked. Aleja fidgeted with her costume, wishing she could vanish into it, while Frances tried to weave some very obvious lies into an excuse.

'. . . and then we followed him through the carnival, but he stopped to talk to a squadron of *soldati* and then they escorted him through the streets and then the city guards set out to begin their nightly patrol and it was just heaving! It was impossible to get close to him . . .'

There was a long silence. The ship creaked gently. Captain Quint narrowed her eyes. 'I'm disappointed to hear this, girls,' she said severely. 'I expect better from you. You know what lies in that safe. Without the key everything we've worked for since we arrived in Ragusa is meaningless.'

Aleja squirmed. It was thanks to her spying that they'd learned what the cartographer's safe held: a map of the impenetrable Fort Lovrijenac, secret passages and all. Aleja had *really* wanted to be the one to hand those essential plans over to the captain tonight and prove once and for all that she belonged on her crew.

Aleja tried not to look at Frances, whose costume was bulging. It was well disguised – the kitten was tiny and Frances's raven costume was layered with ruffles on top of ruffles and a sea of feathers. But out of the corner of her eye Aleja saw it had started to wriggle. And meow.

'And on top of that you're being untruthful,' the captain continued. She paused and stared at Frances, her blue eyes creasing round the edges. 'Is that a *cat*?'

'No,' said Frances.

The kitten meowed louder.

Aleja felt a nervous laugh bubble up her throat, which she buried under a cough.

Penumbra looked on with keen interest, his luminous orange eyes tracking the wriggling shape under Frances's feathers. Frances squirmed. The kitten's head popped out of the neck of her costume. 'Well . . . just a small one. She needed rescuing.' Frances held her head high even as her cheeks flushed round the edges of her mask. Penumbra clicked his beak and Frances hugged the kitten closer to her.

The captain was still staring at Frances. 'You failed in your mission . . . because of a cat?'

There was another long silence, as thick as clotted cream. But if anyone understood taking in a stray, it was the captain. The entire crew of the *Ship of Shadows* was formed of the best and brightest girls and women from around the world, talented strays who had found a home on board the magical ship. Shadows rippled around the deck as Aleja waited for the captain to speak.

Just then Malika appeared on deck. She was wearing a rich emerald dress and matching headscarf and the lantern light set her scarred face aglow. But the missing hand and long scars down the right side of her face weren't the most unusual things about Malika. The first mate of the *Ship of Shadows* didn't have a shadow at all. It had been stolen by the crew's greatest enemy: François Levasseur, also known as the Fury.

Malika paused, assessing the situation. She was the most beautiful woman Aleja had ever seen – and the deadliest. 'I see you've failed in your mission,' she said, her voice silky. Aleja winced. 'And after you'd shown such promise, too.' She gave Aleja and Frances a disparaging look and stalked away.

Aleja felt sick.

'Fine, keep the cat,' Captain Quint said. 'Train it to catch mice. But we need those plans. You'll be going to the cartographer's house at the first sign of nightfall tomorrow, where you will retrieve them. Since you failed to get the key, you'll have to break in. It's not ideal, but we don't have time to sit around waiting for another opportunity. This will have to do. And this time there will be no room for failure. Understood?' Her voice was dagger-sharp and dangerous.

'Aye, Captain,' Aleja and Frances said as one.

'Good. And I expect this deck scrubbed before weapons training tomorrow morning.' She strode off.

Frances groaned. '*Before* weapons training? I'll never be able to hold a cutlass after all that scrubbing!'

'Maybe you should have thought about that before running after a kitten,' Aleja said, their failure still stinging.

'I couldn't just leave it there,' Frances said miserably, making Aleja feel a twinge of guilt.

They climbed down the wooden ladder to the lower decks in silence.

## CHAPTER TWO

### Claws

Below decks, the ship was a dark and magical maze. The vessel lived and breathed shadows, and it was their constant presence on board that fed the ship's magic. A passageway ran between the crew's cabins and the galley, where Aleja could smell something delicious baking. It was lit by dim lanterns, and here and there an owl was engraved in the wall so that emerald eyes glittered and seemed to follow you as you wandered past. On the ceiling the night sky was mapped out in brilliant sapphires that glinted like real stars.

The kitten wriggled wildly in Frances's arms as she jumped over a chained trapdoor. 'Stay . . . *still*.'

'Do you think Quint will stay angry for long?' Aleja asked.

'Nah. She never does.' Frances sounded a bit doubtful and Aleja bit her lip. 'Should we do something to get back in her good books?' she added.

Aleja nodded eagerly. 'Let's solve one of the clues in Thomas James's book. She won't be able to be cross at us then! I'll go and fetch it.' She ran towards her cabin.

'I've got to get this off,' Frances called up the passageway, flapping her feathery wings. 'And then I'll meet you up on deck.' She jerked her head towards the galley, her glasses shining like the emerald-eyed owls. 'Something smells good in there. Bet I could pinch some of it.'

Aleja grinned at her. 'Perfect.'

Back in her cabin, Aleja found Tinta waiting for her, fox-shaped to match Aleja's costume. Tinta was one of the ship's shadows, a small shape-shifting thing that had latched on to Aleja one lonely day and turned Aleja into the only pirate on board who had *two* shadows. Usually Tinta waited up on deck for Aleja to return – but not when the captain was unhappy. Aleja folded her arms. 'How do you always know when I'm going to get into trouble?' she asked it. 'Maybe you can warn me next time.' The shadow-fox scuffed a wispy paw sadly against the floor. Aleja laughed. 'I'm only teasing you.' She ruffled the fur she couldn't feel, watching the little shadow ripple with delight under her invisible touch.

Aleja slipped her fox mask off and placed it on a shelf that Farren – the boatswain – had built for her, next to a stack of books. Books were treasures in ink and paper and Aleja collected them, hunting for legends and tales of explorers like Thomas James. A lantern next to the porthole swung as the ship gently creaked up and down and Aleja looked around her cabin.

Last summer it had been bare but during the months they had spent in the Republic of Ragusa she'd had time to make it hers. On her desk was a jar filled with shells she'd collected from the beaches with Griete and paper bags of sweets that she and Frances had haggled for. Handfuls of sparkling rubies and diamonds were hidden under a plank – Tinta tended to fall into a trance around anything shiny – and her narrow bunk was piled with soft blankets and pillows. Storm-jars were dotted here and there – each one held an entire storm complete with purple-black clouds and crackling lightning. Aleja had found the jars in one of the rooms that had magically appeared in the legendary pirate ship. The shadows might be the heart of the ship, responsible for its magic, but legends fed that magic, powering the crew across the seas, faster than any other ship. Rumours whispered in taverns and ports kept the legends alive and sometimes led to a new room popping into existence. The crew had told her the opposite could also happen – a room could suddenly disappear if it was no longer talked about – but she had yet to see *that* happen.

Aleja slipped out of her fox-coloured dress and poured it into a large trunk sitting on the corner of a plum-coloured carpet dotted with stars. The carpet had been bought by Aleja and Frances in Morocco, during the very first adventure Aleja had had with the pirates. She smiled at the memory as she pulled on a pair of trousers and a tunic. Eager to get to work on a new puzzle, she snatched up Thomas James's golden book from beside her bed and raced out of the door, Tinta following in its fox shape. She found Frances already halfway up the ladder with the kitten leaping up after her.

After Frances spread a blanket out at the bow and sat a plate heaped with baklava on it, Aleja opened the book to its dedication on the first page:

*For my family, in case of emergency.*

*Thomas James*

Tinta shifted down to a small shadow-mouse and the kitten chased it around the deck. Frances sat back on her elbows and watched them, munching on a piece of baklava.

'OK, which page shall we try to crack first?' Aleja asked, dragging her friend's attention back to the book.

*Like Robin Hood*, Frances had described the crew members of the legendary *Ship of Shadows* when she'd explained life on board to Aleja last summer. Pirates with a moral compass, stealing only from the worst of the worst and other pirates – and lining their own pockets in the process. Except when it came to Thomas James's map.

There was nothing Captain Quint wouldn't do to get her hands on that.

Torn in four pieces and hidden in the most secret corners of the world, the map was a magical artefact that, when reassembled, would show all the secrets of the world. Ancient cities, buried treasure, mythological sites lost to time – the map would display them all. It had once belonged to explorer Thomas James, the first owner of the *Ship of Shadows*, and the captain's own great-grandfather. For reasons that still mystified Aleja, Thomas James had torn up the map and created this book, a slim volume of just six parchment pages, as a key to finding each hidden piece. The only problem was that Aleja had still only solved one of its pages.

It had been the sixth page, the very last puzzle in the book. Aleja had worked out that it contained an anagram of '*speak what you seek*', and that the carved world map in the library was the clue. When the words were spoken aloud, the map warmed the continent that held the thing that the speaker sought. After the end of their last adventure, Aleja had asked it where the map pieces were and discovered that one lay in the Americas, another in Europe, a third in Africa – which they'd already found – and the final piece in Asia. But it wasn't much to go on and Aleja needed to solve the other four pages of codes and symbols as soon as possible. The book was like a thorn buried beneath her skin.

'What do you think?' she asked Frances, staring at one of the pages, which was covered in strange dots.

'I think this is the cutest kitten in the whole world,' Frances said, tickling the kitten's stomach.

'Frances!'

'Sorry, sorry.' Frances sat next to Aleja with the kitten on her lap. The kitten batted the parchment and Aleja sighed, whisking the book away before it could be damaged by tiny claws. She stared at the page of dots, concentrating as hard as she could. Then she realized Frances had started speaking again. 'And then the snake squeezed the Sultan until his eyes popped out of his head –'

Aleja poked her. 'That's not helping. And you *do* know your stories always have sultans in them?'

'They do?'

'They do,' Aleja confirmed.

'Huh.' Frances scratched her long nose. 'I've got to throw some more kings in then.'

'Or you could start telling *true* stories,' Velka suggested in her sing-song Swedish accent as she and Farren sat down next to them. Frances shot her an offended look and Aleja giggled. Velka's armfuls of bracelets and cropped emerald hair shone in the lantern light. Her pale arms were inked with a jungle of green vines and leaves.

Farren grinned. 'Perish the thought.' She stretched her long legs out and helped herself to some baklava. Tucking her choppy auburn hair behind her ears, she stuffed her mouth with a piece and slung one leg over the other.

Aleja didn't want to get her fingers sticky with the book on her lap but she couldn't resist one of the honey-glazed pastries. Merchant ships sailed into Ragusa from around the world, their lower decks groaning with spices, fruits and foods she'd never tasted before, and Ermtgen, their cook, had been cooking up a storm since they'd arrived. Aleja popped a piece into her mouth, still staring at the open book.

'Who do we have here?' Velka cooed, stroking the kitten's tiny head. Lantern-bright green eyes stared back at her.

'I've decided to name her Claws,' Frances said proudly. 'She's a ferocious street cat.'

Velka cast a doubtful look at the kitten, which rolled on to its back, purring.

Farren snorted. 'And she's a he,' she added.

Frances flushed. 'How's this for a true story?' she said, changing the subject and leaning forward. 'It was on a night much like this one,' she began in a lower, graver tone.

Aleja peered over the book at the pretty harbour, which twinkled with the reflections of lanterns and stars.

'Deceptively calm,' Frances said pointedly. 'When, all of a sudden, the seas twisted and spat out a monstrous, hulking ship. It was the fearsome *Spectre of the Seas*, the legendary ghost ship, made from the bones of its victims!' Frances paused dramatically.

Aleja sighed and turned the page. *What could this symbol be?* Tinta darted across the book in a kitten shape. Aleja watched it grow into the shadow of a little ship, pretending to glide across the deck. Seconds later, Claws took chase. Aleja thought she preferred shadows to kittens. Frances didn't get so distracted by *shadows*.

'I've never seen a ghost ship,' Velka said, capturing the energetic kitten and scratching him behind his ears. Claws's wide eyes remained fixed on Tinta sailing back and forth.

'I've heard tales,' Farren said, 'but never seen one. Geoffrey's the only ghost I've had the, er, pleasure of meeting.' She glanced over her shoulder, checking their resident ghost wasn't nearby.

'Empty eye sockets stared out from the upper decks!' Frances burst out, determined to finish her story.

'Yes, fearsome phantoms are often missing their eyes,' Farren whispered sarcastically.

Frances threw a piece of baklava at her, but Farren snatched it deftly out of the air and munched on it as Frances cast her a withering stare. Velka giggled and Aleja hid her smile in the pages of the book.

'But most terrifyingly and horrifyingly of all,' Frances ploughed on, 'all who caught a glimpse of the ivory bone-ship were cursed to die a terrible and messy death.'

There was a brief silence.

Aleja turned her attention back to the book. *Perhaps if I try –*

'Aw, a kitten!' Griete said, appearing on deck and coming to coo at the fluffy bundle of fur, her blue eyes wide. She picked up Claws and fussed him, the dark of his fur stark against her golden hair and rosy face. 'Who are *you*?'

Aleja flopped back, the book covering her face. 'I give up,' she moaned.

## CHAPTER THREE

*Magic and Shadows*

Before the sun had peered over the horizon, Aleja and Frances were already up and scrubbing the deck with buckets of seawater. Penumbra was snoozing on the mast. Aleja paused, her hand still on her brush, and watched Claws clamber up the netting towards the owl.

Frances rushed over. 'Come down from there, Claws!' she hissed.

But the kitten ignored her, advancing on Penumbra. It reached out a paw and batted at one of the owl's colossal wings. Penumbra's eyes flew open. He screeched at the kitten, who immediately fell back into the netting in shock. Penumbra closed his eyes once more and Frances climbed up the netting in a hurry to rescue her tangled kitten.

Aleja laughed and looked around for Tinta, wondering if it was watching too. A couple of shadows were dancing round her feet but Aleja knew Tinta wasn't one of them. She couldn't explain how she knew; she just did, as sure as she knew the sun would rise each morning.

The dancing shadows scooted away, pooling under the canvas that hid the kraken bells. Engraved with ancient writing, etched using a tip dipped in old magic and kraken blood, the bells would ring whenever a kraken swam near. The second they had spotted Ragusa on the horizon, the pirates had hidden them, along with any other evidence that their ship wasn't a normal merchant ship. It had been a difficult task; the ship leaked magic and shadows.

Aleja stood up, wondering where Tinta had gone, when a splash of yellow fabric on the other side of the ship caught her eye. Someone was coming aboard. Someone she didn't recognize.

'Frances,' she whispered, 'who's that?'

Frances jumped down from the netting, Claws squirming in her arms. 'I don't know.' She exchanged a worried look with Aleja. 'I'll go and fetch Malika.'

'No – wait!' Aleja said, but Frances was already sliding down the ladder.

Tinta suddenly appeared and puffed up into a shadow-wolf that stood loyally at Aleja's side as the woman walked towards them. Aleja's hand fell to her boot, where her owl-engraved dagger was stashed. She swallowed.

'I have a letter for Aleja,' the woman said in a soft voice.

Aleja stared at her. Her hair was like wildfire, flaming down her sunshine-coloured dress. If she knew Aleja's name and wasn't startled by the magic whispering round the edges of the deck, she could only be one person. 'Are you Caterina? Our shadow in Ragusa?' The *Ship of Shadows* had secret allies all around the world – who Captain Quint called her shadows.

The woman inclined her head. 'I am.' She held out an envelope and Aleja at once recognized her favourite brother's handwriting. Aleja took it with trembling fingers. Tinta nestled closer to her.

'Caterina, it's been an age since I've seen you on board.' Malika had appeared on deck, Frances at her side. 'Would you care to join Elizabeth and myself for some tea?' Malika ushered the shadow towards the captain's quarters.

'What's that?' Frances asked, looking at the envelope.

'It's a letter from my brother. I sent him one through Caterina when we first arrived in Ragusa.' She looked up at Frances. 'But I didn't think we'd be here long enough for him to write back.' She felt so comfortable on the ship now that it was hard to imagine that last summer she had been considering returning to Sevilla and her family. She knew that her father, abuela and two older brothers would have been worried sick about her disappearing, but the *Ship of Shadows* and its crew had burrowed into her heart and refused to let go. Aleja had always dreamed of a world of adventures, of setting out on expeditions and great ocean-crossing voyages. She wanted to explore and see the mysteries and magic of the world for herself. In the end it had been a pirate's life for her and they had sailed straight past Sevilla and on to Ragusa.

'Do you think he's writing to tell you to go back to Spain?' Frances asked worriedly.

Aleja's heart gave a big thump. 'I don't know.' She opened the envelope and slid the letter out. The parchment smelled like Miguel: flour and sugar and lemons. Aleja felt a flash of white-hot guilt. After their mother had died six years ago, they'd become each other's best friend and he was the one she missed most at sea.

'Do you want to be alone to read it?' Frances asked.

Aleja shook her head and started to read out loud. The Spanish words tasted thick and sweet as honey. She hadn't spoken in Spanish for months, had filled her mouth with English and French and Arabic instead. It gave her a pinch of homesickness, as did the news of the tavern, El Puente, and the cakes Miguel had been baking. Then she got to the important part:

We're all fine. In fact, Pablo's gone off to sea too. Padre and Abuela worried for you but I always knew you'd fall into an adventure one day. You always hungered for more than tavern life and it sounds like you've found the right place for yourself.

'It's OK,' Aleja said in English with a sigh of relief.

Frances beamed at her and squeezed her hand. 'Then we'd better finish scrubbing.'

No sooner had they finished than Malika reappeared to usher them straight into weapons training with the other girls. But, rather than taking them to the weapons room as usual, Malika ordered the girls to scale the netting. 'Real battles don't take place in an ordered manner,' she said from below. 'They're fast and unexpected and you must be prepared to fight under the most difficult of circumstances with whatever you're holding at the time.'

She then tossed them a variety of weapons from the trunk she'd hauled up from below decks, which was how Aleja ended up holding a heavy curved sabre as she hooked her legs round the netting and tried to bat away Griete's relentless cutlass attack.

By the end of the lesson Aleja was exhausted.

Velka, Farren and Griete brought up a tray stacked with fruit and pastries, and they ate breakfast together under the bright-blue morning sky. Aleja listened to the others chat, one hand lingering on the shiny coin strung round her neck. It had been the last thing her abuela had given her before she'd run away.

She was trudging back to her cabin, stifling a yawn, Tinta plodding beside her in leopard form, when Frances suddenly appeared behind her.

'Look!' she said urgently, nudging Aleja with an elbow, her hands filled with the sleeping kitten.

Aleja glanced up to see a shadow girl skulking behind a door, watching them pass with blank eyes. 'It's just a shadow,' she said. But something made her look again. 'Wait – is that . . .?'

'Raven,' Frances whispered, wide-eyed.

'We can't let the others see!' Aleja whispered back, hearing the older girls descend the ladder. 'They can't know –'

'That she's Quint's spy on board the Fury's ship?' finished Frances.

Aleja nodded. The crew believed that Raven had betrayed the *Ship of Shadows* and left them for the Fury. Only Captain Quint, Malika, Frances and Aleja knew the truth.

Frances swallowed. 'If they see her shadow, they'll know something's wrong – shadows only take the form of people loyal to this ship. We have to do something!'

Aleja's stomach burned with guilt. She hated keeping Raven's secret from Griete, Raven's best friend. She stared at Raven's half-hidden shadow and then glanced down at Tinta. 'Can you shoo her away?' she asked, dipping her fingers down and grazing them across the shadow-leopard's wispy back.

But at that very moment Aleja felt a strange lurch and the *Ship of Shadows* started to spin. Faster and faster, everything blurred together until Aleja felt sick and cried out, squeezing her eyes shut.

When she opened them again, she was standing on a different ship.

CHAPTER FOUR

*An Impossible Vision*

Aleja staggered backwards on the unfamiliar deck. Two figures were standing in front of her but she was too dizzy to see properly. She blinked hard until her vision cleared . . . and her heart almost stopped.

Raven and François Levasseur were standing in front of her, talking to each other. Aleja swallowed a scream at seeing the Fury so close. Just the sight of his powdered blond hair and eyepatch, marking where Malika had stolen his eye in revenge, made her fingers tremble.

'*¿Qué?*' she whispered to herself, clutching her coin necklace. *What's happening?* She looked around for Tinta but it wasn't there. She was hit with a wave of dizziness and fell on to the deck. A beat later, she realized neither

Raven nor François had noticed her at all. They were still deep in conversation. She listened but the words sounded faraway and faded, as if she was hearing them from underwater.

As François turned to leave, his eye met Aleja's and she let out a yelp. He stepped closer and closer, but Aleja was frozen in place.

Then François stepped straight through her. *This isn't possible*, she thought.

Raven looked miserable, her long ebony hair quivering in the breeze, her eyes moons in her pale face. Aleja opened her mouth to say something but the rushing sickness roared back. The ship swam round her, swirling and tilting in odd directions.

The next thing she knew, she was back in the passageway with Frances staring at her.

'Are you OK?'

Aleja slumped to the floor, still dizzy. Tinta curled round her legs.

'Aleja? What happened?' Griete asked, running towards her, Velka and Farren on her heels.

'I . . . don't know,' Aleja said. 'But for a minute I – I was standing on *La Promesse Lumineuse*.'

Frances looked anxious. 'No, Aleja, you were standing here the entire time. It was like you were in a trance.'

Aleja frowned. 'But it felt so real.' Her head was whirling at what she'd seen.

'Maybe she's hallucinating,' Velka said, kneeling down and looking into Aleja's eyes. She laid a hand against her forehead. 'She hasn't got a fever, though.'

Farren held out a hand and Aleja pulled herself up. 'I'm fine,' she said firmly. She noticed the Raven-shadow had vanished.

'You've had a busy morning. Why don't you get some rest?' Farren said kindly. 'When our shadows on board overexert themselves, it saps their energy.' She pursed her lips. 'I wonder whether having two shadows is doing something similar to you. Have a nap and if it happens again, we'll inform the captain.'

Aleja nodded, her thoughts racing faster than the ship at full speed. It was only when she'd shut her cabin door that she turned and stared at Tinta. 'What was *that*?' But the shadow-leopard tilted its head at Aleja and, as always, said nothing.

Later that day, Aleja was in the sea.

'That's it! Kick harder – no, *harder* – and keep your fingers together. Oh, and don't breathe in the water . . .'

Coughing and spluttering from her accidental mouthful of cold seawater, Aleja glared at Frances, who cackled back at her.

The water surrounding Ragusa was a dream. Crystal clear with tiny fish darting past, it would have been a beautiful place to swim – if it hadn't been winter. *And* if Aleja could swim.

Frances had made it her mission to teach Aleja, declaring in her most stubborn voice that 'pirates need to be able to swim'.

When Aleja had caught her first glimpse of the azure sea that lay flat and smooth around Ragusa, she'd agreed. But learning to do anything at first was hard, made even harder by Frances coasting along beside Aleja wearing a smug grin. Aleja kicked her legs and struck out with her arms, struggling through the water.

'You're trying too hard,' Frances said, swimming effortlessly on her back.

Aleja flicked water at her, but she was finding it hard to concentrate. 'I didn't know the shadows could lose energy,' she said, Farren's comment still playing on her mind.

'Oh yeah,' Frances said. 'When they've been extra magical it seems to tire them out. Once we accidentally sailed into the middle of a battle near Sweden and the shadows hid our entire ship so no one could see it!' Her eyes widened. 'We crawled along at a snail's pace after that, while the shadows regained their strength.'

Aleja's heart beat faster. Could *she* have done something magical?

*

A short time later, they strolled across the rocky shore towards the harbour, trying to wring the water out from their clothes.

'Is that Griete?' Aleja asked, spotting their crew mate walking along the beach in a bright-pink dress.

When they neared, Griete held up a seashell. It was a perfect pearly swirl. 'The spirals are mathematical shapes,' she said happily. 'Look, each swirl represents the Fibonacci sequence!' She dropped it into a basket looped over her arm as Frances shrugged at Aleja, looking baffled. 'And they're lovely sewn on to bodices.' Griete was an inventor, who loved maths and dresses equally.

The three of them ambled into the port. Frances and Griete chatted but Aleja couldn't help her attention straying. Sailors and merchants streamed past tall ships, speaking in dozens of different languages that never failed to thrill her. Ragusa was a melting pot of cultures and the ideal place for a legendary pirate ship filled with women and girls from around the world to lie low and blend in.

'– said it's filled with shadows that can move about like people.'

Aleja yanked Frances and Griete behind a nearby cask of whale oil. 'Listen,' she said.

A second English sailor answered the first. 'I heard tales that the pirate ship carries storms instead of cannons.'

'Aye, and they say it's unsinkable, too . . .'

The voices grew more distant and Aleja grinned at the other two, thinking of the storm-jars in her cabin and how she used them as reading lamps. 'Let's follow them.'

The three girls linked arms and drew closer to the English sailors. 'Did you hear the *Ship of Shadows* even has a bathhouse on board?' Griete asked loudly as they passed, her eyes twinkling.

The pair of sailors did a double take as they strolled past.

Frances groaned. 'You and your bathhouse.'

Aleja laughed. Griete loved baths and was forever trying to stir up enough rumours to create a new room on the ship.

'Why not?' Griete said indignantly. 'A bathhouse would make everything better and stop me thinking so much about –' Her ears pinkened and she clammed up.

Aleja exchanged a look with Frances. 'Is everything OK?' she asked.

Griete fiddled with one of her diamond earrings. 'It's fine. I'm just missing Raven, I guess.' Aleja caught her breath. Over Griete's shoulder she saw Frances cringe. 'I even thought I saw her shadow this morning.' She gave a hollow laugh. 'I must be thinking about her so much that even the shadows are starting to look like her.'

Frances's eyes had turned to globes. Aleja shot her a warning look. She squeezed Griete's hand, not sure what to say. She knew Quint had only told them and Malika the truth to prevent Malika from killing Raven. Captain Quint believed that the more people who knew of Raven's spying, the greater danger she would be in. 'Let's go back to the ship,' Aleja said instead, hoping to distract her. 'You never know – maybe your bathhouse has finally appeared!'

They made their way back across the port to the ship, Aleja and Frances still damp and starting to shiver. Penumbra, perched on the netting slung across the mast, clicked his beak disapprovingly at them.

'It makes me think the captain can see me when he does that,' Frances said to Aleja. 'Like she's looking out through his eyes.'

'Good,' Captain Quint said, materializing and making Frances jump. 'Perhaps then you'll realize that nothing you do on my ship goes unnoticed. Get changed – we're strategizing in the library in a few minutes.' She strode off across the deck to the navigator's room.

Aada, their navigator from the Norwegian Arctic, plotted their courses and stargazed from the large structure that was raised above the deck on long poles. Hers was a curious room, filled with gigantic windows and a glass ceiling that made you feel as if you had suddenly sprouted wings and were soaring above the waves.

Griete, Frances and Aleja climbed down the ladder below decks. Griete gave them a little smile and disappeared into the galley.

'D'you think she's all right?' Frances asked Aleja, finding Claws batting at a padlock on a trapdoor in the passageway. She scooped up the kitten. 'There's my ferocious Claws!'

'I don't know,' Aleja said, 'but I feel horrible not telling her the truth.'

Tinta appeared through the bulkhead shaped like a deer with antlers that trailed off into shadows. It fell into step beside them. The odd burst of gunpowder echoed up from the weapons room and, as they passed Velka's door, there was a small explosion and a yelp.

Back in her cabin, Aleja peeled off her sodden clothes and wrung them out. Tinta morphed into a penguin and waddled under the rain of droplets. The water slipped straight through it, blurring its outline for a second.

'Does that tickle?' Aleja asked it, giggling and flicking water at it. Tinta elongated into a seal shape and flomped through the water, silently clapping its flippers together. Aleja kneeled down on the carpet and looked at her shadow. 'Tinta, was that you this morning? I don't know what happened but it was right after I touched you.' Tinta paused and seemed to look back at her. 'If I touch you again –' Aleja stretched out a hand to Tinta's flipper – 'will you show me something else?' she whispered.

Aleja braced herself for the sickening swirl and spin of the cabin.

Nothing happened.

'Never mind.' She pulled her hand back with a frown. 'Maybe I was wrong,' she muttered to herself, more confused than before.

She dressed and dried her hair in a hurry before racing to the library.

## CHAPTER FIVE
### *The Owl Clock*

Everyone else was already in the library when Aleja rushed in, a seal-shaped Tinta at her heels. The library was a cavernous space hollowed out at the heart of the pirate ship, packed with towering walls of shelves that curved round the portholes, squashy settees for nights of burrowing into books, and a large table that bore an engraved map of the world. Lanterns had already been lit to puncture the gloom and the ceiling sparkled spectacularly – it was covered with giant painted wings edged with diamonds. Because of the magic rippling through it, the *Ship of Shadows* was much more immense than it looked from the outside. Aleja hurried across the Persian rugs, dislodging a little shadow-mouse that ran away, ignoring the globe that was making clunking sounds in the corner of the library, and took her place at the table next to Frances.

Captain Quint plonked a large book down on the table. 'William Pharos,' she announced, tapping a finger on the book.

Aleja didn't need to see the title to know which book it was – *In the Company of the Great Wanderers* by William Pharos. Captain Quint had been talking about it for months. She heard someone sigh and saw Farren roll her eyes at Velka.

'As you all know, Pharos refers here to my great-grandfather Thomas James, when he visited Ragusa many years ago with his crew and mutinous first mate,' Captain Quint said, flipping the book open to a marked passage.

'She's going to read it again,' Farren said in an undertone, and Frances snorted then coughed loudly to cover it up. Across the table, Malika glared at them both.

Captain Quint started reading. '*Though the invitation did not extend to myself, Thomas spent several long afternoons in the company of Senator Prodanelli, whose extraordinary generosity led to Thomas being afforded a tour of the impenetrable Fort Lovrijenac. I recall him being particularly enamoured with the Aurum collection that was kept there . . .*'

'Is there a reason you're reminding us of this, Captain?' Malika asked.

Frances nudged Aleja, grinning. 'Even Malika's sick of her dragging this out at every meeting,' she said under her breath.

Aleja noticed something moving on Frances's lap under the table. A black paw sneaked up and Frances quickly pushed it back down. Aleja suppressed a giggle.

Captain Quint looked up at them all. 'I'm reminding us why we're here. We came to Ragusa to enact a heist at Fort Lovrijenac.'

Though the captain had made enquiries, tours were no longer offered to collectors. A heist was the only way to find what they needed.

'We know. And every minute we lose more time,' Malika said grimly. 'We've already stayed in Ragusa for far too long.' She levelled a glare at Aleja and Frances, and her voice chilled. 'And seeing as you two failed in the scheme you devised . . .'

Aleja wished she could hide under the table.

'It was a brilliant scheme!' Frances said indignantly, pushing her glasses up her nose. 'The carnival would have been the perfect distraction to slip in and –'

'Yes, it would have been.' Malika's eyes glittered. 'And then no one would have known we'd broken into the safe.'

Frances clammed up. She crossed her arms. Claws took the opportunity to pop up on to the table. He padded across the book and stalked over to Penumbra, who ruffled his feathers and screeched at him.

'Unless you want to see that cat eaten, I suggest you remove it,' Malika said.

Frances scrambled to retrieve Claws, who in Aleja's opinion should have stayed safe in Frances's cabin.

Velka set a glass beaker on the table. It was filled with a yellow liquid and stoppered shut. 'Nitric acid,' she said. 'It will melt the steel.' She looked seriously at them all. 'Its fumes can be lethal so do not breathe it in.'

'Excellent,' said Captain Quint. 'Tonight you'll accompany Frances and Aleja and supervise the mission.'

Aleja's face burned. They were perfectly capable of doing the mission themselves! Even though at twelve she was the youngest pirate on board, *she* had been the one to find out about the secret passageways that ran up into the fort from the cliff below. And, after the pirates had tried and failed to locate them, *she'd* learned about the one man who had mapped the passageways out: the cartographer.

Olitiana, the friendly quartermaster with curly hair and dark-brown skin, shot Aleja a sympathetic look.

'Then tomorrow, the heist at Fort Lovrijenac,' the captain announced, 'before anyone realizes the plans are missing.'

Aleja glanced at the large owl-shaped clock that hung down a wall of books, its face buried under a collection of dials and hands that not even Griete could figure out how to work. According to Frances, it had always been frozen. A little shadow trickled down it and on to the shelf below. And then another movement caught Aleja's eye.

'Did the clock just *move*?' she asked out loud.

The rest of the pirates looked up just in time to see a hand slide a notch lower.

Penumbra hooted and Captain Quint leaped up. 'It's *working*? It's never worked!' She looked at Griete but Griete was shaking her head.

'It wasn't me,' she said, looking to Farren, who shrugged.

'That clock has been ticking ever since you returned from the infernal heat of the desert,' a ghostly voice boomed from inside the globe.

Captain Quint strode over and rapped on the equator. 'Show yourself, Geoffrey,' she demanded. 'Tell us what you know of the clock.'

'I do not materialize on command,' Geoffrey said sulkily. 'Though it has amused me how long you've faffed about in harbour while that clock has been counting down.'

'What does this mean?' Frances asked as Claws tapped her glasses with an inquisitive paw.

Malika's eyebrows pinched together. 'Nothing good, I suspect.'

Aleja started to get a bad feeling. 'It must have started ticking when we arrived back with the map,' she whispered. 'That had to be the trigger.'

'Then . . . it *is* counting down,' Griete said. She gave it an anxious look.

'It doesn't seem to be moving at a normal speed,' Farren agreed.

The captain exchanged a sharp look with Olitiana. 'Griete and Farren, I'm assigning you two to calculate precisely how much time we have left. Aleja, Frances and Velka, do *not* fail me tonight.'

Soon after, Aleja slid her trusty dagger into her boot. She was permitted to carry a pistol but pistols were loud and awkward to use so hers was buried in her trunk. She looked at Tinta. 'I wish you didn't have to stay on the ship,' she whispered as Frances tucked Claws into a blanket nest in her cabin and stashed her own knife in her boot. Tinta hopped round Aleja's ankles as a shadow-bunny. Aleja turned to Frances. 'Our shadows have to stay on board the ship. With the magic.'

Frances looked at Aleja like she'd lost her mind. 'I know.'

'So . . . how can François *steal* our shadows?' Aleja asked, thinking of the stone urn that François used to capture shadows. 'What's so special about that urn?'

Frances shrugged. 'I dunno.' She stroked Claws's nose thoughtfully. 'It must be made of something magical, though, because it can capture a whole cast of shadows at once.'

Aleja frowned. 'But where did he get it from?' It seemed the more she learned about the shadows, the more she realized she still didn't know. 'A cast of shadows?' she repeated.

'Yep, that's what I call a group of them,' Frances said. 'It's going to catch on, you just wait.'

Aleja smiled. 'I like it.'

Velka appeared at Frances's cabin door with her small satchel of chemicals. 'Are you ready?'

The rest of the crew whispered good luck as they left the ship, walked down the gangplank and slipped into the city like wraiths.

## CHAPTER SIX

### *The Cartographer's House*

The medieval city walls towered up to the star-spattered sky, curving round Ragusa protectively. Aleja led the way across the cobblestones, Frances and Velka at her back. The night was moon-glow bright but they were dressed in midnight shades well suited to sneaking around old cities after sundown.

And there, between the dark-green trees surrounding the thick wall, was the large townhouse perched high up on the hill, overlooking the rocky bay far below.

'I didn't know there was that much money in drawing maps,' Frances said, looking up at it.

'Thinking about a career change?' Aleja asked.

Frances grinned. 'Nah. Once you turn pirate, there's no going back.'

Aleja thought this might be true – since she'd become a pirate she couldn't imagine life without the *Ship of Shadows*. She walked up the winding stone path and their conversation faded away to just the odd huff of exertion. Ragusa had been forged in steep, twining paths up hills and cliffs, and the cartographer's townhouse sat like an eagle atop it all.

Something small and as dark as a shadow streaked by. Aleja's heart leaped. *Tinta?* She knew it wasn't possible for her shadow to leave the ship but sometimes she caught herself hoping . . .

'Claws? How did you get out of the cabin?' Frances looked baffled. She picked up the meowing kitten and tucked it into her biggest pocket. Only his whiskers poked out.

Aleja swallowed her hopes back down. 'Should we take him back first?'

'Nah, he'll behave,' Frances said and ploughed on.

Aleja bit her lip and followed.

When they reached the top, Aleja's breath caught at the view. The old city was a maze of terracotta roofs surrounded by ancient walls and fortifications in pale stone, polished by moonlight. The odd bit of scaffolding stuck out and Aleja pointed it out to Velka. 'That's from the great earthquake about forty years ago. They lost so many people. So much art and history. I read that in the fire afterwards one of the richest churches burned, turning the streets into rivers of molten silver and gold,' Aleja said, looking down.

'I can't imagine that,' Velka murmured beside her. 'It looks so peaceful now.'

'I wonder –' Aleja turned round. 'Where's Frances?'

Frances poked her head round a tree beside the house and gestured at them. Aleja and Velka darted over. A window had been left cracked open on the ground floor. Frances and Aleja prised it open together. Velka climbed in while they held it open, careful not to knock her satchel with the beaker of acid inside. Aleja clambered through next, and then Frances slipped in noiselessly.

They were in a dining room. A large table and chairs stretched out in the middle, surrounded by dark wooden cabinets displaying china, and old painted maps on the walls. The maps depicted the ancient centre of Ragusa, the harbour jutting out, the curl of the coastline, a city Aleja now knew by heart. She was out exploring the world, city by city, just as she'd always dreamed. The movement of Frances and Velka caught her eye as they tiptoed out of the room. She followed and found that they were in the entrance hall where a large marble staircase swept up to the next floor.

Aleja went first. Trying to make her steps as silent as possible, she melted into the shadows that pooled in the corners of the stairs. She wished they would crawl to life and cover her like a blanket of night, the way they might have done if she'd been on board the *Ship of Shadows*. But here bright slashes of moonlight cut through the windows and there was the sound of someone snoring upstairs. When she reached the top, a large window offered a staggering view. All of Ragusa was at their feet. Winding paths, baroque palaces, moon-dappled water and lantern-lit ships.

Frances poked Aleja and she tore her eyes away. They separated to listen at doors and peek round the curving hallway of the second floor. Aleja pressed her ear to a door and was about to push it open to peer inside when a sudden, especially loud snore sounded. She moved quickly on to the next door. This one was silent. Pulling out the oil-soaked cloth that Griete had supplied each of them with and swiping it down the hinges, Aleja opened the door without a sound.

Inside was a study lined with books she resisted looking at; Aleja cast a quick glance around at the marble desk, framed maps and stiff armchairs, and popped back out to beckon the others in. This was the cartographer's study. Aleja would have wagered a purse of doubloons that his safe was in here. Examining the room while Velka remained at the door as lookout,

Frances and Aleja looked behind books, under the desk and round the chairs. Nothing.

'It's not here,' Frances whispered to Aleja.

Aleja sat back on her heels from where she'd been poking along a dusty fireplace. How did people hide their secrets? The *Ship of Shadows* always hid in plain sight, disguised as a merchant ship.

She leaped up. 'I have an idea.' There were four maps mounted on the walls: the harbour, the walled city, the Adriatic coastline and Europe. Weren't they looking for a kind of map, too? She began sliding each one aside. When she peeked behind the map of the harbour, metal gleamed back at her.

'I found it!' she whispered, holding the map to one side so Velka could hurry over and examine the safe. Frances switched places with her to become the lookout.

'It is steel,' Velka said. She removed the glass beaker from her satchel, then took a deep breath as she unstoppered it. Aleja sucked in a lungful of air. Using a glass dropper, Velka dribbled the acid over the front of the safe. As soon as it began misting and dissolving the metal, Aleja rushed to slide the window open to let the fumes escape before the smell reached those snoring, sleeping nostrils.

A gaping hole emerged in the safe. Aleja held her sleeve tightly in her fingers, careful not to let her wrist touch the acid, and reached inside. Her fingers shook a little and Velka murmured, 'Careful.'

'I'm sure melting skin and bones will smell much worse than metal,' Frances added from behind her shoulder.

'Frances! You're meant to be listening out,' Velka told her.

Aleja ignored them both and concentrated. She touched a roll of crisp parchment. Curling her fingers round it, she began to withdraw her hand, hoping that they'd got the right safe, the right plans. But before she could pull her arm free of the smoking ring of acid, there was a noise behind the shut door. The squeak of a slipper on marble.

The three of them froze.

Claws chose that moment to break free of Frances's pocket with a loud meow.

The door handle began to turn.

## CHAPTER SEVEN

*An Impenetrable Fort*

Aleja whipped her hand out and shoved all the parchments down her tunic as Velka pushed the frame back in place, hiding the safe again and hissing, 'Hide!'

Frances tried to catch Claws but the kitten refused to go back into her pocket. Aleja ran over to the desk. Just as she was about to dive behind it, she spotted a scrap of parchment. A note, written in English:

*Someone tried to rob me last night – who? Suspect that –*

Aleja didn't have time to read any more. She reached out to grab it but Claws meowed again, making her jump and drop it. As the door swung open Aleja ducked under the desk. A draught caught the note and sent it fluttering out of the window.

*The window.* With heart-sinking panic Aleja realized they'd forgotten to shut it. A pair of slippers emerged. Peeking out, Aleja saw Velka's feet under an armchair. Aleja sucked in a breath and pressed her back further against the desk as if she could make herself even smaller. The slippers plodded across the floor. Aleja wondered if they belonged to the cartographer or one of his staff.

Claws suddenly darted out and Aleja almost gasped. That kitten was going to get them all caught! The man in slippers paused, exclaimed something in the Croatian language Aleja could only curse in, and picked Claws up. Aleja's heart rabbited in her chest. The man put Claws outside the window, closed it and plodded back out of the room, shutting the door behind himself with a loud yawn.

Then they heard the scariest noise yet that night. The clunk of a key turning in the door. They were locked inside the study.

'Claws?' Frances called softly seconds later, after they'd all rushed to the window in a panic.

A small meow greeted their ears.

'There he is!' Aleja leaned further out of the window, looking down. 'There's a rail down there.' The fuzzy ball of mischief was perched on it. He seemed fine, despite nearly getting them caught, and Frances sighed in relief. *Is the note down there too?* Aleja wondered.

After a few quiet minutes had passed, Frances was out of the window and standing on the thin metal rail. She scooped up Claws and looked up. 'I think we can climb into those trees.' She pointed to the trees that coated the hill down towards the rest of the city and the coast.

Velka pursed her lips. 'I'm not as good a climber as you two . . .'

'It'll be fine,' Aleja said firmly. 'Frances will go first, then you, and I'll be behind you.'

Like a tightrope walker, Frances crossed the rail, sure and smooth as if the dizzying drop below didn't exist.

Velka sat on the window ledge and swung her legs out. Frances was perched on the other side, waiting to help.

But Velka didn't need any encouragement or steadying hands. She kept her head high and walked one graceful step at a time until she'd crossed the railing and disappeared into the tree. Then it was Aleja's turn. She stepped out on to the rail and cast a look down. The note was nowhere to be seen. Frustration bubbled inside her. First Claws had put them in danger and now she'd lost an important clue.

She took a deep breath and walked along the thin rail, parchment rustling inside her tunic. The sea breeze carried the scent of the city, citrus and rose petals and spices, and gulls whirled above. The ground sloped down on either side of the railing, leaving Aleja treading a higher and higher path, as if she were walking into the night sky itself. Eventually Aleja reached across and climbed into the gentle rustle of the tall evergreen, where Frances and Velka were waiting for her. Descending the tree and going back down the cobblestoned hills through the walled city was easy and it wasn't long before they were racing back up the gangplank to the ship.

'Excellent work,' Captain Quint said after they'd rolled out the parchments Aleja had grabbed and found the plans to the fort.

'There was a note, though,' Aleja said, 'and it was written in English. Somehow the cartographer knows we were after the plans.'

'I'd wager nobody in his household speaks English,' Captain Quint said. 'I'm sure he writes all his notes in English to hide them from prying eyes. But it's of no concern; by the time he realizes the plans are gone, we'll have weighed anchor.' The captain turned her attention back to the plans and Aleja looked too, ignoring the niggling feeling at the back of her mind. That they seemed to have located the second map piece a bit too easily. And the more she thought about it, the more she wondered *how* the cartographer had known they were planning to rob him.

They were in the library, with Aleja standing to one side of the captain at the table, and Malika, Griete and

Velka on the other. Tinta was in its girl form next to Aleja. The crisped edges of the plans kept curling up round the captain's fingers. The fort was built on top of a sheer cliff, over a hundred feet high, its walls were forty feet thick in places and it was defended with huge cannons and a garrison of *soldati*. There was just one entrance in and out: one hundred and seventy-five rickety steps up the cliff. It seemed impenetrable. The perfect place to stash a magical map piece.

Malika, in a sapphire dress and bronze headscarf that matched her skin, pulled a dagger out of her sleeve to hold down one side of the plans. A second dagger shot out of the same sleeve for the other side. Aleja eyed her, wondering just how many weapons she was concealing.

At that moment Frances burst into the library. Aleja bit back a giggle – a black paw was scrabbling under the shut library door. It was like Frances had picked up a shadow of her own. Now that they were safely back on board, Aleja couldn't deny that Claws was pretty cute.

Captain Quint ignored Frances and traced a finger down the plans. 'Here, this passage leads directly down, below the fort and into the caves beneath.' She gave Malika a nod. 'Our point of access will be from the coast. Perfect.' She turned to Aleja who felt almost light-headed with relief. 'Your information about the secret passages was correct, Aleja. Nice work – you'd make a rather exceptional spy.'

Aleja beamed at her, but Quint's mention of spies had made her think again of Raven. She'd looked so miserable in that strange vision Aleja had had of her on board the Fury's ship – but had that even been real? Nothing had happened since. Maybe Farren was right and she'd just been overtired. *Or maybe*, a little voice whispered in her head, *maybe you* did *do something magical.*

A shadow-owl swooped down from atop the golden clock and sat on the plans. It cocked its head as if it were trying to make them out. Penumbra, who was standing on the table next to the parchment, shrieked at it and it collapsed like smoke, sinking into the table and vanishing.

Malika snatched her daggers up and smoothly inserted them back up her sleeve. 'Let's go.'

'No, we'll go tomorrow night as planned,' Captain Quint said, stroking Penumbra. 'I want to allow us enough time. Now let's run through the plan. I want it to be seamless. In and out.' She rolled out the plans again. A blob of shadow ran across it and dived under the table.

Malika tapped the plans. 'This doesn't tell us which room is the exhibitions room.'

Aleja leaned closer to examine it. 'No, but there are only so many it could be,' she said. It wouldn't be in the barracks or kitchens or any of the wide, cannon-lined terraces. 'It's got to be here or here,' she said, pointing out two medium-sized rooms that didn't seem to serve any other purpose.

'Then we'll split up,' Captain Quint said. 'Malika and I shall exit the secret passage first and head to this room.' She pointed to a room burrowed deep in the fort. 'The second group will wait ten minutes to ensure we haven't been noticed, then head directly to this room.' She tapped the other room Aleja had pointed out, a few corridors away from the secret passage.

Aleja was desperate to hear who would be going – she was itching to see the fort and get a chance to find the map piece.

Malika nodded. 'We'll need to carry weapons,' she said, and Frances kicked Aleja's ankle under the table, the corners of her mouth wobbling as she tried not to laugh.

Aleja hid a smile – was Malika ever *not* carrying weapons?

'Yes, but only use them if strictly necessary,' Quint said, her gaze penetrating Malika until she gave a reluctant nod. 'The fort will be crammed with *soldati*. On no account are they to see or hear a whisper of our presence.'

'Will the rooms be guarded?' Griete asked.

Velka shook her head. 'I doubt it; there's no need – the entire fort is protected.'

'I heard talk in the taverns that you'd be crazy to try to rob it,' Aleja said helpfully.

Captain Quint's eyes twinkled. 'I often find my best ideas come with a side of folly.'

Griete opened her mouth to speak but jumped instead. In a silvery mist a translucent body slunk through the bookshelves and formed the features of a pirate captain from several hundred years ago, complete with curly wig, massive hat and more buttons and bits of gold than should be able to fit on to a jacket.

'What's this? Plans afoot?' Geoffrey, their resident ghost, enquired.

'Nothing that concerns you,' Frances told him.

Geoffrey gasped. 'Such rudeness. I'll have you know, in my day, when we were aboard the *Smiling Skull* – such a fine ship, far grander than this heap of wood,' he said, sniffing derisively, 'we would never have tolerated the abhorrent lack of manners that your crew seem to possess.'

'I apologize for your suffering,' Captain Quint said drily. 'Now, I've had the rowing boat checked over and our supplies loaded into it. We leave at sundown. Malika, Griete, you'll both be joining me for backup. Frances, I'll need your particular skills and, Aleja –' Aleja looked up, her breath catching in her throat – 'since you were so instrumental in retrieving the first piece of the map –' Captain Quint's hand fluttered to the glass vial round her neck in which she kept that first precious piece – 'and responsible for discovering the existence of the secret passages, you may come, too.'

Frances grinned at her and Aleja fizzed with excitement. Tinta pooled down into its leopard form and silently roared.

'We ought to be safe until then but, to be certain, I shall move the ship to the far side of the harbour to keep it out of sight,' the captain continued.

A low thunk sounded. Geoffrey had swept back inside the ornate globe, sulking.

'He really is rather delicate for a pirate,' Griete said.

'Geoffrey Edgerton was a fearsome pirate in his day,' Malika said, gathering the attention of the room. Her grin slashed her face open. 'But now he's met his most terrifying battle of all – girls who dare to be pirates.'

## CHAPTER EIGHT
### Lokrum Island

After a long sleep filled with maps and trees and a moon that became a lantern and chased her before she turned into a shadow and flew away, Aleja woke with a start. Something was batting at her hair. She tried to sit up but she was pinned to her pillow.

'Mmph!'

'No, Claws,' Frances said mildly, removing the kitten from Aleja's face.

Aleja sat up. Frances was already dressed. Tinta bounded up on to the bunk in a little cat shape and dashed round the kitten, who wriggled in Frances's hands, his tiny paws trying to catch the shadow.

Aleja rubbed her eyes. 'Am I late for breakfast? Or weapons training?'

'Nope and nope.' Frances sounded much too cheerful. When Aleja managed to prise her eyes open, she realized it was still dark. Thomas James's book was resting beside her, still open after she'd stayed up late trying to solve it. 'I thought we'd get some swimming practice in this morning!' Frances said, almost bouncing around as much as Claws. 'I brought cake.' She showed an oilcloth-wrapped bundle. 'And it's waterproof!'

Aleja groaned and pulled her blankets over her head. Then she heard Frances laugh and peeked out. Tinta had swelled into a huge lion that filled the cabin, and the tiny kitten was now stalking and pouncing on its massive shadow-paws as if he were the same size. Frances left to put Claws in her cabin while Aleja dressed in swimming clothes, Tinta dancing around in her girl form. When Tinta wisped down to the shadow of a single droplet and back again, Aleja paused. 'Can you swim?' she wondered aloud, pushing her washing basin across the carpet to the shadow. Tying up her tangle of light-brown hair, Aleja watched Tinta edge round the basin before morphing down into a duck shape and hopping in. Aleja rushed to look. Her little shadow was resting atop the water, its edges rippling. Aleja smiled at it and rushed off to her own swimming lesson.

\*

Frances and Aleja stood side by side on the beach, watching the first hint of sunrise melt away the night. Frances pointed at a small island some distance across the water. 'I thought we'd swim over there,' she said, raising her eyebrows in a challenge.

Aleja looked at the water. She swallowed. 'I don't know, Frances – I'm not a very good swimmer yet . . .'

'You were great last time!' Frances said confidently. 'I'm sure you can do it.'

Aleja stepped into the water. It lapped round her ankles, cold but refreshing. She looked towards the island. 'OK.'

They swam out together under a honeyed sky, the same shade as the sugared orange peel that Frances had been buying by the bagful since their arrival in Ragusa. But the seawater became colder the deeper they went. 'Remind me why we're doing this again?' Aleja said as she grumpily ploughed after Frances.

'Practice makes perfect.' Frances splashed Aleja. 'And you need all the help you can get.' She eyed Aleja's thrashing arms. 'Try to relax – you're battling too much. Let your body loosen up.'

Aleja watched the clear water ripple. It sparkled in the morning sun like diamonds and she smiled. To her surprise the more she relaxed, the faster she glided along.

'That's it!' Frances beamed at her. 'You're getting the hang of it now.'

Aleja beamed back at her.

The island inched closer. *Casi, casi,* she thought to herself. *Nearly there.* But her lungs were beginning to pinch and her muscles were burning. She gasped for air, suddenly aware of how deep the water was. And how *much* of it there was surrounding her in every direction. 'Frances!' she spluttered, struggling to stay afloat. 'It's too far!'

But before Frances could turn round, Aleja slipped underwater. Panic coloured her view as she tried to blink, reaching for the surface. But it was dim and down was up and up was down and she couldn't think and –

An arm wrapped round her stomach and yanked her up. Aleja broke the surface with a deep gasp. 'Don't worry,' Frances said, holding on to her and treading water, looking not the least bit fazed. 'It happens to everyone.'

Aleja sighed but the island was far closer than the shore so she took a deep breath and swam forward, shutting her nerves out and watching the beach edge closer and closer. After one final push of effort, she was there. She felt a big burst of relief.

The island was lush with greenery, and the shallow waters of the bay glinted in the soft sunlight. Aleja splashed up to the shore and sat on a smooth rock to admire the view of the ancient walled city. Frances popped up next to her, her glasses on a string round her neck.

'I did it!' Aleja said, grinning.

Frances dug out her cake, which was a bit squished now, and passed Aleja a slice. 'Time to celebrate.'

Aleja bit into the almond-and-marzipan cake, hungrier than she'd realized and not even minding that the oilcloth wasn't as waterproof as Frances had claimed. 'Frances?'

'Hmm?'

'When I found myself standing on *La Promesse Lumineuse* yesterday, I saw Raven.'

Frances lowered her cake. 'But I saw you the entire time; you never once left the passageway,' she said gently.

Aleja frowned at her cake. 'I know, but what I saw felt real. Do you know of any kind of magic on the ship that could have done that?'

Frances shook her head slowly.

'What about Tinta?' Aleja asked. 'It happened when I was touching it. Could Tinta's magic have shown me something somehow?'

'I really don't know,' Frances said. 'But it's nothing I've ever heard of before. I'm sure it won't happen again, though, don't worry.'

Aleja didn't tell her that she wished it would. That she had been dreaming about the possibility that she could do something magical. She changed the subject instead. 'What's next?'

Frances's answering grin lit up her face. She shoved

the entire slice of mushy cake in her mouth and leaped to her feet.

A few minutes later, Aleja was learning to swim underwater. Frances claimed that it would help her not to panic while swimming and Aleja had to admit she was right. Down there, it was an entirely different world. Fish flitted in and out of sight, an octopus drifted past, and the floor was fringed with colourful seagrass and speckled with starfish. Aleja wished she could hold her breath longer. Each time she surfaced for a fresh lungful of air, she couldn't resist dipping back down into the turquoise water for another peek.

They ended up setting off a lot later than intended. So much later, in fact, that they were met on the deck by Malika. And a couple of eavesdropping shadows.

Frances gulped. 'Uh-oh.'

Aleja bit her lip. Tinta peeked its head above deck then vanished.

Malika glared at them. 'And where exactly have you two been that was so important it necessitated skipping weapons training?' she asked icily. Her stare trailed down their dripping clothes. Shadows danced round Malika's feet as if they were looking for her missing one. They quickly collapsed down into one small splodge and trundled away.

'I've been learning how to swim,' Aleja whispered,

trying not to watch the shadows. Was it Malika's missing shadow that had scared them – or Malika herself?

Malika's gaze snapped on to her with a ferocity that made her wince. 'And can you?'

'All the way to Lokrum Island,' Frances piped up. 'And even underwater! I've been teaching her.'

Aleja cringed – Frances never could resist showing off.

To her immense surprise Malika was slowly nodding. 'Good,' she said. 'All pirates should be able to swim. And since you two are so *industrious*, you won't mind the three-hour private weapons-training session you'll be having with me after breakfast. We don't know what to expect when the clock has finished counting down and I will not have us unprepared.' She sauntered off, her silky aquamarine dress swishing against the deck.

Aleja stared at her retreating back. 'Three *hours*?'

Frances looked horrified.

## CHAPTER NINE

*Frances's Story*

Breakfast was a glum affair. Most of the pirates had already eaten and dashed off on their own errands. Captain Quint's mood had frayed round the edges after learning that the owl clock had been counting down for months, and everyone was scurrying around on her orders. There was still no update on how long the countdown had left, and the longer Captain Quint had to wait, the worse her mood got. Ermtgen tsked at Aleja and Frances when they appeared in the galley with Claws, hoping for griddle cakes and a bowl of milk. It seemed a long time since the soggy cake and their stomachs were snarling. 'Isn't it a bit early to be getting into trouble?' she asked, and Aleja reddened. But Ermtgen stacked their plates with the thin rounds of sugared batter anyway and they tucked in.

'We'll need it for strength,' Frances said dourly, watching Claws lap up his bowl of milk. 'Three hours of weapons training alone with Malika? She'll kill us!'

Aleja stabbed a griddle cake with her fork. 'Just as long as it's not cutlasses.'

It was cutlasses.

Cutlasses were heavy and difficult to fight well with, and they were Aleja's most hated weapon. It didn't help that after just twenty minutes Aleja's arm was already drooping and Malika was more gleeful than ever.

'Try to breach Aleja's defences,' Malika instructed Frances as she charged towards Aleja, brandishing her cutlass high above her head and swinging it wildly down. Aleja raised hers in a hurry, the smash echoing down her arm and through her bones. Frances stepped forward, slashing away, and Aleja quickly skipped back. She preferred the smoothness of sword fighting, where Malika made them memorize steps and sequences. Cutlasses were fast and vicious and chaotic.

'Switch places,' Malika said, her eyes gleaming.

Aleja swiped her cutlass at Frances, who blocked it again and again.

'Here, let me show you something.' Malika twizzled her own cutlass around. Aleja stepped aside. Malika turned and spun, the blade of her cutlass flashing as she whipped it round, sending Frances's clanging out of her hands.

'Whoa,' Frances said.

'Can you show me how to do that?' Aleja asked eagerly.

Malika repeated the demonstration more slowly. They took it in turns to spin and attack each other. Until Frances twisted too far round and accidentally embedded her cutlass in a mannequin. Aleja rushed over and the two of them heaved it out between them. The weapons-training room was huge, with mannequins hanging from beams overhead and weapons from all over the world mounted on the walls. It was often the noisiest place on the ship between the magical echoes of ancient battles and Farren shooting her pistols, which was why Frances had left Claws in her cabin. Tinta was sitting on the sidelines, a little shadow-fox utterly transfixed by the flashes of light from the cutlass blades.

Aleja twirled at Frances, arcing her cutlass in a tight spiral and down, twisting the blade as it hit Frances's defence . . . and knocked it away.

Frances gasped. 'You did it! That was *brilliant*.'

Aleja stared at the fallen cutlass in amazement.

'Good work,' Malika said, a rare compliment that made Aleja flush happily. Until she opened her mouth again. 'Two more hours to go.'

'Malika?' Frances asked, pushing her glasses up her nose and looking determined.

Aleja widened her eyes at her. Whatever Frances was about to ask, she sensed it was a terrible idea.

Malika's eyes narrowed as she took in Frances's expression. 'Yes?'

'Where did you learn –' Frances waved an arm at the weapons room – 'all this?'

Malika considered her for a moment. 'I had an excellent teacher.'

Now Aleja was curious, too. 'Where? Did you go to a special school or something?'

'In a manner of speaking,' Malika said. 'Now, if you hold your cutlass –'

'What kind of school?' Frances interrupted.

Malika sighed. 'I fail to see how any of this is pertinent to your own training. What difference does it make if I was instructed in the art of fighting by a tutor or in an assassins' guild? I am your teacher and you're here to learn.'

Aleja and Frances gaped at her.

'An assassins' guild?' Frances asked, her amber eyes gleaming.

'Is that true?' Aleja demanded.

Malika blinked. 'I –'

'It *is* true!' Frances crowed.

'What was it like?' Aleja asked eagerly.

Malika caressed her cutlass hilt. 'Two more hours to go.'

By the time they'd finished, Aleja's arms were as wobbly as the soggy cake and she never wanted to see another cutlass again in her life. Frances snatched a tin of sweets from a cupboard in the galley and collected Claws, and they ran across the deck and whizzed down the wooden slide into the cave of shadows. There they found the shadows doing something very odd indeed.

'Oh!' said Griete, pink-faced, shutting her book in a hurry.

'Did we surprise you?' Aleja asked, looking at the shadows nestled either side of Griete, blowing kisses at her.

The cave of shadows was one of the rooms on board the *Ship of Shadows* that they had suddenly discovered last summer. The cave was lined with charcoal-grey rocks shot through with marbled purple veins, creating little hideaway corners. Large smooth rocks dotted here and there made ideal seats. Old silver lanterns hung down crookedly and a few had sputtered to life. Since it had been magically created, the shadows were unusually active here and responded to whatever was happening around them, making it a brilliant place to hear one of Frances's ghoulish stories. It was one of Aleja's favourite magical rooms – not all the rooms rumoured into being were pleasant. Frances was rather fond of a very creepy one containing masks that lined its walls like faces, which made Aleja's skin crawl.

'What *are* you reading?' Frances tried to get a look at the cover before Griete shoved it into a pocket in her tool belt. '*The Duke and the Lady Buccaneer*?' she read sceptically.

Aleja craned her neck at the cover, where she saw a female pirate in a pristine white dress in the arms of a handsome duke.

'It doesn't look very realistic,' Frances continued. 'I've never seen a pirate look that clean on a voyage.' She looked at the grease smudged across Griete's forehead and muttered, 'Or ever.'

'Intelligent women can read romances *and* be engineers,' Griete said, standing up. 'And this is precisely why we need a bathhouse on board this ship.' She stormed out of the cave.

Aleja giggled at the shadows pining at her absence.

Frances looked baffled. 'Do you think I offended her?'

'It's *never* a good idea to disturb a reader,' Aleja said, helping herself to a large meringue from the tin.

After several stories involving heists that went drastically wrong, Frances launched into a fresh tale that made the hairs on the back of Aleja's neck rise.

'*Ro-langs*,' she said, her face shadowed. The cave's shadows crept closer round her to listen. 'I heard a story once about a man who went climbing in the highest, most treacherous mountain peaks in the world. High on the Tibetan Plateau, where mountains are made of snow and ice. One wrong step and –' Frances drew a line across her neck – 'you're finished.'

Tinta inched closer to Aleja, its form unspooling until it shrank down into a hare, black as tar. She automatically reached for it. Claws stared at Frances.

'Well, that man took a friend with him, thinking he wouldn't be alone on those freezing nights, but his friend slipped on a patch of ice and plummeted to his doom, leaving the man all alone on the mountain.'

Aleja shivered.

The shadows formed the shape of the man a hundred times over, climbing up the rocky cave walls around them. Claws hissed, the fur on his back rising in spiky tufts.

'Or so he thought,' Frances said ominously.

Aleja reached into the sweet tin and bit into a meringue without thinking, her eyes locked on to Frances.

'But darker things prowl those mountains and each night the man went to sleep he'd hear his dead friend's voice whispering across the snow and howling winds, calling for him.' A shadow-man peered down at them and Claws yelped and fled into Frances's arms. Tinta, still a shadow-hare, hopped out and flicked its wispy whiskers at it. The shadow-man retreated. A fierce wind struck up instead, but when Aleja watched it she realized it wasn't real – it was made of shadows raging through the cave like silent mist. She couldn't feel it though the lanterns began to swing from the ceiling.

'One day, the man grew tired of waiting for his dead friend to appear and haunt his tent so he went searching for him instead. But when he found him, he wasn't a ghost at all!' Frances cried out, making Aleja start.

'He was one of the undead – a risen corpse, with skin peeling off his face and eyeballs hanging out by their strings!'

The shadow-men re-formed into corpses. Aleja shuddered and scooted closer to Tinta. Even though she couldn't feel it, its presence comforted her.

'I don't believe one word of that,' Farren said, suddenly poking her head into the cave.

Aleja leaped up.

Frances jumped then grinned. 'It's all true.'

'I'm sure.' Farren grinned back at her. 'You need to get changed – it's twilight.'

After returning to their cabins to change and leaving Velka to cat-sit so the kitten couldn't sneak after Frances again, Aleja and Frances met the others on deck. Captain Quint, Malika and Griete were already there. All of them were dressed in night-dark clothes and armed with an assortment of glittering blades.

Captain Quint's smile shone as bright as a sword. 'Now let's go and get the next piece of the map,' she said, and Aleja was hit by a wave of excitement – this was the moment they'd been waiting for.

Olitiana lowered the rowing boat into the water with a splash. 'Good luck,' she said.

One by one they jumped over the edge of the ship.

## CHAPTER TEN

### *The Heist*

Captain Quint and Griete took the oars. Rowing smoothly through the mirrored sea, they cut a course towards the fortress in the west. The cliff grew nearer, then nearer still, the sheer rock face towering above them as if it were trying to clamber into the stars. Just when Aleja thought they were about to row straight into it, a narrow alcove appeared. They glided through the rocky opening with a spark and a hiss as Malika lit a lantern to guide them through the caves. Inside, the water was as black as oil. The oars steadily pushed them deeper into the hushed cave, and they rowed under the cliff until they hit rock. Then Aleja and Frances hopped out and held on to the boat. Malika and Griete joined them on the rocky platform as the captain grabbed a coil of rope and secured the boat.

Frances muttered, 'It's a bit dank, isn't it?'

Aleja looked at the dark cave wall in front of them. It didn't *look* like a secret passage.

Malika held the lantern higher. She stepped forward, patting the rock with her wrist, feeling her way to one side . . . and vanished. Aleja gasped and examined the hidden entrance. A second wall had been built in front of the main wall so that, while it appeared to be one solid wall, it was, in fact, concealing a narrow passage.

'Time to enact our heist,' Captain Quint said, thrilled.

Aleja slid into the rock after Malika. Cold water sloshed round her ankles – she'd stepped straight into a deep puddle. She braced her hands on either side to navigate the passage that curved left then up, up into the heart of the cliff. Her hands sliding on the slick cave walls, Aleja kept her eyes down, on her boots and the uneven rock floor that cut a sharp spiral up. Water dripped down the rock, making everything damp and slimy. Their footsteps echoed in the silence.

Frances suddenly shrieked.

Aleja whipped round. '*¿Qué pasa?*' *What's wrong?*

'Something slimy just crawled over my hand!' Frances said, her eyes and the glint of her glasses all Aleja could make out in the dim light. Then Malika twisted round a bend with the lantern, plunging them into blackness.

'Keep moving,' Captain Quint barked out from the back, and Aleja and Frances stumbled forward over rocks and loose stones until they'd caught up again.

Up they climbed, until Aleja's legs began to burn and the stone passageway grew narrower, clenching in around them. Up, up and up, until it came to an abrupt end.

Malika and Aleja looked at the trapdoor cut into the rock above them.

Malika leaned her hand and wrist against it. 'On the count of three.'

'Shouldn't we wait for the others?' Aleja asked, looking at the rusted hinges. 'I'm not as strong as Captain Quint or Griete . . .'

Malika arched an eyebrow at her. 'One. Two. *Three.*'

Aleja scrambled to push as hard as she could, her arms feeling like they might burst with the effort. The trapdoor didn't budge. Malika shifted to brace her back against it and Aleja copied her, using her shoulders as she was shorter. This time, when they heaved together, a whining squeak escaped the hinges and the trapdoor flew open.

'Right,' Captain Quint said when they were all huddled together in the cramped space beneath the trapdoor. 'Everyone follow the plan. We go in and out, fast and efficient. We'll meet here afterwards. If there's even a *hint* of danger –'

'Get back down here,' Griete finished.

'Without being noticed,' Captain Quint said seriously. 'Any tails you pick up must be shaken off first or you'll not only endanger us – you'll put the ship and the rest of the crew at risk, too.'

Aleja's nerves jangled – breaking into an armed fort filled with *soldati*? This was their riskiest plot yet. She thought of the note she'd found – if the guards knew someone had been after the plans, could this be a trap? She swallowed. Again she had that strange feeling that something wasn't right . . .

Malika slunk through the trapdoor first, followed by Captain Quint. Aleja and Frances looked at each other as Griete counted down the minutes on her pocket watch.

'She seems tense,' Frances whispered, her face ghostly by the lantern light.

'I hope we find the map piece,' Aleja whispered back, thinking of the owl clock counting down. 'If not –'

She didn't get to finish her thought. 'It's time,' Griete said, pocketing her watch.

Aleja scrambled up the rocky wall and through the trapdoor, holding it open for Frances and Griete. It was embedded in the floor of a tiny room with no windows or furniture. A single door led out. Her heart thudding in her chest, Aleja inched it open and looked outside. It was pitch black. She crept forward, reaching out with her hands . . . and walked into fabric. Thick and heavy, it was draped over the entire door. 'The whole room is hidden,' she said. Sneaking out of the door sideways, they emerged from behind a large tapestry.

'Good job the guards didn't redecorate,' Frances whispered.

Griete dashed to the end of the stone passage. She gestured at Aleja and Frances, who darted towards her. Now they'd left the security of the hidden room, a fresh set of nerves gnawed at Aleja. The fortress was an ancient maze of stone and flames. They crept along identical-looking passages lit with wall-mounted sconces and darted past stone arches that led back outside. Aleja wondered how many secrets and whispers the thick walls had heard across the centuries. After several corridors, they paused at Griete's side, listening. The odd footstep, distant voices, the chink of cups. Griete nodded and handed them a small mirror. Aleja and Frances left her at her assigned post to sneak down the next passage and outside the room Captain Quint had had them memorize from the plans.

Aleja positioned the mirror under the thick wooden door and angled it to look inside. 'Velka was right; no one's guarding it,' she said in a sigh of relief.

Frances nodded at Griete and then the two of them slipped inside.

It was a vast dim room cut from stone the colour of sand. Another low door was opposite and Aleja frowned – she hadn't seen *that* on the plans. She darted over to check it. It was just a walk-in cupboard filled with old crates and packing material. She turned her attention back to the main room. There were no windows. A fiery flare from the sconces bounced off the glass cases rimming the room, which were filled with curious artefacts, ancient relics and gleaming bits of treasure.

'Oh,' Frances said, spellbound.

'We're just here for the map,' Aleja said quickly, even though she was captivated, too. She spotted an intricate gold compass with unusual markings, scrolls of old parchments and the tiniest globe she'd ever seen, with all the countries picked out in precious gems. 'Look, they're all displayed with the name of the collection.' She pointed at the little placard neatly mounted beside the tiny globe.

Frances squinted at it. 'They're in Croatian,' she pointed out, 'and, unless I'm mistaken, that's not one of the thousand languages you speak. Cursing doesn't count,' she added as an afterthought.

'Yes, but names are names. We're looking for the Aurum collection,' Aleja said, scanning a row of glass cases. 'And I only speak four languages, but I've been thinking about learning another one.' She spotted a curl of parchment, but it was covered in tiny lines of script, not a map, so she moved on. Roman coins, a cursed opal necklace, an ancient statuette. But nothing that looked like a fragment of map.

'I can't find it,' Frances said desperately, 'and we've already been in here too long.'

Aleja sighed. 'We must be in the wrong room. Maybe Quint's found it.'

The door suddenly burst open. Aleja and Frances twirled round, hands on dagger and knife hilts.

'It's just me,' Griete said, catching the door before it banged against the wall and closing it quietly. 'Someone's coming!'

'Quick, in here!' said Aleja, running to the cupboard. Frances and Griete dived inside and she shut all three of them into the darkness. 'Hide behind the crates,' she whispered, ducking behind one, her eyes on the crack of light seeping under the bottom of the door.

Aleja heard the main door to the collections room open. To Aleja's surprise the men who entered were speaking in English. And they were discussing the very collection that the pirates had stolen into the armed fortress to find.

'What an extraordinary room. As a historian, I am somewhat interested in the Aurum collection – I have been given to understand that it was originally housed in here, is that correct?'

Worst of all was who the voice belonged to. Aleja would have recognized it anywhere. It belonged to the Fury: François Levasseur, infamous pirate hunter, stealer of shadows and the only thing the *Ship of Shadows* feared.

## CHAPTER ELEVEN

### An Old Enemy

Aleja stared at the cupboard door as if she could stare straight through it. She felt Griete stiffen at her side and Frances's jerk of recognition. Hearing François's voice took her right back to that strange moment just yesterday when she'd stood – or maybe not stood – on the deck of his ship. How had he figured out so quickly where the next map piece was?

She had a sudden realization: the cartographer's note hadn't been about the pirates at all – it had been about François. He must have attempted to rob the cartographer the night they'd rescued Claws. But while they'd had to break into the safe, he'd managed to gain access to the fortress. Aleja couldn't understand how – only guards were allowed inside.

She listened as hard as she could, trying to ignore the fear sloshing about in the pit of her stomach like a stormy sea.

'Ah, the Aurum collection. I am afraid that particular collection has been relocated. Perhaps you would be interested in seeing the fourteenth-century Venetian carnival masks? There is one crafted entirely from glass . . .'

Relocated? Aleja's breath caught in her lungs. She looked at Frances, dismayed. Breaking into the cartographer's safe, stealing the plans and planning the heist had all been for nothing. *Where was the second map piece?*

'Very impressive,' François said smoothly. 'May I enquire where the Aurum collection has been moved to? It is of great interest to my patron.'

Aleja was torn between desperately wanting to hear the answer and dreading François finding out.

'It was purchased some years ago by a private collector. One Xú Jì Chéng, if I remember correctly. He owns a veritable museum of artefacts.'

'Jì Chéng . . .' François sounded out, as if he was trying to place it.

He was doing a good job of digging for information, Aleja reluctantly acknowledged, furious that they were stuck in a cupboard while the one man who could destroy the *Ship of Shadows* was about to discover where the map was.

'He's a prominent court official to the Kāng Xī Emperor,' the guide said helpfully.

Emperor Kāng Xī. Aleja bit her lip. Did that mean that the map piece was in –

'His mansion is in Shanghai, China,' the guide continued.

A scrap of light glinted off Frances's glasses as she turned to Aleja, shocked.

'I see,' François murmured. The boots moved to the other side of the room.

Aleja relaxed a little.

Then Griete sneezed.

She muffled it, but in the tiny space it echoed. With her hands clapped over her mouth she looked at Aleja with wide eyes.

'What was that?' François's footsteps grew louder again. Closer.

Aleja shrank back behind the crates, wishing she could make herself smaller, wishing that Tinta was there to hide her. She wrapped her fingers round the coin at her neck for comfort.

The cupboard door was flung open and light streamed through it. Aleja and Frances exchanged a look of horror.

'It's probably just rats,' the guide said. 'Nothing to worry about. Pesky creatures find their way into every cupboard.'

Aleja felt like she was breathing so loud, François must be able to hear it. She held her breath and squeezed her eyes shut.

*Bang!* Someone kicked the crate she was hiding behind.

A rat suddenly scurried out. Aleja felt Griete recoil at her side. She reached out and gripped her hand. They couldn't make a single sound. François was known as the Fury for his vicious temper. If he caught them, there was no telling what he'd do.

'What did I tell you?' the guide said. 'Rats.'

The cupboard door slammed shut, making them all jump. They were in darkness once more. With a rat. Its beady eyes glittered as it stared back at them. A minute later, Aleja heard the door open and the men walk through it, their conversation moving further away before the door shut once more.

Griete leaped to her feet. With one hand on her trusty dagger, Aleja slowly opened the door. The three of them listened hard. The murmur of passing *soldati*, boots on stone floors and distant squawks of seagulls greeted their ears.

'We need to get out of here,' Aleja said. 'We can't let François beat us back to the harbour!'

They fled back through the fortress, pausing between passages and darting past stone arches that led to clifftop terraces. Her mind a blur, Aleja didn't know how they navigated it until the tapestry was before them and they had just one more passage to creep across, one more corner to go round.

'We're nearly there now,' Griete said, leading the way, her mathematical brain the best at translating plans into directions.

When they'd reached the halfway point, a noise froze Aleja in place. Someone was rushing after them. Her palm slick against her dagger hilt, she stared at Frances and Griete – in a few minutes the *soldato* (or, worse, François) would turn the corner and see them. She wondered if he had his stone urn that devoured shadows with him. Her heart leaped into her throat. She couldn't lose Tinta – not when she was just beginning to understand how very special her second shadow was.

Frances whirled round to look for somewhere to take cover, but there was nothing but stone. 'We can't turn back!'

'We're going to have to fight our way out,' Griete said, drawing her sword. 'Silence them however you can. We can't risk the *soldati* sounding the alarm and sending reinforcements after us – better a few now than the entire fortress laying siege to our ship.'

Aleja cast a longing look at the tapestry, but the footfalls were coming from that direction and she knew they'd never make it into the secret room without betraying its location. Griete was right; they had to fight their way out. 'We've got the advantage,' she said, thinking fast and out loud. 'They don't know we're here.'

Frances grinned. 'Looks like it's time for a surprise attack.'

Aleja clutching her dagger, Griete raising her sword and Frances bearing the wickedly curved knife she'd stolen in Marrakesh, the three of them ran forward and round the corner in attack, a silent battle cry of blades and bravery.

## CHAPTER TWELVE

*The Race Is On*

They charged straight into Captain Quint and Malika. The two women had their cutlasses drawn and raised, and they wore terrifying expressions on their faces.

Captain Quint swore and they all lowered their weapons.

'He's here,' Malika spat out.

'We know, and we know where the map piece is, too,' Griete told the captain as the two of them shifted the tapestry aside for Frances and Aleja to run through.

Malika paused. 'He's here alone. No crew. Give me five minutes. I'll end him.'

Bootsteps sounded in the distance. They were heading their way.

'No crew, just an entire fortress of *soldati* who will discover us if you don't move. *Now*,' Captain Quint snapped.

Malika stormed into the hidden room and leaped down into the secret passage. Griete and the captain moved the tapestry back and shut the door. Aleja held the trapdoor open for Frances to jump down while Griete pulled out a twist of metal from one of her pockets and shoved it under the door to jam it. 'Just in case,' she said, jumping after Frances.

'Go,' the captain said to Aleja, who dropped down into the secret passage like a cat. Captain Quint was quick on her heels, pausing only to shut the trapdoor, scoop up the lantern and pass it to Malika, who charged ahead in a murderous rage. The way down was far more treacherous than the way up and the mood had turned rotten.

'The map piece has been moved to Shanghai,' Aleja told Captain Quint, stumbling over a pile of loose stones. She wondered if she should mention the clue in the note that she'd missed, but Captain Quint was already in a terrible mood.

'I thought the library table revealed that the second piece was in Europe,' Griete said from further back in the tunnel.

Captain Quint's sigh was almost lost in the crunch of boots on stone and the sudden splash of someone plunging into a deep puddle. 'Ugh,' Aleja heard Frances mutter quietly to herself. Aleja stepped over the puddle, her fingers resting on the slimy stone on either side. The air was seaweed-thick and murky.

'Yes, a piece is in Europe,' Captain Quint said, marching straight through the puddle without noticing. 'But apparently we're currently chasing a *different* piece. With no clues as to where the European piece is, it would be a waste of time to hunt through the whole continent. Not when we need to beat François to China. Meanwhile that confounded clock is counting down each minute that passes.'

Aleja ducked under a low jut of rock, trying to puzzle it all through. 'The table did say that there's a piece in Asia.'

Malika suddenly growled from where she was forging ahead. 'I don't care if we have to sail to the bottom of the world to get this piece. We must get it before François and before that clock runs out.'

'The *Ship of Shadows* is the fastest ship on the seas,' Captain Quint said. 'We *will* get there first.'

They rowed back to the ship in silence. Aleja couldn't shake the image of François appearing on their ship to gobble up their shadows. She kept imagining Tinta dragged into his urn, shifting and struggling and helpless. She gripped the handle of her dagger. *No, I'll never let that happen*, she told herself fiercely. Beside her, she noticed Frances was paler than usual – she wasn't the only one afraid of what else they'd find. Something else niggled at her, deep and insistent. She thought about the time she'd opened her eyes to find herself standing on François's ship – had that been a warning?

The *Ship of Shadows*, bobbing softly on the water, all cosy with lantern light, was a comforting sight. Aleja and Frances climbed up the side of the ship and hopped on to the deck. The rest of the crew had already assembled there and Ermtgen had baked a cake. Aleja felt a pang when she looked at its icing, a bright and hopeful pink, then Tinta popped up at her heels and she smiled down at the shadow-squirrel. Farren and Velka winched up the rowing boat and the captain and Malika stepped out to address the pirates.

'It seems we were mistaken. We didn't find the second map piece,' Captain Quint said, calmer than Aleja felt. And definitely calmer than Malika, who was pacing, her midnight skirt whipping round with each turn she made like a storm. 'We also have company.'

At this Aleja glanced down at Tinta, who hopped up and perched on her boot. 'Were you trying to warn me?' Aleja asked her shadow in a tiny whisper. Tinta's squirrel tail twitched.

'Don't tell me François has found us again,' Olitiana said, eyeing Malika cutting a path across the deck again and again.

The captain inclined her head.

Velka exclaimed, Farren shook her head angrily, and Olitiana closed her eyes.

Tinta scurried up to Aleja's shoulder and huddled there. Aleja dipped her fingers into its shadowy body, just in case that same strange magic wrapped round her once more and whisked her away. If she could see François without his knowledge . . . She shivered at the thought, but it would help. She waited.

Nothing happened.

Captain Quint waved her hand, quietening them. 'He has also discovered the true location of the piece we sought tonight. It is imperative we claim it first.' Her expression turned as ferocious as Malika's and Aleja felt a sudden chill. 'Olitiana, Ermtgen, how are our supplies? We'll require enough for a long voyage.'

A spark of excitement flared up in Aleja and, despite their defeat, she couldn't help the smile that spread across her face at the promise of adventure.

'We have plentiful supplies,' Olitiana said, 'and more than enough barrels of fresh drinking water to last a month at sea.'

'I've been stockpiling the galley since we arrived in Ragusa,' Ermtgen added.

'Good. Aada, set a fresh course. We're setting sail.'

'Aye, Captain,' Aada said. She looked as if she'd been touched by moonlight with her pale skin, almost white hair and light-grey eyes. 'Where shall I chart the course to?'

Captain Quint looked to the skies, where Penumbra was floating in lazy circles on an updraught against the bright orb of the moon. She gave a loud whistle and held her arm out. The eagle owl immediately returned to the captain, swooping across the deck and settling on her arm. Captain Quint turned back to the waiting crew. 'China.'

The race was on.

## CHAPTER THIRTEEN

*A Hiding Place*

'All hands on deck,' Olitiana called out after Captain Quint had retreated to her quarters.

'Is it wise to cross oceans in winter?' Farren asked, glancing at Velka. 'The risk of storms –'

'We'll have to count on the shadows to protect us,' Olitiana said in a tone that brooked no argument. 'Now, we need to leave swiftly and quietly. Everyone to your posts.' The crew ran to their stations, everyone slotting into place like a well-oiled machine. 'Untie the dock lines. Weigh the anchor. Hoist the mainsail.' Olitiana turned to Frances and Aleja, pushing her sleeves up to reveal her owl tattoo on her right forearm. Now that they were leaving Ragusa, their merchant disguise was rolling back, baring them as pirates once more. Pistols and cutlasses were openly worn, the cloth draped over the magic kraken bells was removed, shadows surged around the deck. 'Be my eyes,' Olitiana ordered them.

'Aye, Quartermaster,' Frances said.

Aleja looked up at the impossibly high crow's nest. Once she had struggled to climb the netting as fast as Frances. Now she led the way. She climbed up until there was nothing between her and the stars. The fear of the pirate hunters and the taste of a brand-new adventure whirled together in her head. *China*. All she knew about China was that it was a huge country with a fascinating history as ancient as its mountains and rivers. She couldn't wait to dive into the library and find out more. She pulled herself into the basket, Frances jumping in after her, and the two of them stood back to back, spyglasses clamped on, scouring the harbour for François.

The lantern-lit ship crawled out of the harbour, gliding past other slumbering ships, its sails glowing in the moonlight. Tinta materialized through the bottom of the basket and took the form of a great seabird.

There was no sign of François or *La Promesse Lumineuse*. '¿Dónde estás?' Aleja muttered. *Where are you?*

'I can't see him either,' Frances said. 'Maybe he's in another harbour? That would explain why he hasn't seen our ship.'

The sails puffed up with wind as they inched away from Ragusa, its medieval fortifications lit up like a beacon. Aleja stretched out over the basket's rim to see round the curve of the city. 'There.' She trained her spyglass on the gilded ship, the shiniest one anchored there. Seeing it gave her a stab of fear. 'He's still in harbour.'

'Is he weighing anchor?' Frances asked anxiously.

'His sails are unfurling,' Aleja said, turning to exchange a panicked glance with Frances. 'They're setting sail, too.' She craned her neck for another look just as the *Ship of Shadows* swept out into the fresh sea wind, taking flight like an albatross. The Republic of Ragusa swung out of view, taking the pirate hunters' ship along with it.

'He'll never catch us now,' Frances said confidently, scurrying back down the netting to relay the information to Olitiana.

Aleja stayed in the crow's nest, keeping watch as they picked up speed and headed into deeper water. She felt a prickle of unease. How did François keep cropping up in the same places as them? They were lucky he hadn't spotted them. Almost *too* lucky . . . She felt she was missing some key information – something wasn't right here. Surely Raven couldn't be double-crossing them?

She held out her arm for Tinta to perch on. 'Show me François's ship,' she whispered to the shadow-bird, stroking its silhouette. Tinta ruffled its shadowy feathers and Aleja closed her eyes, thinking hard. But when she opened them again, she was still in the crow's nest.

That night Ermtgen cooked a humongous pot of macaroni and all the pirates sat round the wooden table in the galley, laughing and chatting as Ermtgen ladled out bowl after bowl of the creamy pasta. Aleja sat between Frances, who was shovelling macaroni into her mouth at an alarming rate, and Aada, who was weaving tales of wild narwhals in her native Arctic Norway.

'*Narhval*,' she told Aleja, who repeated it after her, committing the word to memory. 'It is quite something to witness a pod of them among the ice floes.'

'Just wait until we hit the Indian Ocean,' Farren said, leaning her elbows on the table opposite Aleja. She was wearing her red bandana and silver hooped earrings along with her two pistols, and her owlish face glowed happily now that they were back at sea. 'We'll probably find some whales there. Humpbacks or blue whales maybe.'

'I read that a blue whale's tongue is as big as an elephant!' Aleja said, unable to imagine seeing something that huge swimming peacefully alongside them.

'We've seen a kraken bigger than that!' Frances said, and half the pirates groaned. Aleja shuddered at the thought of kraken. The ship suddenly felt a lot smaller, rocking and creaking around them. Just a thin wooden shell between the pirates and the might of the ocean. Then Tinta grew from the fox perched round her ankles into a dolphin frolicking around the galley, and Aleja smiled to herself. She wasn't on any old ship; she was on a *magic* ship. Claws leaped up on to the table and sniffed Frances's pasta. Tinta popped up in front of him as a squirrel, waving its fluffy tail back and forth in front of the kitten. Claws lunged to catch it and Tinta raced up the galley wall.

Remembering the macaroni with a start, Aleja dug in. Velka, Farren and Griete were debating the merits of a complicated mathematical formula at one end of the scarred table, and Olitiana and Malika were sitting next to the captain at the other end, who was drinking rum and reminiscing about their last voyage to China. 'And then I said, that's not *your* sword!' the captain said, guffawing. Olitiana snorted with laughter.

Tinta ran under the table, Claws streaking after it. When Aleja looked down, she spotted Malika sneaking bits of fish to Penumbra, who was standing next to her chair, his beak reaching up to her knee. Aleja giggled quietly. Then she noticed Farren reach for Velka's hand, but a large thud on the table made her jump and she bobbed back up to see what it was.

Ermtgen had seated herself next to Malika and plonked down a bowl of oranges. 'I'll not be having any scurvy in my galley,' she said pointedly, eyeing them all, her grey hair frazzling out of her bun. Everyone reached to grab an orange in a hurry. Even the captain.

As Aleja peeled her orange and bit into the first segment, Frances leaned closer and whispered into her ear. 'I've just had the most brilliant idea.'

'Are you sure this is a good idea?' Aleja asked doubtfully, following Frances's frenzied plunge past the cabins.

'Sure it is!' Frances said, pushing open the door into the mask room, a bag of sweets in one hand. 'The best disguise of all is someone else's face. And if we're wearing *these* in Shanghai, François won't recognize us.' She swept a hand out at the large rectangular room lined with mannequins, each wearing a different – and very lifelike – face. Suits of armour wandered about by themselves and in one corner a wig of blue curls was trying to climb up the wall. Aleja shuddered. Only Frances and Malika tended to frequent this room; everyone else found it too eerie. Wearing one of the masks would turn you into a different person for an hour and Aleja had only tried it once to know she never wanted to do it again.

Frances turned to her. 'Honestly, I don't know why we didn't wear one of these in the heist in Ragusa. Or at the consul's party in Marrakesh. Or at the carnival,' Frances continued. Claws meowed at her and she set him down. At once he took off after the blue wig, which squeaked and tried to climb up a suit of armour that was stuck marching in a corner.

Aleja tore her eyes away. 'Because it slips off after only an hour? Or because you'd be too clumsy in someone else's body to fight or run? Or even walk?'

Frances waved her off. 'Small inconveniences.'

Aleja blinked. 'Is it just me or is it a bit . . . misty in here?' It was as if someone had suddenly dragged a layer of gauze over the room. She stared at it, realizing it was getting harder and harder to see.

Frances jerked her head up from examining a mask she held. She frowned at the ambling suits of armour, which were now being devoured by fog. Then her expression shifted. 'Oh no!' she wailed.

'Is – is the room vanishing?' Aleja yanked open the door, relieved that the rest of the ship was as solid as ever beyond it.

'But I don't want it to go,' Frances said, the mask still in her hands as Aleja dragged her out, Tinta hurrying in a shapeless blob at her side. 'Oh, bother,' Frances said grumpily as they watched the room – door and all – fade away, until they were left standing in the passageway, staring at nothing. Frances sighed. 'And I left my sweets in there.'

There was a pause and then Frances's bag of sweets was spat out into the air.

Frances looked down then grabbed Aleja. 'Claws!'

Aleja stared at her. 'He didn't come out?'

Frances ran towards the space where the room had been. Claws suddenly flew out of the air, all four legs stretched out, yowling. Frances gasped and caught him. Claws immediately ran off. 'Poor thing,' Frances said. She scowled at the empty passageway. 'I can't believe people stopped telling stories about that room. I hope the cave of shadows doesn't go next.'

'You still have the mask, though.' Aleja looked at Frances's now empty hands. 'Oh.'

'At least give us something good in return!' Frances told the ship, picking up her sweets and shoving them into a pocket.

Aleja bit back a smile at Frances's indignation. 'I don't think it works like that.'

A staircase suddenly appeared in front of them and Frances grinned. 'Aha!'

'That was a coincidence,' Aleja said, gaping.

The staircase was solid oak with huge scrolling banisters carved either side of it and wide steps. It led up into a hole in the ceiling that hadn't been there before. Next to the hole, a massive chandelier dangled down in tiers of shimmering crystals and candles. It bounced around with the motion of the ship, sending spangles of light darting around the staircase.

Aleja took a lantern off a hook on the wall and stepped on to the stairs at the same time as Frances. Tinta wisped into a shadow-rabbit that frolicked round her ankles. They ventured up the staircase, which gleamed with polish, and into . . . blackness.

'Did the lantern go out?'

Aleja heard the frown in Frances's words but couldn't see her. Couldn't see anything. Not even the light from the chandelier. She waved her hand over the lantern and felt the flames tickle her palm with heat. 'No, it must be the room.' They were standing in a darkness thick enough to gobble up every speck of light.

'Is it filled with shadows?' Frances bumped into Aleja. 'Oops, sorry.'

Aleja squinted into the dark, though it made no difference. 'There probably are shadows in here, but I think the darkness is something else. Some kind of magic.' She wished she could touch or hear Tinta just to make sure her little shadow was still by her side.

'What is this place?' Aleja heard Frances shuffle around and knock into something. 'There are shelves here!' she exclaimed.

Aleja felt her way round the perimeter of the room. It was smaller than she'd expected – the blackness seemed to stretch on forever, but they were in a small room, lined with empty shelves.

All at once, Aleja realized what the legendary pirate ship had rustled up for them. 'It's a hiding place.'

A voice boomed out at them. 'In my day pirates weren't lily-livered hiders; they were ferocious cutlass fighters!'

Aleja nearly dropped the lantern. 'Where did you hide your gold, then?' she asked Geoffrey once her heart had stopped racing.

There was a disapproving sniff and Geoffrey fell silent.

Not knowing if the ghost was still lurking in the darkness, Aleja and Frances left quickly.

## CHAPTER FOURTEEN

*Sailing, Sharks and Shadows*

In their first few days they sailed out of the Adriatic Sea and into the Mediterranean. It felt like an age until their planned stop in Melaka, Malaya, where Olitiana had announced they'd restock supplies en route to China. Aleja busied herself with another puzzle in Thomas James's book, which was now more important than ever with the owl clock counting down.

The book held four unsolved puzzles across four pages. One for each piece of the map. Luckily Quint had already known where the first piece was without the need for a clue, but now they were relying on the coded book. Yet every time Aleja sat down to try and work it out, something else happened. Sometimes it was Frances bursting into her cabin, Claws bundled up in her arms. At other times it was one of the other girls inviting her to a picnic up on deck or a midnight feast in the cave of shadows. And sometimes it was Aleja sitting in front of the book and staring at Tinta, her head crammed with questions she didn't know how to ask.

This time the sun was setting outside, sending a blaze of gold through Aleja's porthole and on to her carpet, where she lounged, studying the book. Tinta was curled up in a panther shape next to her.

'Mira,' Aleja said to her shadow. *Look*. 'I have two options. Either I try to solve the entire book before we reach China, or I figure out which page we need and focus on that.' Tinta cocked its head lazily at Aleja, who carried on voicing her thoughts. 'One page would be best. I've been trying to crack this book for months now and I haven't got anywhere.' She let out a puff of frustration. She flipped to the fourth page, which was a leaf of parchment covered in dots.

Her cabin door thudded open. '*There* you are,' Frances said impatiently. Claws ran in on her heels and over to Aleja. 'Ermtgen's baked us a cheesecake, and Velka's hung sheets and lanterns under Aada's cabin so we can sleep up on deck tonight!'

Aleja fussed Claws behind his ears until he purred. She glanced down at the page of dots. 'But –'

'Bring it with you,' Frances said, darting back out of the cabin and calling back, 'Come on!'

'Frances, wait!'

Frances poked her head back round the door and Aleja gestured at the book. 'We're already on our way and the clock in the library is counting down fast – what if I can't solve it?' she whispered. The sun had now set and her cabin was lit by the crackling and glowing storm-jars. Another day had sunk below the horizon. Another sweep of hands round one of the mysterious dials on the clock face.

Frances softened. 'It's not just *your* job to solve it,' she said, wandering back in. She picked up one of the shells Aleja had collected with Griete. It was pink and shiny in the storm-light. 'Remember how Griete got all excited about these shells? With the Fibosnacky sequence?'

'Fibonacci,' Aleja said automatically.

'Different people see different things. Maybe you should work on the book with someone else.'

Aleja stared up at her. 'You don't think I can solve it?' The words felt sticky in her throat.

Frances grinned. 'I think you can do anything, but everyone gets a bit stuck now and then. Maybe someone else will notice something that gets you . . . unstuck.' She scooped up Claws, who was climbing up a stack of books and batting at Tinta with a tiny paw. 'Now let's go. Ermtgen's cheesecake is the best thing you'll ever taste and I left it up there with Farren and Velka.' She looked worried. 'And I still need to fetch Griete . . .'

Aleja smothered her laugh. 'Go and rescue the cheesecake,' she said, grabbing the book. 'I'll get Griete.'

A few minutes later, she burst into Griete's cabin and explained her problem. 'I was wondering whether the dots were some kind of pattern,' Aleja finished. 'Maybe you can see something in them that I can't.'

Griete, who had been munching on a honey tart and cleaning the rust off a spanner while listening to Aleja, set her tart down. 'Let me see,' she said, wiping her fingers on a rag.

Aleja passed the book to her and looked around; she'd never been in Griete's cabin before. Her bunk had towers of silk pillows, and shelves beside it held tools, a collection of unfinished inventions and a battered stack of romance novels. Her desk was huge and covered in sweets, scraps of metal and velvet boxes of jewellery. Dishes overflowed with needles and pins, bright glass beads and turquoise feathers. Reams of silks were bursting out of her trunk, and her tool belt, cutlass and sword swung from hooks. Her cabin smelled of sugar and jasmine and grease. A white-painted wooden board was mounted on one wall and covered in neatly inked equations and sketches of strange circles. A language of numbers Aleja couldn't navigate. With a burst of hope she turned back to Griete.

Griete shook her head. 'Sorry, Aleja, I can't make out what this could be. Raven was always the best at figuring out puzzles and mysteries.'

Aleja nodded, biting back the secret she kept. 'Do you want to sleep up on deck tonight?' she asked instead. 'We have cheesecake.'

'Ooh, I hope it's vanilla,' Griete said, picking up an armful of silk pillows and wrapping a fluffy blanket round her like a cape.

Aleja dropped the book off in the library for someone else to have a turn and went up on deck, too. With every step she took her thoughts sank deeper and deeper, Griete's words echoing in her head. *Raven was always the best*. Did Frances think that too? Did everyone?

That night Aleja couldn't sleep. She lay awake in the glowing tentlike structure Velka had constructed, watching the sheets around them flutter like sails. After a while, she got up, smiled at seeing Claws fast asleep in Frances's arms, and wandered up the deck. Tinta trailed after her, half hidden by the night.

Olitiana was guiding the ship through the dark sea. She stood at the helm, the huge wooden wheel in her hands, her tri-cornered hat perched on top of her mass of hair, and smiled at Aleja. 'I'd missed being at sea,' she said. 'There's nothing like it.'

'Can you teach me how to steer the ship?' Aleja asked.

'Come and stand here,' Olitiana said, gesturing to the helm.

Aleja stood in front of her and Olitiana planted Aleja's hands on the wheel. 'The wheel is one of the most important things on the ship. Before you learn how to steer, you need to understand how it works. Take a good look at it.'

Aleja looked. It was polished wood with spokes jutting out around it. A second wheel was connected to it by a thick bar of wood with a coil of rope wound round it, the ends vanishing into two holes in the deck. 'The wheel is connected to the rudder outside the hull at the stern of the ship. When you turn the wheel starboard,' Olitiana said, using Aleja's hands to turn the wheel right, 'the left side of the rope pulls up, coiling round the wheel, and the right side drops below. When we steer port –' their hands turned left – 'the opposite happens.'

'Where do the ropes go?' Aleja asked, watching them move.

'Below decks, where they connect to the tiller, which moves the rudder. When we turn the wheel starboard, the ship moves starboard. Here, you have a turn.' Olitiana took her hands off the wheel and Aleja suddenly felt the entire power of the ship at her control. 'Relax your grip and keep the ship on a steady course,' Olitiana said, watching Aleja. 'Eyes on the horizon. That's it.'

*

Aleja began waking up early to take the wheel, steering the *Ship of Shadows* through the Mediterranean each day as dawn teased the horizon. It felt like a magical hour, when only she and Olitiana were awake and the slumbering ship was calm and still. But it never lasted for long, and those early mornings were chased by Malika's weapons training, which was an hour of clanging metal or the sulphurous bite of gunpowder. Then there were griddle cakes, best eaten hot, sugary and stacked to the sky, while the girls chatted and Tinta experimented with forms, a shadow-panther one moment, a dusky hippo the next. Aleja might sneak to the library or her cabin to take her turn in trying to decode the book before Olitiana set them all to work scrubbing the deck or cleaning the passageways. After dinner, their time was theirs and Aleja loved it best when they spent it together up on deck, laughing and telling stories, Claws and Tinta playing, Penumbra soaring up above the ship as the sunset glazed the sea with gold.

They passed a pleasant few days in this routine until something exciting happened to disrupt it.

One morning, Aleja had awoken to find land nestled close on either side of the ship. A new shadow, Anippe, had come aboard in the night to help guide them through the ancient waterways that ran through Egypt and into the Red Sea. She was a historian, a petite woman with light-brown skin and a headful of glossy black hair. She had dark eyes and a headscarf as blue as the sky trimmed in gold.

Over the next few days Aleja helped guide the ship through Egypt and chatted away to Anippe in Arabic, peppering their conversations with questions about her country and the pyramids (and mummies when Frances joined them – 'Is it true that mummies' brains are pulled out of their noses?' she'd asked in horrified glee). Anippe was friendly and patient and thrilled Frances when she'd informed her that the Ancient Egyptians worshipped cats. 'Did you hear that, Claws?' Frances had said, lifting the protesting kitten up. On those nights the pirates stayed up late in the galley, exchanging stories and laughter and memories over Ermtgen's Egyptian-inspired feasts held in Anippe's honour. Aleja missed her when they dropped her off, but not for long – the Red Sea was beckoning them.

'What's that?'

'What's what?'

Aleja pointed out the frothing water in their wake. Their ship often attracted curious sea life. Aleja's favourites were the dolphins that had leaped out of the water in playful patterns on their way to Ragusa. She often looked to see if there were any. Today she had glanced out to find several sleek dark shapes in the water, following the ship without coming up for air. Aleja shuddered and pulled her thick sleeves down over her fingers. Despite its warm climate, the Red Sea still had cool winter nights.

'Maybe they're sirens,' Frances said dubiously, looking at them.

Aleja stopped staring at the water to stare at Frances instead. 'Sirens are *real*?' Every time she thought she was used to the wild and wondrous magic that whispered through the world, a new surprise popped up.

'Oh yes.' Frances gave a knowledgeable nod and pushed her glasses up her nose, a signal she was about to break into a fresh story.

'They are real but incredibly rare,' Velka interrupted before Frances could string her imagination into words, 'and I wouldn't expect to see them in these waters.'

Frances shut her mouth, disappointed.

'Have you ever seen one?' Aleja asked Velka.

'No, but I'd like to.'

'Sirens are dangerous beasts.' Malika appeared behind them, drawn over by their interest in whatever was tailing the ship. 'I wouldn't recommend meeting one.'

'I thought sirens sang to lure men off their ships?' Aleja asked, her questions stacking up sky-high.

Malika gave a long-suffering sigh. 'Men always think they're special. Sirens aren't picky. Any human flesh will do.' She narrowed her eyes at the shadows underwater.

'Those aren't sirens, though. They're sharks.' With that she stalked off before Aleja could ask the rest of her questions.

The mention of sharks distracted Aleja and she leaned over the taffrail to get a closer look. But the taffrail was slick and Aleja slid further than she'd intended. She yelped and scrabbled to hold on, teetering over the edge. Tinta flew around her in a shapeless blob, too quick to take shape. The water loomed close and choppy.

Farren grabbed the back of her tunic and hauled her backwards. 'Careful –' she nodded at the sharks – 'they're even less picky than sirens.'

'Thanks,' Aleja said weakly, smoothing down her tunic.

Aada was the next person to float over to peer at the sharks. 'Some sailors say sharks sense death,' she said, her eyes orb-like. 'They follow ships when they know one of us will die soon, hopeful to get a bite out of the fresh corpse thrown overboard.'

This thought horrified Aleja more than the sharks.

'Let's get out of here,' Frances murmured to her and Aleja readily agreed.

The sharks stuck around for weeks. They tailed the *Ship of Shadows* out of the Red Sea and into the Indian Ocean as if they were hunting them. Their constant presence kept the pirates casting looks back, Aada's superstitions echoing around all of their minds. And then one day, as suddenly as they'd appeared, they were gone. Frances sighed in relief but Aleja found something eerie in the way they'd vanished. It was like they knew something worse was hurtling towards the *Ship of Shadows*.

## CHAPTER FIFTEEN

### *The Storm*

Aleja was flung on to her cabin floor.

She lay there for a moment, confused at what had woken her. Then she heard people racing past her door and Olitiana shout, 'All hands on deck!'

She rushed over to her porthole, her cabin tilting and swaying around her. Tinta shrank down into a moth that flapped at her face in a panic. Seconds later, that same panic seized hold of Aleja as she saw what was outside. Huge waves were stacked to the horizon. The ship lurched down, forcing her to hold on as a massive wave slammed into the ship, submerging Aleja's porthole until the ship rose again on a fresh wave.

All her books flew off their shelves – including Thomas James's. Aleja grabbed it and shoved it into her biggest pocket to keep it safe.

Automatically clutching the coin round her neck, Aleja struggled into her boots and wrenched her cabin door open. The lanterns lining the passageway were swinging madly and shadows flitted past, retreating deeper into the ship. Crashes and bangs echoed as everything on board was flung around. Doors opened and slammed and she heard Frances yell.

Aleja raced towards the sound. She found Frances inside Griete's cabin, shaking her awake.

'I'm up, I'm up,' Griete grumbled as Frances tossed her boots on to her bunk. She suddenly sighed and rubbed her eyes, muttering, 'I must be half asleep,' to herself.

Aleja turned. It was Raven's shadow. Her face was peering out behind a silken drape. Tinta flew over, flapping its shadow-wings at it until it seeped back into the wall. The ship gave a huge rattle, shaking Aleja back to her senses.

'Come on.' Aleja grabbed Frances, who was staring at where Raven's shadow had been, and pulled her into the passageway. 'They need help.'

Frances blinked. 'We haven't hit a storm this big since –' She was cut off as the ship gave a bone-shaking jolt and smashed into another wave, knocking them both over. 'Never,' she said instead, her eyes huge.

'*Dios*,' Aleja whispered to herself as they got back to their feet and raced over to the ladder. Velka and Farren were running and tugging their boots on behind them.

They emerged into chaos. The horizon was invisible through the thick grey hemming them in. Rain thundered down and the water-coated deck was treacherous. Captain Quint was battling through the storm at the helm, steering the might of the ship away from it. 'We have to get out of the storm's path,' she yelled as another monstrous wave loomed.

Aleja ran across the deck to the mainsail, where Olitiana was struggling alone. Aada rushed over too and between the three of them they furled it before the storm could shred it. The mainsail was thick and heavy and the wind kept trying to rip the ropes out of their hands. Aleja held tight until Farren ran over with more ropes and the four of them secured it.

Aleja peered through the rain to see Frances and Griete furling the smaller sails higher up. Ermtgen and Malika were securing the rest of the ship, tying everything down. The deck bucked and Aleja skidded across it. Tinta flapped at her, struggling through the wind. 'Go below decks,' Aleja shouted at it, grabbing on to the boom to steady herself.

Velka materialized out of the gloom. 'Tie yourself to the ship,' she shouted, flinging a bundle of ropes at Aleja. Aleja scrambled to separate them, handing half to

Frances and Griete as they clambered back down the netting. They tied themselves to the mast. But Aleja's fingers were stiff and wet and she fumbled, dropping the rope. The water cascading over the deck stole it away at once and another wave crashed down around them.

Tinta flapped harder, fighting its way to Aleja's shoulder. She clamped a hand over it, even though she knew that wouldn't, couldn't, do anything. The ship groaned under the ocean's attack. Aleja shut her eyes and clung on to the mast as hard as she could. The icy wave rushed across the deck and hit Aleja, loosening her grip. A spear of lightning shot through the sky and a great crack of thunder bellowed directly above. Aleja scrabbled to hold on tighter as another wave swelled before them, her feet sliding on the slanting deck.

*The book!*

She suddenly realized it was still in her pocket. She blinked through the rain at the nearest barrels, which were roped to the ship, and half ran, half skidded over to one. She yanked the lid off, sighing in relief when she saw its sparkling contents: jewels. *The book will be safe in here*, she thought, putting it inside to keep dry.

When the next bolt of lightning illuminated the ship, Aleja saw Captain Quint turning the prow into the storm, struggling to sail through the raging waters.

She staggered to the helm to help. But thunder and lightning raged above her and she began to slide down the deck. When she shouted for help, the storm devoured her voice. In another flash she saw the captain reaching out for her. Quint pulled her towards the wheel and Aleja hung on, desperately looking for Tinta. So far she'd never seen her little shadow get hurt by anything, but she'd never witnessed a storm like this and she couldn't help worrying. Could shadows be killed? Why had she never thought to ask?

The next wave rolled over them.

'We need to turn her a notch starboard!' Captain Quint yelled.

Gulping in air and blinking the water out of her eyes, her hair plastered over her face, Aleja added her weight to the wheel. A tiny shadow-moth fluttered weakly back up and perched on Aleja's nose. 'Go below decks!' she told Tinta, her stomach clenching at the rain gushing down the shadow, turning its edges droopy. '*Please!*' Instead Tinta flapped to her shoulder and vanished up her sleeve.

Aleja helped the captain steer the ship. She tried to remember everything Olitiana had taught her, but she'd practised sailing on calm waters, not through a raging storm. The ropes moaned and strained and panic trickled down Aleja's neck along with the rain – what if they snapped? Then Captain Quint cursed and Aleja suddenly realized the deck was moving strangely. She jerked her head up just as the entire ship hurtled down sideways into the ocean.

The *Ship of Shadows* was capsizing.

## CHAPTER SIXTEEN
*Skull and Crossbones*

Aleja stared at the ocean rushing up towards them. Tinta flew out of her sleeve and Aleja tried to wrap her fingers round it, wanting it nearby. There was a sickening swirl, and suddenly everything was calm and blue and peaceful.

Aleja blinked. She was back on the gleaming deck of *La Promesse Lumineuse*.

She turned round. Raven was standing before her. 'Raven!' Aleja cried out. 'I don't know what's happening to me but –'

She fell silent. Raven couldn't hear her.

The dark-haired girl glanced over her shoulder before sneaking into the captain's quarters. Aleja swallowed and followed her. Walking felt strange. She couldn't feel her feet on the deck but she kind of floated in the right direction as if she were walking through a dream. When she entered the Fury's quarters, Raven was desperately rifling through the papers on his desk. Aleja crept closer to look but at that very moment she felt a great lurch as she was whisked back to the *Ship of Shadows*. Which was still falling.

Aleja screamed as she flew down the deck, heading straight for the open ocean. She knew if she fell into those writhing waters, there'd be no rescuing her. She'd be lost forever. A sudden pinch round her ankles made her slam down on to the deck. A white-faced Frances was holding on to her. Digging her nails into the sodden planks, Aleja watched the *Ship of Shadows* fall down, down, down.

'Brace yourselves!' Captain Quint shouted.

The ship paused for a heart-shattering second, its wooden bones creaking a protest, the crew hanging on to it.

A few barrels of treasure cracked under the pressure, and precious jewels arced into the water like glittering rain. Others broke free of their ties and began to roll.

'No!' Aleja shouted.

The barrel she'd put the coded book into to keep it safe and dry was tumbling faster and faster across the deck. She struggled to free herself from Frances, to try to stop it somehow, but Frances held on tighter. 'Don't be stupid!' she yelled at her.

One by one the barrels fell into the ocean. Aleja gave a choking cry. The ship shuddered as if it knew something terrible had just happened. Then a whispering sigh rushed round the edge of the deck.

In a flicker of lightning Aleja saw shadowy tendrils wisp across the deck and wrap round the taffrail. More and more shadows gathered, streaming up from the lower decks like a river of night. They surrounded the deck, forming a protective barrier, and the ship began to right itself.

Aleja slid back into the helm, Frances crashing into it alongside her. Captain Quint pulled them both up. Aleja stared at the shadows in wonder. And then the kraken bells rang.

'Not again,' Frances moaned. 'I've only just forgotten what the last one smelled like.'

Aleja had not forgotten. Neither had she forgotten how terrifying their last battle with the sea monster had been. But all she could think was *I lost the book*.

The bells didn't ring again.

'Just a kraken brushing past, nothing to worry about!' Captain Quint called out cheerfully. The sky sparked to life with a roll of distant thunder, lighting up the captain, drenched and holding on to her hat with a kraken-sized grin, steering them away. Aleja suspected she'd secretly enjoyed the storm. Which made what she had to tell her much, much harder.

The shadows slipped across the ship and back below decks. The pirates watched them recede in silence. Captain Quint doffed her hat to them.

'I didn't know they could do that,' Aleja said in an aside to Frances. She wondered once more what gave the shadows their magic and why they couldn't leave the ship.

'It's the first time I've seen it,' Frances whispered, wide-eyed, fumbling to dry her glasses.

Aleja squeezed her hand. 'Thank you for saving me. Again.'

Frances smiled. 'Who would I tell all my stories to if you drowned?' She paused, more serious. 'I saw what happened, Aleja. You need to tell Quint now so we can look for it.'

The mountainous peaks slumped down into watery hills as the ocean slowly calmed and the storm began to fade into the background like a bad dream. Before they could sail too far away, Aleja went to the captain.

'I lost Thomas James's book,' she told her in a small voice.

Captain Quint stared at Aleja.

'I'm so sorry. I brought it up on deck, so I put it into a barrel to keep it safe and when they fell overboard –' Aleja swallowed, imagining the coded book lost in the ocean. The rest of the map forever a mystery.

'Olitiana, Malika, lower the rowing boat,' Captain Quint snapped. 'Search the seas.' She turned the wheel, steering them back.

Farren was looking through a spyglass. 'There's a ship there,' she said before the captain's orders could be acted upon. 'We must have drifted further than we'd thought in the storm – look.' She passed it to Olitiana.

'Aye, looks like they've found our bounty,' Olitiana said grimly. 'They're hauling up barrels.'

Aleja scrambled for a spyglass to see for herself. One of the barrels was glimmering in the sunlight – their lost jewels! 'They must have the book then,' she said.

'You'd better hope they don't realize what they've found,' Captain Quint growled, glaring through her own spyglass. 'That's the Pirate Lord's ship. But if he's got it, we can retrieve it. Unfurl the sails!'

But Olitiana shook her head. 'After using that much magic, you know too well it will be impossible to match their speed. We'll never catch his galleon now.'

Captain Quint cursed. 'Then this will have to wait. Resume our course to China, by way of Melaka. We cannot allow François to get there first.' She rubbed her forehead with a knuckle. 'We'll locate the Pirate Lord when the map piece is in our possession. The book's pages will be concealed now it's off the ship – protecting its secret. The map remains our priority.'

Aleja's eyes prickled. She stared at the deck. This was all her fault.

Aleja was drenched, her clothes stiff with salt. She trudged miserably into her cabin. Tinta sat on her desk and poked up a small nose at her.

'*Mi ratoncito*,' Aleja said, stroking the shadow. *My little mouse.* It stood up on its hind legs and twitched its whiskers at her. 'What are you trying to show me?' Aleja asked it, her fingers trembling as she stroked it. 'I saw Raven again. Are these visions things that are really happening?' Tinta twitched its whiskers more frantically. Aleja breathed in sharply. 'Is that a yes?' She waited for another sign but Tinta was still. She sighed. 'I wish you could talk. I don't even know if you understand me . . . but if you can, Tinta, I'm scared. I accidentally lost the book and now the captain's cross with me.' Tinta ran on to Aleja's lap and nestled close to her. 'Can you show me a vision of the Pirate Lord? I need to see if he's got the book.' She waited but nothing happened. Tinta peered up at her like it was worried and Aleja wished she could hug it. She stared fiercely at the little shadow-mouse. 'I'm going to find out how François can carry shadows off the ship and then we'll always be together.'

Tinta laid its shadow-head on Aleja's hand.

Aleja yanked her clothes off with numb fingers and dried herself. She pulled on her warmest trousers and a thick jumper that Griete had knitted for her and padded to the galley.

Fighting a storm was hungry work and she wasn't surprised to see half the crew already there. Ermtgen had returned to her stove and was now busy frying up stacks and stacks of hot griddle cakes. Frances was first in line, her plate already mountained with griddle cakes and scattered with sugar. They smelled delicious and Aleja's stomach rumbled. She grabbed a plate and joined the line behind Farren, shooting her a nervous look – was everyone angry at her for losing the book?

Farren passed her a fork. 'Stop worrying,' she said. 'It was an accident. And in a storm like that everyone panics and makes mistakes.'

Aleja bit her lip. She wasn't sure Captain Quint would agree.

'We'll get it back, just you wait and see.' Farren winked and went to sit with Velka.

'There you are,' Ermtgen said, stacking Aleja's plate as high as possible. The top griddle cake began to slip down the tower and Aleja nudged it back up. Ermtgen added thick slices of butter and several large spoonfuls of sugar on top and Aleja went to sit beside Frances, her eye on the butter melting down her griddle cakes and the sugar glittering in the lantern light. Even Frances was too exhausted to speak and the pair of them sat there and ate and ate and ate until they couldn't manage another bite.

Aleja flung a bucket of water over the deck and scrubbed it until it foamed clean. Beside her, Frances picked up another glob of seaweed with a disgusted expression and added it to her bucket. Aleja was privately glad she'd been assigned to scrub the deck; Frances's bucket stank of fish guts and seaweed from the storm debris. They'd already spent the morning pumping out water from the bilges – weapons training had been cancelled in favour of getting rid of the water the ship had taken on in the storm – and Aleja's arms ached. Captain Quint hadn't punished her for losing the book but she'd barely spoken to her other than ordering her to clean, and Aleja hadn't stopped worrying since.

The horizon was blue once more, with tiny islands dotted along it. Aada had informed her they were skirting the Maldives and Aleja couldn't stop staring as they nudged closer. Frances glared at the sky as if it was brewing another storm. They had sailed into a patch of the Indian Ocean with turquoise water so clear you could see straight down to the coral reefs. Brightly coloured fish swam by and, as the islands neared, Aleja kept pulling out her spyglass to gaze at their white-sand beaches.

'I wish we could stop,' she said for the thousandth time, desperate to swim in that water and wondering what it would feel like to sink her toes into the sand.

'Haven't you seen the clock?' Frances asked, sitting back on her heels to watch Claws stalk towards a clump of seaweed.

Aleja snapped her spyglass down. 'No, why?'

Frances grimaced. 'It's running down. Fast. Griete and Farren are in the library now, calculating how long we have left but . . .' She looked behind her before dropping her voice to a whisper. 'We'd better hope the last two pieces of the map are a lot closer than this one or we won't have time to get them, and then who knows what will happen.'

Aleja's guilt flared. She brushed her fingers against the coin at her neck. 'I delayed us even more by losing the book.'

Frances flapped a hand at her. 'It was an *accident*. Everyone knows that and Quint'll come round, you'll see.'

Aleja frowned at the sails. They were practically crawling along as the ship rekindled its magic. The shadows seemed to be hiding and even Tinta was nowhere to be seen.

She thought about the book, about how it worked as the key to the ship, unlocking rooms and puzzles hidden on board. Aleja wondered if it was worth searching the ship itself in the absence of the book. Maybe then Captain Quint would be impressed with her again.

Claws reached out a paw and touched the seaweed. He jumped a foot in the air and ran behind Frances, who laughed.

Aleja managed a weak smile. 'What do you think will happen when the clock runs down?'

Frances shrugged. 'No clue. But it can't be good, can it? Maybe the ship will magically explode.'

Aleja stared at her in alarm. 'Or if it's linked to the map, maybe the other map pieces will vanish or something . . .'

'Let's hope we're sailing at full speed again soon. Before Quint loses it even *more*,' Frances said.

When the sun sank down in the sky, it set the world aglow. Aleja sat on a barrel of grog on the upper deck to watch by herself. But she wasn't alone for long. Penumbra rustled his wings and flew up on to the tip of the mast, where he stretched his wings out against the pink sky. Tinta shifted into a great albatross beside Aleja as they watched the sunset together. Griete soon ambled up to watch with them, Claws sleeping in her arms, followed by Frances with a tin of biscuits, Velka with her iguana, Peridot, and Farren with a fiddle.

'I didn't know you could play,' Aleja said as Farren stood with one boot on the rigging.

Farren winked. 'Don't get used to it.'

Frances handed out the biscuits and Farren broke into a sea shanty of murder and mutiny. Griete harmonized with her and Aleja admired her singing voice – the last time *she'd* sung anything her father had joked she sounded like a drowned cat. Her fingers fell to the coin at her neck. Sometimes she heard her mother singing her to sleep in her dreams. She didn't know if that was memory or imagination, and her family wasn't here to ask.

Aleja's gaze drifted out to sea as they neared another white-sand tropical island. But this particular island already had company. A large galleon was in its waters. Its sails were black.

Aleja scrambled for her spyglass. The ship had a flag hoisted high. On it was a skull and crossbones.

## CHAPTER SEVENTEEN

### *The* Cursed Cutlass

Aleja gaped at the flag. Could she be so lucky? 'Sails!' she shouted, interrupting Farren's shanty.

Frances appeared by her side. 'Where?'

Aleja handed her the spyglass and turned to the others. 'It's another pirate ship,' she said. 'Do you think it's the Pirate Lord? Have we caught him up?' Hope fizzed in her stomach and Tinta hopped up and down at her side as a rabbit.

Farren ran for the captain.

'It *is* the Pirate Lord,' Captain Quint said a few agonizing minutes later, peering through her spyglass. She snapped it down and put it in her pocket. Penumbra flew down from the mast to sit on her wrist guard.

Now that Aleja wasn't storm-weary and panicked, she remembered reading about him back in Sevilla. One of her favourite books, *The Most Dangerous Pirates Who Sail the Seas*, had called him 'an elusive but masterful treasure hunter'.

Malika fingered her scimitar. 'Their galleon is anchored. I suggest we wait until dusk before making our move.' She smiled, her scars stretching across her face.

Aleja almost felt sorry for the other pirates. Almost.

'It's sitting heavy in the water; it must be loaded with treasure besides ours,' Aleja said, thinking out loud.

The other pirates stiffened like hunters catching sight of prey. Penumbra let out a shriek and nipped the captain's ear.

'We don't have time,' Captain Quint said. 'I know we need the book but the clock is moving and François –'

Olitiana interrupted the captain. 'François also doesn't have the book, but nor do we want him to discover it if other pirates are gossiping about it. Reclaiming it is a matter of urgency.' Frances sucked in a breath at her side. 'Besides which, François appears to be magically funded. Whereas we are running low, as I warned you in Ragusa. Even more so since we lost several barrels of jewels.'

Captain Quint surveyed her, her face a blank mask. Penumbra ruffled his feathers. 'The map comes first.'

'We won't find the rest of the map if we don't have either the book or the treasure to fund sailing over the world looking for it,' Olitiana snapped back. 'Not to mention paying your crew who faithfully follow you around countless lands in your quest. Would you repay them by neglecting their wages?'

Captain Quint rubbed her temple. 'I suppose we are the fastest ship on the seas,' she said at last, 'or we will be soon again.' She patted the mast. 'Maybe a short rest will help it recover faster. All right. Let's get our book back.'

Olitiana steered them out of sight behind the island. There they readied the rowing boats and awaited nightfall. When the island was bathed in velvety moonlight, Aleja slid her dagger into her boot, strapped a cutlass to her waist and hopped into one of the boats. Farren, her pistols at her hips, leaped in after her, along with Frances and the captain. Malika, Griete and Aada took the other boat while the others stayed to guard the ship. Captain Quint paused to consider Aleja. 'There's no need for you to join us if you'd rather stay.'

Aleja's face burned. 'No,' she said firmly. 'I made a mistake and I'm going to fix it.'

Captain Quint nodded and took up the oars. There was a familiar gleam in her eyes.

The water rippled like silk as they rowed round the island. When Aleja glanced back, she saw Tinta waiting on the taffrail for her. The air was balmy and warm, and Aleja let her fingers trail in the water, wishing she'd had time to take a dip in it.

The pirate galleon was huge and hulking. It had three masts, rows of gun decks and a mermaid skeleton carved into its bow. THE CURSED CUTLASS was painted on the side. Aleja's fingers grazed her coin as they approached.

The captain and Farren tied their boat to the ship quickly and quietly. Further up, Griete and Aada were doing the same.

Laughter, cheering and the odd burst of song wafted out of the creaking ship. It blazed with lantern light. Captain Quint nodded and, as one, Aleja, the captain, Frances, Malika and Aada silently climbed up the side of the ship. Like a shadow, Aleja clambered up the curving hull until she reached the taffrail, where they all stopped. With just her eyes peeking over, Aleja surveyed the deck. The *Cursed Cutlass* was anchored, and it sounded as if most of the crew were below decks. Other than a single pirate keeping guard, it was empty. They clearly hadn't expected the *Ship of Shadows* to find them.

Malika vaulted over the taffrail. Silent as a secret, she slunk up to the guard and struck him on the head with the hilt of her scimitar. He fell down, unconscious.

Aleja and the others launched over the taffrail and on to the deck.

Malika's eyes glittered. 'Dead men tell no tales.' She raised her scimitar above the guard and brought it crashing down.

Aleja winced but Captain Quint lashed out, her cutlass a blur, and blocked Malika's blow. 'They leave evidence, though.'

Disappointment flitted across Malika's face.

'D'you think that's because she used to be an assassin?' Frances whispered loudly to Aleja.

Aleja batted her away. 'Shh!'

On the deck were the remains of the barrels from the *Ship of Shadows*. A loose sapphire glittered, stuck between the planks.

Aada dragged the guard behind a barrel. 'His crew will think he drank too much grog,' Captain Quint chortled. 'No one will know we were ever here. Now. Where is my book?'

Malika tightened her headscarf and gestured to Frances. Aleja watched the two of them steal down a ladder below decks, in search of Thomas James's book. Her heart thumped, hoping desperately they'd find it. Aleja, Aada and the captain were left to keep watch on deck. Farren and Griete were minding the rowing boats and keeping an eye on the water.

It was hard not knowing what was happening below decks. 'Should we go and help them?' Aleja asked Aada, who was holding her battleaxe and staring up at the moon.

'Too many of us would be more likely to attract unwanted attention,' she said.

Captain Quint busied herself with pacing the deck. 'Their ship isn't as clean as ours,' she said to herself, running a finger over the taffrail.

A few minutes later, a sack popped out above the ladder. Aleja ran over to help Frances heave it out. Seconds later, Malika appeared with a second sack.

'And the book?' Captain Quint asked impatiently.

Frances held it up. 'Got it!'

Aleja felt a rush of relief. She grinned at Frances. Quint put it into a large pocket and patted it. 'Excellent.'

They worked together to lower the sacks on to one of the rowing boats, which Griete immediately rowed back to the *Ship of Shadows*.

Before the captain could object, Frances and Malika disappeared back below decks.

'How did you recognize the Pirate Lord's ship?' Aleja asked.

'I make it my business to know the most notorious pirates who sail the seas,' Captain Quint said, her voice a little muffled as she stuck her head into a barrel. 'Aha! I found a secret stash.' She reappeared with her hat knocked askew and a dusty bottle of rum.

Frances and Malika emerged with more sacks groaning with treasure. Before they could be loaded on to the rowing boat, there was a sudden roar.

Pirates streamed up on to the deck, yelling and brandishing cutlasses.

Aleja drew her own cutlass in a hurry. She saw Farren vault over the taffrail, pistol already in hand, then the first cutlass clashed against the captain's and she felt a wave of panic. A man came at her, growling and baring gold teeth. Aleja raised her cutlass and waved it menacingly at him. At her side, Frances grabbed handfuls of treasure and flung them into the men's eyes. Aada whirled through the fight wielding her axe and Malika was a storm of destruction with her scimitar. If they could be brave, then so could she, Aleja decided. The man swung his cutlass at her.

Aleja jumped back. Again and again he dived for her and Aleja danced out of the way each time. Until he began panting and sweating in the balmy night and she sensed her opportunity. Arcing her cutlass high above, she looped it round and brought it crashing down on his with a deft flick of her wrist at the end that sent his cutlass flying out of his hands. Aleja quickly kicked it away. The man gaped at her. Aleja growled back at him. He backed away in a hurry. Before Aleja could smile, she heard someone sneak up on her from behind.

She spun round, swinging her cutlass down fast. The boy she'd attacked took a startled step back, fumbling to block her with his cutlass. He looked down at her and froze.

'Aleja? ¿Qué haces aquí?' *What are you doing here?*

Aleja gasped. 'Pablo?'

It was her brother.

He gave her a cheeky grin and lowered his cutlass. Pablo was two years older than Aleja and a head taller. His olive skin was as sun-bronzed as hers, his hair wild, and he wore striped trousers with a shirt and bright-red sash. His ear was scarred from where she'd bitten it during a particularly nasty argument years ago. All around them, the pirate battle raged on.

The door to the captain's quarters slammed open.

Still gripping her cutlass, Aleja tore her eyes away from her brother to glance at the Pirate Lord. He was tall and broad, with light-brown skin and dreadlocks falling past his shoulders. His jacket was black and gleaming with gold, and blades were stuffed into the wide belt he wore.

'Avast!' His shout boomed out across the deck like a cannon shot. The battle paused.

His piercing glare raked the pirates, their weapons stilled, mid-fight. His huge crew outnumbered that of the *Ship of Shadows*, but, as Aleja looked around, she realized her fellow pirates were holding their own.

The Pirate Lord's gaze fell on Captain Quint. 'Ah, Elizabeth. I might have known this was your doing.'

Aleja and Pablo looked at each other in disbelief. Aleja felt a tug of betrayal – Quint hadn't said she knew him personally. Had she stopped trusting Aleja?

Captain Quint sauntered over to him, twirling her cutlass in her hand. 'Hullo, Bancroft, you old marauding cur. You ought to have known better than to rob us in a treacherous squall. Surrender your treasure and my girls might let you live to tell the tale.'

The Pirate Lord tipped his head back and roared a laugh.

Captain Quint waited patiently for him to finish. 'Very well then,' she said mildly. 'Shadows, take no man alive.'

Aleja raised her cutlass. Pablo looked alarmed. Frances swung her cutlass in the air, eyeing Aleja and Pablo with interest. Aada lifted her axe with a cry and Farren aimed her pistols.

'Very nice, Elizabeth, but you're still vastly outnumbered,' the Pirate Lord said.

Malika materialized behind the Pirate Lord as if she'd stepped out of thin air. She laid her scimitar against his neck.

'Wait,' he commanded.

Captain Quint arched an eyebrow at him.

He grinned, revealing several golden teeth, and spread his hands. 'Elizabeth, I know you too well. You're robbing me blind to distract me from that rather interesting book of yours. The one that's now missing from my quarters.'

'I have no idea what you're referring to,' Captain Quint said.

Aleja's fingers tightened round her cutlass hilt.

'Did you ever tell your crew how we met?' the Pirate Lord asked, as if Malika's scimitar wasn't still pressed to his throat.

Aleja and Frances exchanged curious looks.

'I met Elizabeth in Persia,' he continued. 'I was just about to sell a priceless yellow diamond, the Light of a Thousand Stars, to the shah when I stumbled across your captain about to be hanged for crimes of piracy.'

Aleja stole a look at Captain Quint.

'I would never have been hanged,' Quint said with a dismissive snort. 'I had a dagger stashed down my shirt. I was seconds away from cutting myself free and making a dash for it.'

The Pirate Lord grinned at her. 'After my daring rescue, your captain repaid me by running away with the Light of a Thousand Stars one night and setting sail before I could catch her. And since then I've been trying to get it back.'

'Brilliant,' Frances said in awe.

'Amazing,' Aleja whispered.

Captain Quint leaned towards him. 'And you can keep trying for all the good it will do you. It's mine.'

The Pirate Lord suddenly moved his hand, fast as a snake, and grabbed the bottle of rum poking out of Quint's pocket. 'Like this?' He uncorked it with his teeth and took a swig.

'Does this little story have a purpose?' Captain Quint asked impatiently.

'Ah, I'm glad you asked that. Yes. Return the Light of a Thousand Stars and I'll turn a blind eye to whatever you're up to with that book of yours.'

Malika pressed the blade of her scimitar harder against his throat.

He winced.

'Surrender,' Malika said. 'Or I will take your life.'

'Fine,' the Pirate Lord growled. 'But, mark my words, the day will come when we rob you back. And I will find out what you're up to.'

Captain Quint's smile was slow. 'We'll be waiting for you when you do.'

Cutlasses were begrudgingly lowered and pistols tucked away. The *Cursed Cutlass*'s pirates grumbled and stood around the deck wearing sulky expressions as Captain Quint vaulted off the galleon into the rowing boat.

Frances jerked her head at Pablo and whispered, 'That one keeps looking at you strangely.'

'He's my brother,' Aleja said.

Frances's mouth fell open.

Aada and Malika sauntered after Captain Quint with suspiciously bulging pockets.

Pablo gave Aleja a rueful grin but Aleja still had a hundred questions tumbling around her head and that didn't answer any of them, so she grabbed his arm and whispered, 'Meet me on the beach before sunrise.' She didn't know exactly what hour it was but she'd been a pirate long enough to read the time in the sky, and the first hints of dawn were already pinkening the horizon.

He nodded and melted back into the Pirate Lord's crew. Most of their crew went below decks but Aleja noticed a significant number of guards had now been posted on deck. Her lips twitching, she climbed back over the taffrail.

'How are you going to climb with your hands full?' Aleja asked Frances, who was climbing down at her side, a collection of gemstones in each fist.

'By being spectacularly talented,' Frances said as she inched down.

Aleja looked down. 'We're a bit far off from the rowing boat; we'll have to climb sideways.'

Frances sighed. Her glasses slid down her nose and she jerked her head to jolt them back up. They flew off her face. 'No!' Frances cried, trying to grab them. The jewels in her hands fell like sparkling raindrops and her glasses vanished into the sea with a splash.

'Why didn't you tie them round your neck?' Aleja said.

'I only do that for swimming!'

Aleja climbed down faster. 'Don't worry, we'll find them.'

'But I can't see!'

Aleja glanced across just in time to see Frances miss her footing. She tumbled down the side of the ship and plunged straight underwater. Aleja waited for her to bob up again. No one in the rowing boat seemed to have noticed – they were talking among themselves.

Frances didn't reappear. Her heart thudding, Aleja let go of the ship and jumped in after her.

The water rushed over her head. Aleja blinked hard, trying to clear her eyes. Frances was floundering nearby. Aleja swam over and tugged her up, but she was heavy. Too heavy. Frances urgently gestured at her foot, bubbles streaming from her mouth as she shouted. Her trouser leg was caught in the anchor chain. Aleja dived deeper and pulled at Frances's leg until it loosened, and Frances was freed. She kicked up to the surface. Aleja was about to follow when something glimmered at her a little lower down the chain. She swam hard and fast towards it, hoping and hoping. With a big smile she plucked the object from the chain and swam up, her lungs bursting. She popped up beside Frances and waved her glasses. 'I found them!' she said, gulping down air and beaming with pride.

Frances's eyes were red. 'Thank you,' she said, holding tightly on to them. 'I don't know what I would have done without these.' She looked panicked at the thought. Aleja wanted to hug her but Captain Quint chose that moment to appear in the rowing boat and hauled them in.

Aleja was first off the rowing boat and up on to the ship, where she found Tinta pacing in its girl form. 'I'm back – but I have something I need to do,' she whispered to it.

'Where have you been?' Griete asked, running over with Velka. Olitiana rushed over, one hand on her cutlass as Frances and the other pirates climbed over the taffrail. 'We were about to come after you,' she said.

'We got the book!' Frances said happily, dripping on to the deck.

The shadows rippled round the edges of the ship. They were wispier than usual and didn't take shape – Aleja guessed they were still overtired. Penumbra was circling high above, searching for Captain Quint. When she reappeared, Penumbra hurtled down from the skies with a shriek and settled on her shoulder.

'Yes, the book is once more in our possession,' she said, 'but it has interested the Pirate Lord. We'd better hope he doesn't decide to act upon that interest.' With that she disappeared into her quarters.

Aleja waited until the attention had redirected on to the sacks of treasure that Olitiana and Griete were sorting through. Then she took Frances aside. 'Don't let Quint set sail until I'm back,' she said.

Frances's eyes widened. 'Where are you going?'

'To find out how my brother became a pirate.'

## CHAPTER EIGHTEEN

*The Golden Lantern*

Aleja sneaked over the taffrail, clambering back down the side of the ship. She entered the warm water with a splash and swam for the tropical island. Though it was nearly morning, the water was still bathed in moonlight and little fish and turtles swam past her. When the water became too shallow to swim, she stood up and walked on to the white sand. It shone like a pearl. Palm trees rustled behind her, the jungle at the heart of the island humming with a life of its own. Aleja wandered up and down the beach, digging her toes into the silky sand and hoping Pablo would come soon. She kept casting glances back at the *Ship of Shadows*, checking to make sure it was still there. The moon drifted across the sky.

A sudden splash had her whipping her spyglass out and training it on the water. It was Pablo.

'So how did my little sister become a pirate?' he asked, ambling up the shore.

Aleja laughed. 'That's what I was going to ask you!'

Pablo grinned. 'I was jealous of you going off on an adventure.' He sat beside her on the sand. 'I never guessed you ran away on a pirate ship! Though you always were the wild one.' He tapped the ear she'd nearly bitten through.

Aleja's smile felt too tight on her face. She touched her coin. 'When I left, were Padre and Abuela angry or –'

Pablo shook his head. 'I write to them often. Miguel is happy, and now they've heard from you they've stopped worrying. They still miss you, of course,' he said, nudging her. 'But anyone could see you were destined for the sea. I went not long after you did – just as a shipmate to start with, then I hopped ships when the Pirate Lord docked nearby.'

'Being a shipmate too boring for you?'

Pablo pulled a face. 'They made me clean out the bilges.'

Aleja laughed. 'Pirates have to clean too!'

Pablo's eyes lit up. 'But not as much and there's better food. And a *lot* more treasure. At least the treasure makes up for sleeping in a hammock below decks –

it was much worse, crammed in with all the other shipmates.' He shuddered.

Aleja tried not to laugh. 'Want to be even more jealous?'

Pablo narrowed his eyes.

Aleja stretched back on the sand. 'I have an entire cabin to myself.'

He groaned and flicked some sand at her. '*Qué suerte.*' *How lucky.*

Aleja felt even smugger when she told him about the hunt for her in Sevilla last summer, when she'd discovered counterfeit coins, and the places she'd been since. She was careful not to mention the magic map or Tinta. Some things were too secret to share, even with her brother. When she noticed the first rays of sun breaking over the horizon, she stood up in a hurry, brushing sand off her damp trousers.

'I'm a pirate. But, first and foremost, I'll always be your brother,' Pablo said, serious for possibly the first time in his life. She looked at him and an impish grin wandered over his face. 'Though I am going to rob you back.'

Aleja grinned back at him. 'You can try, but I don't like your chances!'

She ran back up the beach and waded into the water, which was twinkling with sunlight peeping over the horizon. 'Hey, Pablo?' she called back before she swam out, suddenly thinking of the memories Griete's singing had brought back last night. 'Did Madre use to sing to me?'

He hesitated for a beat, then said, 'Every night. Songs of explorers and ships and mermaids. She would have loved that you became a pirate.'

Aleja swam back to the *Ship of Shadows* with her heart full.

Olitiana and Captain Quint were waiting for her on deck. Frances was shuffling her feet beside them. 'You *never* leave the ship again without permission, is that clear?' Captain Quint said, stony-faced. 'You've delayed our departure. Again.' She turned and marched back into her cabin.

One hand on her coin, Aleja stared down at the deck. 'I'm sorry,' she whispered.

'You can spend tomorrow pumping out the bilge,' Olitiana said. She rested a hand on Aleja's shoulder for a beat before following the captain.

'I had to tell them you'd gone; they were about to weigh anchor,' Frances said miserably.

'It's OK,' Aleja said. But really it wasn't. 'Do you think she still wants me on her crew?' she asked quietly.

'Of *course*! She'll have forgotten all about this by next week. Now tell me everything. Biscuit?' Frances dug a handful out of her pocket.

*

The very next day, Farren figured out the clock.

'I've been watching it several times a day, studying the patterns of its movements as time passes, every day since Aleja noticed it back in Ragusa –'

'How long do we have left?' Captain Quint interrupted, her mood growing darker.

'By the time we reach Shanghai, we will have eight months left,' Farren said grimly. 'It must have started at sixteen months, so at that point we'll be halfway through its countdown.'

The library exploded with noise as Geoffrey poked his head out of the globe to look. Shadows scuttled away and hid among the books.

Aleja gasped – just eight months to collect three of the map pieces? It took two months just to sail the distance from Ragusa to China! And there was still a piece to find in the Americas . . .

'Silence!' Captain Quint ordered. 'We cannot change the past. Turn your eyes onwards, to the horizon. This is a matter of urgency now.' With that she marched out of the library, accompanied by Penumbra.

A week later, the shadows were back to their full strength: wandering the ship, slinking up through floors and bookcases, darting around as shadow-mice, and lurking round the edges of the pirates' conversations. The *Ship of Shadows* was at full speed and they were soaring across the Indian Ocean to Melaka when Aleja heard an eerie whisper.

*Alejaaaaaaaa.*

She froze. She'd been strolling down the passageway to her cabin with an armful of books, trying to snag a few minutes' reading time. She'd redoubled her efforts to figure out the book in order to try to impress Quint.

She looked around but couldn't see anything. The passageway was dim and shaky, lit by swaying lanterns on the bulkheads and speckled with light reflecting off the sapphire constellations above. Chains over trapdoors clunked, the ship groaned, and shadows melted in and out of the walls like ghosts. 'Is that you, Geoffrey?' Aleja asked.

*Alejaaaa.*

Aleja stepped back and frowned at Tinta. Her second shadow tended to shrink down in a panic when danger was afoot and now and then plummet her into a strange magical vision, but here it was, standing next to her in its panther form, licking a shadow-paw. The next time the creepy whisper came, Aleja followed the sound. It was coming from the nearest owl engraved in the wall. Its emerald eyes stared blankly back at her and Aleja suppressed a shiver. What had Frances told her last summer? *When you whisper into one, it will spill out of all the others.* Aleja followed the whispers. They hissed out of each owl, rippling through the dark underbelly of the ship, until she located their source.

Frances doubled up in laughter. 'Your face!'

Aleja narrowed her eyes.

'OK, OK, I'm sorry. I brought cake.' Frances held up an enormous tin that smelled of vanilla and sugar. Claws was wriggling in her other arm. 'Or were you going to read?' she asked, looking at Aleja's stack of books.

Aleja looked at her books. It was hard to read with Frances around but she'd been looking forward to starting a book about patterns that she hoped would explain the strange page of dots in the book. 'Erm . . .'

'Let's do both,' Frances said confidently. She was leading Aleja up the passageway towards the galley, where the entrance to the underwater room was hidden, when something snatched Aleja's attention. A fizz and a glimmer. She glanced down a ladder that led deeper below decks. 'What was that?'

'What was what?' Frances looked up from the cake tin with frosting around her mouth. The same frosting was on Claws's whiskers, too.

Aleja plunged down the ladder. And there, between the weapons room and the library, the passageway had magically stretched itself out to fit . . . Well, Aleja wasn't quite sure what it was.

It looked like a huge golden lantern, big enough for ten people to squeeze inside. Its walls were bronze glass and a wooden sign flapped down like an afterthought, with THE GOLDEN LANTERN scrolled on it.

Frances read it aloud. 'What is it?'

'It looks like a tavern,' Aleja said, going inside.

The floor was paved in a mosaic of doubloons, and the dark-wood framing was painted with a pattern of tiny golden owls – the mark of Athena. Wooden stools perched round old barrels and hundreds of minuscule lanterns hung above them, setting the whole tavern glittering. A golden fountain bubbled and sparkled in the centre like a witch's cauldron.

'That must be some kind of drink,' Aleja said, unsure.

Frances set Claws down and scooped up a goblet of the bubbling gold liquid. 'Let's try it.'

Before Aleja could voice a warning, Frances had taken a large gulp. Aleja sucked in a breath. Claws dived back into the cake tin and Tinta seemed to freeze.

Frances swallowed and licked her lips. 'Well, that was *delicious*.' She scooped up two more goblets and plonked them down on a barrel. Aleja put her books next to them and sat down. Sipping the drink, she found it tasted sweet, like spices and cream and vanilla.

'I'm going to call it starshine!' Frances announced, watching it shimmer.

The Golden Lantern fast became a popular spot for the crew. Aleja and Frances grew fond of sitting there with a spread of books in front of them. Frances would chatter away to her non-stop and Aleja only managed to read in the gaps when Frances tried to get Claws to catch mice or learn tricks. And often Aleja let herself be distracted by Tinta, who liked to perch next to the fountain in a little hedgehog shape with its nose twitching at the bubbles.

'Ah, good morning, Aleja. Cup of tea? Biscuit?' Captain Quint was spread out on one of the settees in the library with her feet up, half buried beneath a ginormous map, a teacup balanced in one hand. A biscuit tin and Penumbra were wedged in beside her.

Aleja accepted a biscuit, wondering if the captain had forgiven her for delaying the ship's voyage. Maybe Frances was right and she'd already forgotten all about it. She sneaked a look at the map. It covered most of eastern Asia, from islands speckling the page to great lumbering mountain ranges. She opened her mouth to ask a question about China but a little shadow ambling over the map distracted her and a different question popped out instead. 'Where did the shadows come from?'

Penumbra clicked his beak at the shadow and it fled through the page and out of the back of the settee.

Captain Quint glanced up at Aleja. 'They've always been here, I think. I inherited them along with the ship.'

'Did Thomas James mention them in his journals?' Aleja asked.

There was a faint *schloop* and a new ladder burst into existence, rattling against the bookshelves. Captain Quint narrowed her eyes at it. 'Many more of those and we're going to be burning them for firewood,' she grumbled. Penumbra ruffled his feathers in agreement. 'Ah, the journals. No, not that I can recall.'

Aleja frowned. 'What about a person having a second shadow?' She looked at Tinta, who was chasing the little shadow across the Persian rug.

'As far as I know, you're the first,' Captain Quint said, digging in the biscuit tin. 'Hmm, looks like someone's beaten me to the shortbread . . .'

Aleja tried not to sigh. 'Do you know why they can't leave the ship, though? And why François is the only one who can take them and what his urn is made of?'

'Ah, found one!' Captain Quint closed her eyes as she bit into a segment of shortbread. 'Ermtgen is truly talented.' She opened her eyes. 'You all are, of course, but I do enjoy an edible talent.'

Aleja was still staring at Tinta. If having two shadows made her special . . . 'What about Malika?' she asked quietly. 'How does it affect her, not having a shadow?'

Captain Quint dunked her shortbread in her tea, sloshing some on to the map. 'Your shadow contains a spark of your essence. Losing it dulls your senses, your talents. Malika trains hard to compensate for this.' Captain Quint rummaged in the biscuit tin again.

'Other than that, I am as clueless as you. We still have much to learn about the shadows and their magic. Though I do remember Raven asking me some of these questions before I sent the poor girl to her current appointment. What a shame you never met her; perhaps she could have helped you solve these mysteries.'

Aleja left the library more frustrated than before. Her head down in thought, she almost ran into Frances, who was chasing after Claws in the passageway, holding a heap of shortbread. She slowed when she saw Aleja. 'What's wrong?'

'I just spoke to Quint and –'

'No, Claws, not down there!' Frances suddenly sprinted after the kitten, who had his head in the weapons-training room, which was echoing with pistol shots.

Aleja shrugged at Tinta and trudged back to her cabin. She opened the coded book and glared at it. 'If I can solve this, then maybe people will stop saying Raven could have helped me,' she said to Tinta, who crept closer like it was listening, one rabbit ear flopping sympathetically. But the dots on the page refused to make sense and Aleja slammed it shut again. 'Why can't I figure it out? Maybe Raven *was* smarter than me.' She flopped on to her bunk and stared up at the wood above her, her eyes stinging. Tinta darted over to the cabin door and back again.

Aleja sat up. 'Have you got something to show me?'

Tinta melted through the door. Aleja got up and yanked it open, looking down the passageway. A stream of shadows were trickling by. 'Where are they going?' Aleja whispered to Tinta. 'Do you know?' Tinta twitched its nose at her.

Aleja crept down the passageway, following the shadows.

## CHAPTER NINETEEN

*The Underbelly of the Ship*

The shadows wound up the wooden ladder to the next deck and into the galley. By the time Aleja had run after them they'd vanished. 'Where did they go?' Tinta slunk down into a butterfly and fluttered at her, flapping its wings impatiently. '*Vale, vale*,' Aleja said. *OK, OK.* 'I'm coming.'

Tinta vanished through a cupboard door. Aleja yanked it open and climbed down the steps hidden inside. Down and down she went, until she'd reached the secret passages sneaking through the underbelly of the ship. Here the *Ship of Shadows* glittered with magic. Spots of green light, as bright as limes, flickered like fireflies in the air, while magical fountains sputtered out tiny dragons made of gemstones, and clouds drifted along the ceiling. The shadows glided along the narrow passageways, deeper and deeper into the ship, until Aleja heard the pounding of the ocean through its wooden walls. Still she followed, making herself as small and quiet as she could, Tinta stealing along with her as a shadow-mouse. The clouds began to snow. Soft puffs fell on Aleja's hair and eyelashes. She picked one up and it fell apart in her fingers. She looked back at the passageway, which seemed to have changed without her noticing. The walls were no longer wooden but carved from stone that was marbled with purple veins. She had turned to watch the shadows massing above her when the passage suddenly echoed with a great rumbling and grating. Aleja stopped and stared.

A large stone statue of an owl was slowly rising up before her. She stepped back as the stone screeched to a halt. Her fingers reached for Tinta. The owl's beak opened wide and kept opening, until the lower portion of the beak crashed on to the stone floor. 'It's a door,' Aleja whispered to Tinta, and climbed through.

She emerged in the cave of shadows. Tinta swirled its tail. Aleja crouched down and trailed her fingers across its wispy head. It was like touching mist. 'What are you trying to tell me?' she asked eagerly. But Tinta scurried away from her touch.

A little hurt, Aleja followed it up the ladder on to the deck. Salt spray flew up from the bow, and the speed of their shadow-assisted voyage snapped the sails. A few shadows sneaked past Aleja and curled round one of the posts that supported Aada's cabin high above the deck. Tinta followed them.

'Where are you going now?' Aleja watched them melt through the underside of the cabin and disappear. Tinta vanished into Aada's cabin, too. So Aleja climbed Aada's ladder and knocked at the trapdoor.

'You may enter.' Aada's voice sounded muffled through the wood.

'I think Tinta came in here,' Aleja said, climbing up and looking around.

Aada's cabin was filled with squashy purple armchairs, snowy furs, maps of the stars and a trunk of battleaxes. It smelled of coffee and the memory of snow. There was a table and chairs cosied up in one corner, surrounded by navigational tools and huge glass windows. The ceiling was glass, too, offering views of a cloudless day that stretched to the distant horizon. A hammock swung gently in one corner.

'I often find myself visited by our shadows,' Aada said, appearing from behind the giant telescope in the centre of her cabin. 'They seem to enjoy accompanying me with my morning coffee.'

Aleja frowned. 'They do? Why? Do you know where they came from? Why they're attached to the ship's magic?'

Aada chuckled lightly. 'So many questions. Perhaps if you sat still with them, the answers would occur to you.'

Tinta appeared in its fox shape atop Aada's table. 'You share an unusual bond with the shadows, Aleja. It does not surprise me you find yourself so intrigued by them.' She pulled a chair out for Aleja, who sat down.

'I just want to know how François can steal them when we can't even move them off the ship.' Aleja watched the shadows wisping along the cubbyholes built into the wall of the cabin, where rolled maps and star charts were stowed.

Aada's gaze was knowing. 'You wish to carry your shadow with you always,' she said.

'Yes,' Aleja said, then she hesitated. 'And I think Tinta can show me things – I've had a few visions of François and his ship. I think they're real.'

A faraway look flickered across Aada's face. 'How curious,' she murmured to herself. 'Perhaps . . .'

The shadows swirled past Aada's collection of teacups and mugs, breaking apart into a cluster of tiny stars then reforming as a single wave that rushed over a chunk of stone.

'Do you know, I do believe that –'

'Why are the shadows here?' Aleja interrupted.

Aada's brow creased. 'You already asked me that.' She peered at Aleja. 'Are you quite all right?'

'No, *here*. In your cabin,' Aleja said impatiently, standing up and leaning over to watch Tinta dance back and forth.

'They enjoy my collections,' Aada said. 'I often watch them play while I lie in my hammock, before the night closes over us.'

The shadows danced, thicker and blacker, through rolled-up maps and over a compass before returning to the stone. Aleja reached out a hand and picked it up. It was charcoal grey with strands of purple cutting paths through it. 'It's the stone,' Aleja breathed. The shadows shattered into a cloud of tiny moths that fluttered round the stone as she held it, encompassing Aleja in a shadowy orb. She laughed. 'It's the stone!'

Aada stood slowly, her figure blurred by the shadows flying round Aleja. 'We're going to the captain.'

Aleja held the stone up in front of the entire crew, who were amassed in the library at Quint's order. 'This stone matches the stone in the cave of shadows *and* buried deep in the passageways in the bottom of the ship. Both places are the most shadowy and magical on board.' As she spoke, shadows seeped out from the bookshelves and trickled down ladders, drawn towards the stone Aleja held.

'Of course,' Olitiana said to herself.

Captain Quint's eyes bored into Aleja. Frances was listening so hard she'd forgotten the shortbread in her hand and Claws was licking it. A few pirates whispered excitedly to each other.

'And,' Aleja said as the shadows misted around her, 'it's exactly the same stone that François's urn is made from – charcoal grey with purple veins.'

The library hushed into silence.

Malika caressed her scimitar. 'How can it be destroyed?'

The rest of the pirates turned to her. 'We will *not* destroy the source of our magic,' Captain Quint said sharply.

'Not our source – his,' Malika said impatiently.

'Gunpowder,' Farren said at the same time as Velka chimed in with: 'Acid.' They met each other's eyes and smiled.

Frances looked aghast. 'We're lucky you haven't blown the ship up between you by now.'

Captain Quint stood up, reclaiming the crew's attention. 'Yes – let's not be hasty.' She took the stone from Aleja and passed it to Aada. 'This belongs in your cabin. Farren, Griete and Velka, I am placing you in charge of examining the properties of the stone and learning more about it. Do try to avoid any unnecessary explosions. And, Aleja, I am indebted to you for your discovery.'

Aleja felt all the eyes of the crew on her. Farren winked at her and she grinned back. Finally she'd done something right!

'I am bequeathing you a boon,' Captain Quint said, pulling out a single black pearl from her pocket and placing it in Aleja's hand. 'You may exchange this for one favour from me in the future. Anything your heart desires that's in my capabilities.'

Aleja stared at it. 'Thank you,' she said, her throat thick.

Frances ran over and nudged her excitedly. 'What are you going to use it for?'

Aleja closed her fingers over it. 'I'm going to save it.'

Captain Quint nodded. 'A wise decision. Now onwards we go!' She clapped her hands. 'To your tasks, crew.'

The next week passed in a blur. Aleja's days were taken up with sailing into the blue-skied horizon at the helm with Olitiana, weapons training, griddle cakes and midnight feasts up on deck.

Aleja had put the pearl into a silk pouch, along with the golden telescope the captain had gifted to her after their desert adventure. 'We've solved part of the mystery,' Aleja told Tinta, lying on her carpet beside her shadow. 'You showed me the way to the shadows. But I still don't know where you came from or how you're showing me visions.' Tinta seemed to stare back at her with coal-black eyes. 'Maybe soon I won't have to leave you behind on the ship.' She picked up the golden book with THOMAS

JAMES stamped on the cover in bronze letters. 'Now I *have* to figure this out.'

But Tinta was in the mood to play.

After the fourth time Tinta had plodded over the book as a shadow-hippo, Aleja pulled a raw-cut ruby out of her pocket and sat it in the sunshine beaming through the porthole. It sparkled, throwing spangles of light around her cabin. Tinta collapsed down into a little hedgehog and watched it, spellbound.

However, much to her frustration, Aleja still hadn't solved any of the mysterious codes in the book or worked out what was happening with Tinta by the time the shout sounded. 'Land ahoy!'

## CHAPTER TWENTY
### *Melaka*

On the approach to Melaka, Aleja was about to run up
the netting to the crow's nest when she hesitated.
Captain Quint was at the helm, the sunlight dancing
over the freckles on her face, her sleeves rolled up, baring
her owl tattoo on her tanned forearm.

'Can I sail us in?' Aleja asked, Tinta bouncing round
her heels as a shadow-hare.

Captain Quint beamed and stepped aside. 'Guide us
into port, Aleja.'

Aleja steered the ship from the Straits of Melaka into
the Melaka river as Captain Quint gave orders to the
rest of the crew to adjust the rigging and reef the sails,
slowing their speed down to glide up the narrow river.

Tinta unfolded into a shadow-albatross that shielded the sun from Aleja's face. The ropes creaked as Aleja kept them on course, smiling at the sights and sounds of a brand-new land.

The air felt sticky. Wooden houses bordered the river, teetering on stilts, and palm trees and tropical plants were crammed in everywhere. In the distance the Portuguese–Dutch fort loomed over the city in forbidding stone as Aleja manoeuvred the ship towards the port. With the rest of the pirates manning the sails, then dropping the anchor and jumping ashore to tie the dock lines, the *Ship of Shadows* was brought safely in between the crew. Frances shouted down the all-clear from the crow's nest and Aleja sighed in relief. Her hopes flared like a match. Even with the shadows recovering and the owl clock counting down, it had taken them just under six weeks to reach Melaka. There was no way François and his ship could match that. The second piece of the map would be theirs.

Aleja ran down the gangplank and set foot on land. She'd expected it to feel sturdier than ever after they'd crossed an entire ocean but it felt like it was rocking.

She looked down at her boots. '*¿Qué?*' *What's happening?*

'You've got your sea legs now.' Frances sauntered past. She wobbled, betraying her own struggle with the sudden switch to land.

'How strange.' Aleja wandered after her, still feeling the buck and sway of imaginary waves underfoot. She looked around in wonder. There were Portuguese churches and Chinese temples, and fruits and spices she'd never seen in jewel-bright colours. When she looked up, she saw a pair of monkeys chattering in a tree. Frances had to reach back and tug at her arm to keep her moving. She wanted to stand still while Melaka ran amok around her and soak the flavours of the city into her skin. But it wouldn't be long until the *Ship of Shadows* set off again, further east, to China.

Aleja broke into a piece of eight for two tangy curries served on banana leaves that she and Frances ate beside the river and washed down with freshly squeezed pink guava juice. On their walk back Aleja spotted a tiny hat shop. 'What do you think?' she asked Frances, trying on a small black tri-cornered hat that looked like the hats Captain Quint and Olitiana wore.

Frances cocked her head and grinned. 'Like you'll be giving the captain a run for her money,' she said.

Aleja grinned back and flicked a coin on to the table for the hat.

On the way back to the ship they passed Griete and Ermtgen chatting in Dutch to the market sellers, and Velka and Aada ordering barrels of drinking water. Aleja was dragging her feet, casting one final look around the tropical harbour, when she stopped dead and clutched Frances.

'Look!' she hissed, yanking Frances behind a palm tree and pointing down the river.

There, hidden behind a colossal fishing ship, was *La Promesse Lumineuse*.

'How is that possible?' Frances said disbelievingly. 'They'd have to have sailed the secret way through Egypt *and* outrun the storm we hit, but even then it's not possible.'

For a second Aleja was overrun by the memory of standing on the deck of *La Promesse Lumineuse* on calm waters while the storm seized the *Ship of Shadows*. 'It *must* have been real,' she said to herself.

'What?'

'Nothing,' Aleja said. 'And he definitely doesn't have magic?'

Frances frowned. 'Not that I've ever heard. But he can steal our shadows; who knows what else he can do?'

Aleja sucked in a breath. 'They're already leaving – look.' She watched in dismay. Men scurried up and down the gangway with the last of a stack of boxes and barrels beside the ship. 'They'll reach China first!' Her bright flare of hope guttered and died.

Frances opened her mouth but Aleja didn't wait to hear what she said – she was already running back to the *Ship of Shadows* to tell the others.

Most of the crew hadn't yet returned. Malika and Farren were on deck, left guarding the ship.

'We need to stall them,' Malika said immediately, a fierce glint in her eyes. She twisted to look across the river. Aleja looked too, but the pirate hunters' ship couldn't be seen from here, not with the water heaving with ships and boats coming and going. And, once more, François hadn't seemed to notice them either. Aleja was about to comment on how suspicious that was when Malika said, 'Follow me,' and jumped over the side of the ship.

Farren looked at Aleja and Frances. 'Did she really mean . . .?'

There was a splash and an impatient command from the water. 'Now!'

Frances and Farren both leaped overboard.

Aleja's brain caught up with her first. Running to snatch up a coil of rope, she tied one end to the taffrail and let the other drop into the water. They'd need it later. If the Fury didn't catch them first.

A rush of warm air whooshed past Aleja and she plummeted straight underwater. She quickly arrowed back up.

Malika set a challenging pace. Swimming with the deadly intent of a shark, she hurtled underwater and emerged a couple of minutes later in the flat expanse of water before *La Promesse Lumineuse*. There she waited.

'Told you pirates needed to be able to swim,' Frances said with a cheeky grin, before filling her lungs and diving down to avoid the same stretch of cluttered water Malika had swum beneath. Farren followed her. Aleja took an extra-deep breath and plunged underwater, too. It was murky and shadowed with hulls. She swam past fish and round anchor chains until she saw three pairs of legs treading water. Her lungs stretched tight, the need to breathe becoming an ache then a pain, but there was a little boat silhouetted above her that she needed to swim under first and then . . . she was there. With a gasp she broke the surface and flooded her lungs with air.

'You must have one hell of a swimming teacher,' Frances said, smiling.

Malika turned away, her focus dagger-sharp and trained on the pirate hunters' ship.

'What are we going to do?' Aleja asked when she'd caught her breath.

'We're going to stop them,' Malika said, striking out across the water towards the ship.

The pirate hunters' galleon was even larger when you approached it from below. Aleja trod water, staring up at the huge wooden beast above them. Was François in there right now? She shivered at the thought.

Malika whipped out a dagger with a low chuckle and dived down into the depths of the rippling water.

'That wasn't terrifying at all,' Farren remarked while Aleja tried to keep sight of Malika. Farren raked her auburn hair back. It clung to the back of her neck, the golden hoops in her ears dripped and her hazel eyes looked greener than usual in her tanned face. 'I suppose we'll have to follow her.' She inhaled and dived down.

Aleja breathed in and swam down the slope of the ship. Malika was treading water round the hull as she attacked it. Unsheathing her dagger, Aleja joined her in hacking away at it, hoping they could spring at least a small leak in the ship. But the wood was thick and her dagger barely scratched it. Farren joined her, pulling out a chisel. And then Frances appeared with her Moroccan knife. Between them, the scratches poked deeper until they'd scored a row of shallow dips in the hull. Regularly popping up to refill their lungs before ducking back down, they kept at it. Her chest aching now, Aleja stabbed her dagger harder into the wood, wriggling it around to ease it deeper before tugging it back out with her feet braced against the ship. A few bubbles appeared. They'd penetrated the hull! Aleja waved her arms and pointed before swimming back up, Frances and Farren at her heels. Malika broke the surface beside them.

They swam back to their ship and climbed up the rope Aleja had left trailing in the water, Farren clapping her on the back when she spotted it. When they crashed down on to the deck, one by one, in a sodden heap of brine and wet clothes, Captain Quint was standing above them. 'Care to explain?' she asked mildly.

'Just a spot of light sabotaging.' Malika gave her a slow smile before strolling off.

Thunderclouds rolled over the captain's face. 'I saw François's ship in harbour, too. It's taken care of?'

'We'll be first in China now,' Frances boasted.

'Excellent,' said Captain Quint, peering at the harbour through her spyglass.

Farren wrung her shirt out, picked up her matching pistols from the deck and slid them back into her belt before striding off. Frances followed her, eager to find Claws, after whispering to Aleja, 'Meet me in the Golden Lantern at midnight. I'll bring snacks.'

Aleja looked at the captain.

'What is it, Aleja?' she said without putting her spyglass down.

'Are you going to meet Raven?' Aleja asked her quietly, checking no one was close enough to hear her. Tinta crept closer on the deck. A few shadow-mice trickled over and watched them from the taffrail.

Captain Quint collapsed the spyglass and turned to Aleja. 'I had considered it.'

'Maybe she can tell us how François knew to look in the fort for the second piece of the map,' Aleja said more confidently. 'Or how he knows about the map in the first place. Or how he managed to beat us here? The

*Ship of Shadows* is the fastest ship on the seas because it's a magic ship. We need to know what's happening on board *La Promesse Lumineuse* . . .' And she was willing to bet that Raven would have noticed their ship, even if the pirate hunters hadn't.

The captain tapped a finger against the spyglass. 'It's risky. We're lucky he hasn't spotted us. To stay here while we hold the advantage could put us in danger.'

'But that's twice François hasn't seemed to see us in the same city as him; don't you think that's odd?' Aleja shuffled from foot to foot. She glanced at Tinta, who stood at her side, a strong and silent shadow-panther. 'And there's something I haven't told you,' Aleja added. Captain Quint waited patiently. 'I think – in fact, I'm *sure* – that Tinta's shown me visions. I've had two now. I was standing on the deck of *La Promesse Lumineuse* in both of them. And Raven was there.'

Captain Quint stiffened. 'Was she all right?' she asked softly.

'I think so,' Aleja said, relieved that the captain had believed her at once. 'But she looked sad in the first one and in the second she was going through papers in the Fury's quarters.' She swallowed and glanced down at Tinta. 'I don't know how or why the visions work but I think it's a warning.' She felt a pinch of guilt that she'd ever considered Raven had been double-crossing them.

Captain Quint still stared out across the water, her brow furrowing. 'It seems when I brought you on board this ship, I set into motion a chain of events I could never have foreseen.'

Aleja dipped her fingers into Tinta's panther form. 'Me neither,' she said quietly.

The captain turned her piercing eyes on to Aleja. 'In that case I shall meet with Raven.'

Aleja put her new hat on. 'I'll be your eyes and ears in the harbour.'

CHAPTER TWENTY-ONE

*The Spy and the Poison*

Aleja's lips twitched as she leaned back against a wooden beam, watching the crew bustling aboard *La Promesse Lumineuse*. They must have noticed they'd sprung a leak. Crew mates rushed on and off the ship, looking for fresh wood. But the day was already dusking to a close and they'd be lucky to find everything they needed to patch up their leaking ship. Aleja grinned to herself, pulling the brim of her hat down low to hide her face. It didn't disrupt her view of the harbour and she soon spotted a figure sneaking off the pirate hunters' ship.

Like a shadow in the night, her black hair trailing down her back, Raven stole past the wooden houses on stilts towards Aleja. She stood up straighter, tipping her hat back. Something was wrong. Raven was moving oddly. As Aleja watched, Raven inched closer to the noisy tavern, which was beaming with light. Then she stopped and looked up, meeting Aleja's eyes. With a start Aleja realized she'd been recognized.

Raven moved in Aleja's direction, but, as she neared, Aleja was alarmed to see the girl's skin was white and clammy, her black eyes sunken. Raven staggered towards her and Aleja grabbed her, switching places so the other girl could lean against the beam. 'What's wrong?' Aleja asked her urgently. 'Should I fetch the captain?'

Raven rasped for breath and shook her head. 'No time. Too . . . dangerous.' She held her hand out. In it was a neat square of parchment folded up small.

Aleja took it. 'What's this?' She looked back at Raven just in time to see her slip into unconsciousness. Raven slid down the wooden beam and into a heap at Aleja's feet. 'Oh no . . .' Aleja shoved the parchment into her pocket and crouched down. She looked around. 'Hey! You there!' she called across to a nearby boy with dark eyes and a mop of unruly hair.

He wandered over warily and eyed them both.

'Can you fetch someone for me?' Aleja flashed a coin at him. He nodded and she gave him instructions to retrieve Captain Quint from the tavern. To her immense relief he reappeared a minute later, the captain striding alongside him. Aleja tossed him the coin and he ran off. Captain Quint rushed to her side.

Aleja gnawed at her lip. 'Is she ill?'

Captain Quint gave a slow shake of her head. 'I don't know,' she said grimly, looking up. In the dull light from a dirty lantern overhead Aleja saw the frown lines between her eyebrows ran deeper than usual. 'But we can't let her return to the pirate hunters now. Help me get her home.'

With one of Raven's limp arms drooped round Aleja's shoulders and the other round the captain's, they half carried, half dragged her back to the *Ship of Shadows*.

Captain Quint laughed off the suspicious glances. 'Too much rum!'

Aleja forced herself to smile along until they reached the gangplank.

'Straight to the quartermaster's room,' Captain Quint said as they stepped on deck. She ignored the shocked gasps and widened eyes that fixed on Raven; most of the crew believed she'd defected to the Fury, abandoning them in their hour of need. Tinta appeared as a miniature shadow-mouse that vanished into Aleja's boot.

As they took Raven below decks, Aleja looked back in time to see Griete emerge, drop her cutlass and start towards them. They hauled Raven past the crew's cabins and the gleaming staircase to Olitiana's room.

Captain Quint kicked the door open and Olitiana flew to her feet.

'This girl needs urgent help,' Captain Quint told her, laying Raven down on a spare bunk along one wall.

Olitiana's hand crept to her mouth. 'That's our Raven.'

'Aye. And she's never stopped being our Raven. She's been acting under direct orders from me. Can you save her?'

As Olitiana began to examine Raven, Aleja stepped back to give her space, casting an eye around the room. Shelves and cupboards lined one wall, filled with glass bottles, medical books and journals, and curious instruments. She hadn't realized that Olitiana also acted as the ship's doctor.

A few shadows trickled on to Raven's pillow and reached out wispy tendrils to her. Raven sighed and Olitiana nodded. 'The shadows are easing her pain.' Olitiana gently pressed a cloth against Raven's waxy forehead and glanced up at the captain. 'I think this could well be a case of poison.'

Captain Quint closed her eyes. When she snapped them open again, she turned to Aleja and barked out, 'Fetch me Velka. Run!'

Aleja ran.

She didn't have to run far – the passageway between the cabins was packed with the curious and worried crew and thick with shadows. 'Velka, you're needed inside,' Aleja said in one hurried breath. 'Griete, you'd better come too,' she added.

When the three of them burst back into Olitiana's room, Raven's eyes were open. And she was talking.

## CHAPTER TWENTY-TWO

*Sky Lanterns*

'Couldn't tell you.' Raven's whisper was a husk, rough and quiet. Her eyes were pools of black ink fixed on Griete.

Griete went to sit beside her. 'Shh, it's OK, I understand,' Griete said, stroking Raven's hair.

'Important . . . you know about . . . him.'

Aleja looked up and frowned.

'Don't try to talk, save your energy,' Griete said, her voice catching. Aleja bit her question back; now wasn't the time to interrogate poor Raven.

Velka handed a vial to Olitiana. 'Try that,' she said in an undertone. 'I don't have high hopes, but maybe . . .'

Aleja couldn't look away.

'Drink this for me,' Olitiana murmured to Raven, scooping up her head and tipping the liquid past her lips.

There was a knock at the door. Aleja opened it.

'Captain, Aada's charted the course to Shanghai and we need to leave if we're to pursue our advantage,' Malika said, her eyes darting between the captain and Raven. 'Before François sees us and mounts an attack.'

Captain Quint looked tired. 'Very well,' she said, following Malika to the door before pausing and glancing back. 'Keep me informed, Olitiana. You all ought to know that Malika, Frances and Aleja unwittingly discovered the truth last year – they were under my orders not to inform anyone else. And, Raven?'

Raven slid her gaze to the captain.

'You did brilliantly,' Captain Quint told her, her voice cracking.

Aleja hovered awkwardly, unsure if she should stay. The scene felt too private to watch. Then when the captain left, Frances and Farren rushed in and sat round Raven, either side of Griete and Velka.

'I missed you so much,' Griete whispered, holding on to Raven's hand.

A tear slipped down Raven's cheek. She smiled at Griete.

Aleja crept out into the passageway where she stood for a moment, holding on to her coin and trying to catch her thoughts. Shouts echoed down from the upper deck and there was a sudden, strong pull underfoot. They were on their way to China.

Then another volley of shouts erupted and Aleja glanced up as if she could see straight through the ship. Tinta burst out of hiding in the form of a huge shadow-horse. Aleja peered round it. A sudden darkness was rushing through the passageway. Shadows were flooding the ship, pooling across the floor and up the walls, whispering and weaving through the entire ship. Aleja ran and climbed the ladder, Tinta galloping with her. On deck she ground to a halt. The entire ship was clothed in shadows. Captain Quint and Malika were at the helm, blades out and silent. The captain met Aleja's eyes and raised a finger to her lips.

They were gliding past *La Promesse Lumineuse*. Aleja's heart hammered as the *Ship of Shadows* inched by the pirate hunters' ship. The Fury stood on deck, one shining boot on the rigging, scouring the harbour with a spyglass. They were passing close enough to reach out and touch his gleaming jacket but it was as if their ship had been devoured by sea fog. François couldn't see them.

That evening Aleja ate a quiet supper in the unusually solemn and half-empty galley. 'How's Raven?' she asked when Frances appeared.

Frances shook her head. 'She's getting weaker . . .' She trailed off and stared hard at her bowl of spicy stew.

Aleja laid her spoon down and hugged her.

Raven was buried at sea.

Aleja couldn't stop thinking about the sadness she'd seen on Raven's face in her very first vision. She was appalled that they hadn't been able to save her.

Griete stood further up the deck, flanked by Farren and Velka. It had taken time for her to smile again when she'd first thought her best friend had betrayed them, and now Aleja was worried it would fade away again.

Against the first streaks of dawn appearing on the horizon, the crew stood in a line along the deck to pay their respects. In a flicker and a wisp of darkness, shadow-figures lined the ship. Aleja looked at them, recognizing them as the shadows themselves – former crew members and allies from all over the world. She spotted a shadowed version of Anippe, as well as Habiba – Malika's partner who lived in Morocco. It was an ethereal sight.

They hadn't lit the ship's lanterns. Instead, Frances had rummaged around the hold, unearthing a bundle of sky lanterns. She'd handed them to the captain, saying, 'These were all I could find. I know they're usually used for festivities . . .' Frances had stopped talking and swallowed hard. Captain Quint had reached for the bundle and said, 'Then today we shall celebrate Raven.'

Now each of them held a sky lantern.

Captain Quint's voice was a beacon of strength against the darkness. 'We live and we love through happiness and tragedy alike. Today we mark the loss of one of our own, Raven Blackbrook. We grieve that her life was cut short, but on this ship we shall remember her for evermore.'

'For evermore,' the pirates echoed.

Aleja felt Frances's fingers reach out and softly touch hers. She held Frances's hand tightly, holding on to her paper lantern with the other. At her feet Tinta was a shadow-fox wrapped round her ankles.

There was a moment of silence. Then, as one, they let their lanterns go. Aleja let the paper slide through her fingers, the little candle at its base lifting the lantern up, up, up. They stood on the shadow-filled ship, watching the lanterns glow against the inky sky. Aleja touched her coin, holding on to it like an anchor. Though she'd never known Raven properly, it was because of her supposed betrayal that Aleja had been welcomed aboard. Witnessing the others' grief wasn't easy: Griete's tears, Captain Quint's barely concealed guilt and Malika's tight-lipped anger. Aleja didn't really remember losing her mother; she'd been so young. But that sadness had belonged to her. Now she felt like she was trespassing.

The lanterns dwindled away into pinpricks, as small as the distant stars. Ermtgen ushered everyone below decks for the breakfast feast she'd prepared in Raven's honour. Captain Quint excused herself, followed swiftly by Malika. Aleja sat in a little huddle with Frances, Velka, Farren and Griete. It was the only time she'd seen Frances refuse cake. Instead she sat, stroking an unusually subdued Claws. When they began exchanging stories of Raven, digging up old memories, Aleja fidgeted, feeling more and more uncomfortable for sitting there in Raven's place. She took advantage of Aada and Olitiana sitting down to sneak away. She was meant to have met Frances last night in the Golden Lantern, but it was unlikely Frances would remember that now – it was best to leave her with the others who knew Raven as well as she did.

On the way to her cabin, Tinta slinking along at her heels in a small unidentifiable blob, her hand fell from her coin to her pocket. It crisped at her touch. *Raven's note.*

## CHAPTER TWENTY-THREE

*A Coded Message*

Secreted away in her cabin, Aleja unfolded the parchment with trembling fingers. It was the last thing Raven had written. She decided to take it to Captain Quint later. Since the captain had left the galley to have a moment alone, Aleja didn't want to interrupt her grieving. With a deep breath she smoothed the note out on her bunk and sat down to read it by the light of a storm-jar.

There was nothing on the paper.

But Aleja was no stranger to invisible messages. When she sniffed the parchment, she smelled lemon. After a few minutes of carefully heating it with her lantern, the invisible ink appeared. But the message was in code.

P57L29

# A Coded Message

*

Aleja paced the length of her cabin a few times, thinking hard enough to make her brain throb. But it wasn't enough. To crack this code she needed to think like Raven.

She slid her door open a little, listening. Faint conversation echoed down from the galley and the odd clunk came from the weapons room below, but other than that the ship was quiet. Aleja picked up her lantern and tiptoed up the passageway, Tinta an inky fox trailing after her. She headed towards the empty cabin between Frances's and Griete's that she'd never given a second glance before now. The jewelled owl eyes seemed to watch her. The cabin door opened automatically on its mechanized design. Aleja darted inside and shut the door behind her before anyone found her sneaking around.

Raven's cabin was dark and dusty. Captain Quint had ordered it to be left alone and the crew had presumed that had been for Griete – in case she wanted to visit it when she missed her best friend. But Aleja, Frances and Malika had known the truth: it had been left waiting for the day when Raven returned.

Aleja sat her lantern down on the desk and sifted through some leaves of parchment. It looked like Raven had been mid-translation of some ancient text before she'd left to become the captain's spy. Looking at the symbols, Aleja felt a stab of guilty panic – would Raven have been able to solve the key to the ship by now? She trailed her fingers along Tinta's outline. 'Can you help me? Show me another vision? You showed me Raven before; now we're in her cabin and I don't know where to look . . .'

A silvery mist slithered through the wall in front of Aleja, making her jump.

Aleja sighed. 'What do you want?'

'No one's been in here for months,' Geoffrey said, his head floating above the desk, his white curls bouncing. The rest of his body appeared to be on the other side of the wall. 'Is the littlest pirate up to something wicked?'

Aleja glared at Geoffrey. 'I'm not little,' she said, hating that since Frances had turned thirteen last September she was the youngest on board.

Geoffrey cackled and disappeared.

Aleja turned her focus back to Raven's cabin. It was organized and tidy. Leather-bound volumes filled one wall, papers and fountain pens were heaped on the desk and a large dark-grey painting of ravens hung next to the porthole. But there were no clues about how to decipher Raven's coded message. Defeated, Aleja slumped down on to the neatly made bunk. She sat on something hard. Rummaging under the knitted blanket, Aleja came up with a small book. Its title was *Storming the High Seas* – a novel. She opened it, curious, and a scrap of parchment fell out.

# A Coded Message

*Dearest Raven,*

*Now you have no excuse not to read my favourite novel!*

*Love, Griete*

A lump stuck in Aleja's throat. She snapped the book shut.

'I wonder,' she said aloud to Tinta, who cocked its fox-head at her, wispy ears twitching.

She opened the book again. *P57L29.*

She flicked to page fifty-seven. Counting down to line twenty-nine, Aleja read:

> And that was the moment I was filled with fresh panic as it was apparent that the admiral was not acting of his own volition, but rather there was an even greater power operating behind the scenes, controlling him. Our enemy was more dangerous, more powerful than we had realized.

The cabin door flew open and Aleja jumped guiltily to her feet, snapping the book shut.

Griete stood in the doorway, her eyes red and swollen. 'What are you doing in here?'

Aleja felt her cheeks grow warm. 'I – I'm sorry, I was just trying to –'

'Well, *don't*,' Griete said. 'I can't believe you'd dare come in here!'

Aleja swallowed.

Griete closed her eyes and rubbed her head. Her golden hair was frazzled. 'I just want to be alone.'

Aleja nodded. 'Can I borrow this?' she whispered, holding on to the book.

'Fine,' Griete said.

Aleja crept out with the book.

A few minutes later, she flew breathlessly into Captain Quint's quarters. This was too important not to tell her immediately.

Captain Quint was staring out to sea from her chair, a forgotten glass of rum in her hand. The ship's log lay on the table before her. There was still no entry for today's date. Penumbra gently nipped her hand. Aleja paused. The captain wasn't herself.

'Aleja. It's been a while since you last came bursting in here,' she said listlessly.

Aleja stood there awkwardly. 'Raven gave me a coded message in Melaka.'

Captain Quint sat up, meeting Aleja's eyes.

'I'd forgotten it when – with all that happened,' she continued cautiously. 'But I've just figured it out. Look.' She placed the book, open to the correct page, on the table and rested the note on top.

Captain Quint quickly read both. Then she sat back, kneading her forehead with a knuckle. 'A greater enemy operating behind the scenes? I've often wondered if this was the case myself,' she said, sounding wearier than usual. 'The way François has found the location of the map pieces, how he can access prohibited places. The mystery over how he can afford to sail his own ship around the world without turning to piracy or a crown's patronage. How he beat us to Melaka – that should never have happened.'

Aleja nodded. 'And how he discovered the map to begin with.'

'He's toying with us,' Captain Quint said in a low voice. 'Poisoning Raven before she came to meet me? François must have known we were there all along. He didn't fail to notice us; he was just in too much of a hurry to get to China first to engage in a battle with us. So he took the lowest move he could. Killing a child. A child I was responsible for. Who I sent into the lion's den.'

Aleja didn't know what to say. Raven's death was haunting her too. Her head ached with heavy thoughts. She glanced at the chain round the captain's neck. 'Even if he wants the next map piece first, he'll have to come back for the one we have,' she said, thinking aloud. 'But he'll do it when he knows he can win. Whoever sent him after the map must want it as badly as you do . . .' She thought about the way Quint had chased down the map no matter the cost. 'Why *do* you want it so much?' she asked. It *had* to be about more than treasure.

Captain Quint's head snapped round.

Aleja flinched, wondering if she'd be told off for digging into the captain's affairs. But Quint's face was as open as a book.

'In this world all the power is held by just a few men. I think every lonely, lost or angry girl should have some of that power too. The power to make their own decisions, to be whoever they want to be. I want every shadow to have their time in the sun. And this map, Aleja? It's not just treasure. It's knowledge. It's *power*.'

Aleja's heart thrummed harder at her words.

'There's no other information as to who this mystery person is?' Captain Quint asked.

Aleja shook her head. 'Raven just said it was important we knew about him,' she said.

'It's likely Raven didn't know either.' Captain Quint stared out to sea again and, after waiting to see if she'd speak again, Aleja quietly let herself out.

Aleja mooched back through the passageway to her cabin, Tinta at her heels.

'There you are,' Frances said. She looked annoyed. 'You didn't meet me at the Golden Lantern.' She stared at her. 'Why did you leave the feast earlier?' she asked before Aleja had a chance to reply.

Aleja couldn't admit how she'd felt about Raven's death, not when Frances had been her friend. Realizing Frances was still looking at her oddly, waiting for an explanation, she fumbled for one. 'I . . . don't know,' she said at last.

'You don't know?' Frances echoed. 'Do you want to come to the Golden Lantern with me, Farren, Velka and Griete?' she asked, but her tone was stiff and Aleja knew that they wouldn't really want her there. She was an outsider to their private jokes and memories of Raven. Like Griete had said, they wanted to be left alone.

She shook her head. 'I've got something else I need to do,' she said awkwardly.

'Fine,' said Frances.

'OK,' said Aleja.

They split in different directions. Frances back to the rest of the pirates and Aleja to her silent cabin. 'Do you think she's cross with me?' she whispered to Tinta. Tinta grew into a panther shape and wrapped round Aleja, who curled up on her bunk and wished, not for the first time, that she could feel her shadow.

CHAPTER TWENTY-FOUR

*A Parliament of Owls*

The next morning dawned bright and early. Griete had shut herself away in her cabin and now and then sounds of hammering drifted out. She'd pinned a note to her door instructing them all to keep out and even Malika hadn't summoned her to weapons training. Malika wore a shade of murderous red and swept them into a particularly challenging session: knife throwing. Aleja kept sneaking looks at Frances, who stood next to her, hurling her blades into the wooden target with her lips pinched together. She hadn't said one word to Aleja. When Malika announced the end of the lesson, Aleja threw her last knife then turned to see Frances already leaving the room. Aleja tugged her knives out of the target board, eyes stinging. She threw her knives back in their trunk.

'Respect your weapons,' Malika snapped at her, and Aleja trudged miserably back to her cabin with Tinta.

Since she wasn't speaking to Frances and no one seemed to have noticed her missing at breakfast, Aleja found she had loads of reading time for the first time in a while. But every time she tried to read, she didn't get further than the first page, glancing up at the door, wishing that Frances would burst in with her kitten or cake or some fantastical story she just had to share right now. 'Maybe I'll solve the key to the ship instead,' she told Tinta, pulling out Thomas James's golden book and opening it to the page of dots. She stared at it until she went cross-eyed but nothing new came to her. When her stomach growled, she realized it was lunchtime already.

She cracked open her cabin door and peered out. Further up the passageway she saw Frances and Claws wandering up to the galley. She shut the door again quickly. Tinta leaped up on to the door handle as a squirrel and reached out a paw to Aleja. Aleja's fingers passed through it and she felt that sickening jolt that had become familiar to her now, but no vision accompanied it. When the mists cleared, she was still in her cabin, clutching the door.

'Why didn't that work?' Aleja stared at Tinta, whose squirrel tail wisped from side to side. Aleja went to look out of the porthole. 'We're moving slowly,' she said, watching the waves. Tinta popped up at her side and she turned to it. 'You're not at full strength after hiding the ship the day before yesterday. But I wish I knew when and why you decide to show me things.' Tinta looked at her, but there were no answers to be found in its shadow-eyes so Aleja curled up in her bunk again and ate a bag of sweets, her mind whirling. She had never considered power before but after Quint's words she saw that the world was run a certain way and the more she thought about it, the greater she disliked it. 'But are we too small to make a difference?' she whispered to her shadow. When dusk fell around the ship, she fell asleep, one hand on her coin, loneliness rushing in like a storm.

After weapons training the next day, when Frances still wasn't talking to her, Aleja rushed back to the library. It was impossible to feel lonely when surrounded by books, so Aleja made good use of them. She started learning Mandarin.

Curled up on one of the squishy settees in the library, Aleja studied the characters that made up the language. She soon discovered they were like building blocks and each character held patterns and clues to help puzzle out their meaning. The character *mù* looked like a little tree so it meant *tree* or *wood*, but two of them together would be *woods*, plural, and then three *a forest*. She whispered the words to herself, careful to swoop her pronunciation up and down to try to reach the correct tones. Her voice echoed around the silent library. The lanterns rocked with the ship's slow wandering over waves, with shadows nestling in the bookcases and even Geoffrey quiet inside his globe. The library smelled like old books, wood and salt. Aleja read deep into the night, Tinta lazily shifting forms every now and then. When the ship drifted through a patch of sea fog and the air chilled, Aleja pulled a blanket over herself. Plunging straight into another book, she read ancient tales of revenge inflicted by ghosts and smiled, making a mental note to tell Frances about them. Then she remembered they weren't speaking and her chest grew tight. She set her book down on the stack she'd created on the Persian carpet and looked at Tinta. 'I'm scared I'm not wanted here any more,' she whispered to her little shadow.

Tinta cocked its owl head at her. In a silken wave shadows poured across the library towards Aleja. Aleja sat up straight. Before they reached her, the shadows separated into a parliament of owls. Aleja slowly stood up, watching the shadow-owls. They had assembled in two long, curving lines with a path between them. Tinta hopped at her feet, inching away a little before returning to her.

'You want me to follow you?' Aleja asked, letting Tinta guide her down the shadow-owl path. It ended next to a wall with a tiny golden owl carved into it. Fizzing with anticipation, Aleja pushed the owl. Part of the wall rolled back, revealing a hidden nook inside. On a reading stand a large book rested, its ink shadow-dark. Aleja peeked at the spine and saw it declared itself the ROSTER OF SHADOWS. Her finger came to rest on the latest entry the book was open to: *Alejandra Duarte. Twelve years old. Exceptional linguist and voracious reader.* She gasped. 'That's me,' she whispered to Tinta, who had flown on dusky wings to perch atop the book. 'I'm just like you – a shadow.' She watched the shadow-owls melt back into the shelves of books. 'Thank you,' she whispered after them, her eyes falling on her second shadow again. 'I know I belong on this ship – I can feel it – but I still haven't solved the book so I *must* not be good enough.' Her fingers fell to her coin. 'Sometimes I miss my family,' she added in a whisper as secret as the deepest pockets of her heart. 'At least I knew they always wanted me.'

When she looked up, Tinta was swooping straight at her. Its shadow-wings spread wider and wider until she was caught up in their invisible touch, and all at once she tumbled into another vision.

CHAPTER TWENTY-FIVE

*The Ultimate Weapon*

There was no sickening swirl, no slamming jolt. This time the transition was as simple as when one dream shifts into another. Aleja opened her eyes to a small island. It was misty and swamp-like and the air seemed thick. She could see a dark substance around it like water and other islands in the distance. Creepers hung down from trees and, when she looked around, she realized she wasn't alone. There were shadows everywhere, thicker and darker than she'd ever seen them, as though she could have reached out and touched their silhouettes.

One of the smaller shadows seemed oddly familiar. She gasped. 'Tinta?' She wandered over, breathing faster with excitement as she saw that Tinta was with a small flock of other shadows, all bigger than it. The vision shifted and distorted like she was in a vanishing room on the ship and, when she blinked, Aleja realized she was being shown something else. A ship was slowly sailing along the oily black water. Its wood was fresh and new and its sails white. Aleja wished she had a spyglass to see it better. She caught a twinkle of gold from near the prow and her heart almost jumped into her throat. 'The *Ship of Shadows*!' When she glanced back at Tinta, the vision ripped apart at the seams and Aleja was left blinking in the lantern light in the hidden nook back in the library.

She stared at Tinta. 'You weren't always on the ship.' Tinta stared back. 'Where did the rest of your cast of shadows go?' Aleja asked softly. Tinta slipped back into its squirrel form and inched closer to Aleja, nestling against her. 'It's OK,' Aleja told it, wrapping her arms round it. 'We'll be each other's cast.'

The following week, Griete remained locked in her cabin. Aleja continued to avoid the galley at mealtimes, instead sneaking bits of food and spending her nights in the library with Tinta. Frances still wasn't talking to her.

Early one morning, when Aleja skidded into the weapons room, there were no trunks revealing a gleaming assortment of weapons and no targets awaiting them. Aleja looked about curiously, wondering what they'd be taught today. Frances rushed in a second after her. They caught eyes and Frances turned away, going to stand with Farren and Velka. Aleja felt a lump rise in her throat.

Malika strode in, her jade dress and headscarf flowing behind her. 'Today I'll be instructing you in how to fight using the ultimate weapon.'

'I bet it's a scimitar,' Frances whispered to Farren. 'Malika loves fighting with those. One time –'

Aleja heard someone shush her. She focused on Malika.

'Furthermore, it's one you'll always have on you.' *It's a riddle*, Aleja thought to herself, catching Malika's eyes glimmering with the challenge. 'Anyone care to hazard a guess?'

*What do you always have with you?*

'Nature?' Velka suggested.

Malika looked intrigued. 'A possibility, but not the one I'm thinking of. This is faster.'

'Throwing things,' Frances promptly said.

Malika sighed.

The memory of Captain Quint punching François popped into Aleja's head and before Malika could answer Frances, Aleja blurted out, 'Your body.'

Malika paused. 'Go on,' she said, her voice smooth as silk.

'Well, fighting with your arms and legs. Punching and kicking and . . .' Aleja tried to think what else.

Malika nodded. 'The one weapon you can always rely on to be just where you need it. Yourself. Today will be the first in a series of sessions in which you'll be learning the ancient martial arts.'

'What are martial arts?' Farren asked.

'It's a tradition of combat where you use your body for self-defence,' Aleja said straight away, thinking of the books she'd read. 'In Mandarin it's called *wǔ shù*.'

'Precisely,' Malika said. 'And since we're heading to Shanghai, we'll start with the Chinese style. Pair up. Farren and Velka, Frances and Aleja.'

Aleja reluctantly turned to face Frances, who was glaring at her as if she'd been the one to suggest pairing up. Aleja's cheeks flamed. She didn't know how to escape the angry silence between them.

They spent the next hour learning how to stand in the horse and bow stances and how to punch someone – never, ever with your thumb tucked inside your fist or you'd break it – and how to kick by raising your bent knee before propelling your foot out.

Geoffrey materialized through a wall, watching them and grumbling to himself. 'Call yourselves pirates! No pirate *I've* ever seen pranced about throwing their arms and legs around. This is what you get when women think they can fight.'

Malika spun round and launched herself into the air at Geoffrey. He yelped in shock and vanished down through the floorboards before her leg lashed out in a flying front kick.

Aleja and Frances gaped at her as she landed neatly, her jade dress rippling back into place.

Farren grinned. 'Nice.'

Frances opened her mouth to say something to Aleja but seemed to remember they were fighting and snapped it shut again. Aleja frowned at her.

After demonstrating three different blocking techniques for punches and kicks, Malika put them in their pairs again to practise.

Frances came barrelling towards Aleja, her hands clenched into fists, her face scrunched up in determination, hair shooting off in all directions like straw. Aleja raised her fists in a hurry, prepared to block, one leg bent in front of her, the other stretched out behind in bow stance.

'Centre your focus on your opponent,' Malika called out as she patrolled the room. 'Don't watch her arms,' she said to Aleja, who was keeping a wary eye on Frances's fists. 'Watch her core.' Aleja shifted her attention to Frances's stomach instead, catching her raising her knee just in time to swipe one arm down, knocking her kick aside.

Malika jabbed Aleja in the ribs. 'Never let your guard down,' she said severely.

Aleja raised her fists in a hurry. When Frances tried

punching her, Aleja swung her block to the side like Malika had taught them, leaving her other arm protectively in front. When Malika tried to poke her again, Aleja was ready for it and blocked.

'Good. Switch places,' Malika said, and the lesson rolled on.

When Aleja tried to punch Frances, Frances blocked hard.

'Stop frowning at me,' Frances hissed under her breath.

'I'll stop frowning when you stop glaring!' Aleja said, launching another punch, which Frances snapped away.

'I'm glaring at your frown!'

'That's enough,' Malika called out with a sharp clap of her hands.

Frances stalked back to Farren and Velka without a backwards glance. Tinta curled down into a tiny shadow-snail that sat on Aleja's boot. Aleja looked at it sadly.

'Everything OK?' Velka asked kindly, coming over.

Aleja hesitated. She had the horrible feeling that if she said anything, it would all come pouring out. Besides, how could she tell Velka she was upset about Frances ignoring her when their friend had just died? She shook her head.

Olitiana strode into the weapons room. 'All hands on deck,' she said. 'Captain's orders.'

## Chapter Twenty-Six

*Griete's Invention*

When Aleja appeared on the upper deck with the rest of the pirates, she wasn't sure what she was looking at.

Captain Quint was standing before them, Penumbra perched on her wrist guard, her chestnut hair blowing out under her tri-cornered hat. More surprising than the spark in the captain's eyes was the fact that Griete had emerged from her cabin. Her silk dress was rumpled and stained with oil and she looked like she hadn't brushed her hair in a week, but her eyes were dry and the tiniest smile lingered at the corners of her lips. Most surprising of all was the giant wooden basket sitting on the deck.

Aleja looked at it as the other pirates murmured between themselves. Tinta shifted into a fox, crept towards the basket and sneaked inside. Ropes and bags of sand were strapped to it and six pirates could have comfortably sat inside. Beside it was what looked like a collapsed sail, strewn across the planks in a kaleidoscope of blues and purples. Claws ran forward and climbed up into the basket. Aleja bit the inside of her cheek, trying not to laugh as the kitten fell in. She heard a muffled snort from Frances, too.

Captain Quint ignored Claws. 'As you all know, we make a habit of celebrating each other's achievements on this ship. In that spirit Griete has invented a –' She gestured at the basket.

'It's a hot-air balloon,' Griete said.

The captain nodded. 'Ah, indeed.'

Aleja took another look at the material puddled on the deck. 'It's deflated,' she realized.

'Exactly,' Griete said. 'A few years ago in Portugal, a priest invented a passarola – like a giant sky lantern that he could raise himself with. I've been tinkering with the idea of flying for some –'

'Flying? We're going to fly?' Frances interrupted, almost gleaming with excitement. Aleja ached for Frances to turn to her, nudge her and whisper in her ear but Frances didn't even look at her. And Tinta was still in the basket – along with the rest of the shadows on deck, Aleja realized, watching a current of shadows trickle towards the basket. Penumbra hooted softly at them and they dribbled apart, reforming into owls that lined the basket like sentries. Claws popped his head up and meowed at them, batting the nearest shadow-owl with a paw that swept through it like smoke.

'Yes, it flies,' Griete said, reclaiming the pirates' attention. 'This burner will fill the balloon with a combination of hot air and hydrogen – Velka, I'll need your help with that.'

Velka nodded. 'It'll be flammable, though.'

'So this hasn't been tested yet?' Farren asked, shooting a concerned glance at Velka.

'Of course not,' Griete said impatiently. 'Have you seen me flying a gigantic balloon off the ship?'

Farren fell silent.

Griete puffed out a sigh. 'When the balloon's filled, the basket will lift – yes?'

Velka was waving a hand at Griete to get her attention. 'If the basket's wooden, the balloon will have a hard time getting that lifted, never mind carrying passengers . . .' She trailed to a stop at the expression on Griete's face.

'The basket's embedded with fragments of the stone that Aleja discovered attracts shadows.' Griete gestured at the shadow-owls surrounding the basket. 'I believe that if we remove the balloon from the ship, the shadows will be carried with it. By harnessing their magic we can fly.'

The pirates broke out into excited chatter. Flying felt like an impossible dream. Aleja looked up at the sky, bright and blue and vast, like a second ocean above them. What would it feel like to soar up into its heights, alongside birds and clouds, and see the earth from above? She glanced at Frances, who was looking up, too. When Frances looked over to her, Aleja quickly looked away. She felt a stirring of anger in the pit of her stomach.

'Excellent work, Griete,' Captain Quint said. Her eyes twinkled. 'Perhaps we can test this once we have reclaimed the second piece of the map.'

Griete held her chin high. 'It will work,' she said in a blazing voice.

Captain Quint gently laid a hand on her shoulder. 'Of that I have no doubt.'

'If we're not planning on flying soon, why on earth did you suddenly decide to build this?' Frances asked.

Aleja had been wondering this too.

Griete sighed. 'I'm an inventor, and inventors invent. Besides, I thought it would be a good idea to have a big project to take my mind off . . .' Her lip wobbled a little.

Captain Quint squeezed her shoulder. 'Now, Ermtgen, I believe my nose detected a whiff of griddle cakes?'

'Aye, Captain,' Ermtgen said, knotting her apron tighter and descending the ladder first.

Farren and Frances went to Griete, the three of them talking quickly and quietly as Aleja looked in the basket for Tinta.

'Are you coming to breakfast?' Velka asked, appearing behind Aleja with a tinkle of her silver bracelets.

'Erm, I –' Aleja cast around for an excuse.

'Come on,' Velka said firmly, and Aleja began to follow her, Frances, Farren and Griete slightly ahead. When they reached the galley with its hum of conversation and the splash of hot oil as Ermtgen flipped griddle cakes, Aleja hesitated. Her boots felt glued to the deck. Tinta pressed against her leg. She couldn't bear the thought of sitting in the galley with Frances ignoring her and everyone else wondering what she'd done wrong.

'What is it?' Velka asked.

'I just remembered I forgot something in my cabin,' Aleja lied and dashed away.

'Aleja!' Velka called after her but she kept running until she was back in her cabin with her back pressed against the door, breathing hard.

She stayed in her cabin, alone with her thoughts, all day. The sun eventually grew tired and gave the sky over to the moon. Her stomach rumbling, Aleja wandered along the dark passageway to the galley. When she pushed the door open, she found the galley was dim, deserted and smelled of freshly baked bread. She scurried over to tear the crust off a steaming loaf and stuffed it into her mouth.

'I wondered when you'd finally appear,' a voice said from the shadows.

## CHAPTER TWENTY-SEVEN

### *Ermtgen*

Aleja started – she'd thought the galley had been empty.

Ermtgen creaked to her feet from the corner. 'Sit down,' she ordered.

Aleja sat at the big table. Tinta crept under the bench as an otter. Was she in trouble for the food she'd been pinching?

Ermtgen clattered about, lit by a single glum lantern. A fire roared to life. Ermtgen cut thick slices of the loaf and speared them above the flames. Shadows rustled silently in the corners, creeping past in unidentifiable shapes. Ermtgen walked through them and put a plate of toast in front of Aleja. 'Eat this,' she said in a tone that brooked no argument. 'I know you've been avoiding mealtimes.'

Aleja bit into the toast. It was hot and crisp and dripping with melted butter.

Ermtgen nodded approvingly. 'Now, are you going to tell me what this business is between you and Frances?'

Aleja's cheeks warmed. 'She's not talking to me,' she said into her toast.

'Mm-hmm. And have you been talking to her?'

'I –' Aleja looked up. 'I didn't think she'd want me to.'

Ermtgen looked at her sharply. 'Is that why you've been avoiding her?'

Aleja toyed with her food.

'So that's why she's been moping around, then. I did notice my cupboards have been unusually full lately.'

'She's upset about Raven dying,' Aleja said quickly. 'You all are. I thought it would be a good idea to give everyone some space since I didn't know her and now Frances is angry at me . . .'

Ermtgen gave Aleja another shrewd look. Her grey hair was straggly and pinned up in a bun and her tawny eyes were hawkish. Her apron was streaked with flour. 'I grew up in a fine *bakkerij*, selling the people of Amsterdam the best breads and cakes and pastries they could dream of with my three sisters at my side. But we used to bicker something fierce.' She chuckled and rose to rummage in a cupboard.

'About what?' Aleja asked curiously, watching Ermtgen cut a large slice of iced four-layered spice cake, serving it with a mountain of cream.

'Oh, anything and everything. Which boy we had our eye on, who made the airiest pastries, who oversalted the dough . . . It used to drive our poor mother crazy!' She slid the slice of cake over and Aleja dug in.

'*Make amends*, our mother used to tell us. We each had our own unique set of abilities but it was by working together that we were at our strongest. Now, I'd wager Frances is just as hurt and lonely as you've been. Do you even *know* why you're fighting?'

Aleja fidgeted. 'Well,' she began before closing her mouth again.

Ermtgen nodded. 'I thought as much. This ship is your home, Aleja – its crew your family. And sisters fight. But they never stop loving each other.'

Aleja realized then that Ermtgen saw and heard everything that happened on the ship, even the words that had never been spoken aloud. 'The shadows showed me the roster in the library,' she said and Ermtgen nodded, listening. 'But even if I belong on this ship, I'm not as good as Raven was. I'm sure she would have been able to solve the puzzles in the book. She died for this ship; she's a hero.'

'Dying doesn't make you a hero,' Ermtgen said sternly. 'Do not forget everything you've done for this ship. Captain Quint certainly hasn't – that's why she granted you that boon.'

'But I lost the book and delayed our departure.'

'Accidents can happen to anyone, even the captain. And making mistakes is human nature; it's how we learn.'

Aleja gave her a small smile. Tinta poked its head out from under the bench. She finished her cake and wiped her fingers on her trousers. 'What happened with your sisters? How did you come to join this ship?'

'They're all happy with their families in Amsterdam. For me things weren't the same after my husband died. I was selling loaves at the market when the captain discovered me.' A smile spread across Ermtgen's face like honey. 'She said she was in need of a cook who would make her forget she was at sea.' Ermtgen exchanged a conspiratorial look with Aleja. 'Fed up with hard tack biscuits she was. And that's how an old widow became a pirate. I never thought I'd get a second chance at life, a chance for adventure. I might not be the best sword fighter or sailor but I bake the finest bread you'll ever taste.' She chuckled. 'Now you go and find Frances and make things right between you. Something tells me she's skulking down in the tunnels.' Ermtgen raised her eyebrows and pointed at the cupboard.

Aleja lit a lantern and climbed down the secret back of the cupboard, into the labyrinthine tunnels that twisted round the bottom of the ship and fizzed with magic.

It didn't take her long to spot the glow of another lantern ahead. Frances was wandering along, looking at the shadows whispering down the narrow wooden passages. Tinta shifted into a frog and hopped alongside Aleja's boots.

Aleja lowered her lantern. 'Hello.'

'Talking to me again, are you?' Frances said sourly.

Aleja winced. 'I thought you weren't talking to me,' she admitted. 'I thought you were cross with me.'

Frances crossed her arms. 'I am.'

The magic sparked around them. Aleja's stomach swooped like they'd just hurtled down a big wave. What if Frances didn't want to make up?

'I'm upset because my friend died, and since she died you've been avoiding me for no reason.'

Aleja hadn't expected that. 'No, I – I thought you'd want space to be with the others. I didn't want you to feel like you had to spend time with me.'

'I never feel like that. You're my best friend; I *like* spending time with you. You're the one who doesn't want to spend time with me.' She looked down, where the magic was now swirling into ominous storm clouds. Shadows flew in and out of the emerging squall as seabirds.

Aleja stared at her. 'What are you talking about?'

Frances shrugged. 'I'm always interrupting you when you'd rather be reading. I see the look on your face sometimes.'

The shadow-storm raced up the wooden walls, crackling furiously.

'I had all the time in the world to read in the last week,' Aleja said, and Frances's mouth drooped, 'and it was *horrible*.'

Frances looked up at her. 'It was?' she asked hopefully.

'Yep. I missed you. I like books but I like you more. Well, when you believe me, that is,' she couldn't help adding, her bottled-up frustrations spewing out like seafoam.

Frances blinked. 'I always believe you.'

Aleja fidgeted with her lantern. 'Not about the visions Tinta's been showing me.'

Purple lightning flashed and the sound of thunder rolled towards them. Aleja glanced up – the magic was always strange and wonderful in the tunnels.

Frances grabbed her arm. 'You've had more of them? And they're definitely from Tinta?'

'Yes,' Aleja said, seeing purple lightning bolts reflected in Frances's glasses.

'Why didn't you tell me?' Frances wailed. 'I only wasn't sure about the first one because you had turned so green I thought you must have been ill.'

Aleja gave her a small smile.

Frances narrowed her eyes at Aleja. 'But all this still doesn't explain why you've been hiding away from everyone. What's really going on with you?'

Aleja hesitated. Frances raised her eyebrows. 'I thought that everyone must be thinking that I was a failure of a replacement for Raven and that they wished she was still here . . . instead of me,' Aleja finished in a whisper.

It began to rain giant glowing bubbles. They floated down and popped, releasing bursts of vanilla-sweet scented glitter.

Frances flung her arms round her. 'You idiot,' she said affectionately. 'You're your own person and we love you for it.'

Aleja hugged her back. 'I'm really sorry I hid away from you all.' She pulled a face. 'Griete found me in Raven's cabin when I was cracking the note and she was cross.'

Frances shook her head. 'She's been angry at everything; it's not just you.'

The glitter rained down on them as they hugged in a sea of bubbles.

Aleja peeked up at her. 'And we're OK?'

'We're perfect.'

Aleja hugged her tighter. 'Are you all right?' she asked.

Frances gave her a sad smile. 'I will be,' she said. 'Wait – what note?'

Aleja was about to explain when the magic splattered, breaking off from the swirling storm clouds into a thousand glowing pinpricks.

'Pretty,' Frances said, watching them dance into constellations.

Aleja gaped at them, at what had been dots but were now . . .

She grabbed Frances's arm. 'They're not dots – they're stars!'

Frances gasped. 'Of *course*!'

And Aleja knew exactly where to find stars on board the *Ship of Shadows*.

They broke into action. Aleja ran to fetch the book from the library and Frances yelled, 'I'll get the cake; don't solve it without me!'

## CHAPTER TWENTY-EIGHT

### A Star Hunt

The ceiling above the passageway between the cabins and the galley was studded with a fortune's worth of jewels. Constellations were mapped out in sapphires that twinkled in the lanterns' gleam. Entering the lower deck was like stepping into a treasure-filled cave. Thomas James's book in her hands, Aleja wandered up and down, staring up at them.

Now that she'd recognized the dots were stars, constellations leaped off the page at her. She traced them with a finger. Here was Ursa Minor – four stars formed the body of the Little Bear, with another three for its long tail trailing across the night sky. Looped round it was Draco, the Dragon. And here was Ursa Major, the

Greater Bear, sprawled across the page. Aleja had spent so many nights gazing up at these constellations from the rooftops of Sevilla that they were like old friends. But she saw why she hadn't immediately recognized them – the space between the stars was thick with random ink dots, disguising the stars in a sea of speckles.

Aleja spotted Draco first. 'There it is!' she said excitedly to Tinta, who bounded up the passageway after her in wolf form. 'And there's Ursa Minor . . . and Ursa Major,' she said, running to stand under them. 'But now what do I do?' She frowned, glancing down at Tinta. To use the engraved map in the library table she'd had to speak. What action did she need to take here? The book was the key to the ship because it interacted with the ship itself, revealing hidden rooms and secrets that Thomas James himself had built into his ship. She lay down on the wooden planks to examine the ceiling and its patchwork of jewelled stars. Holding the book above her face, she tilted it until the constellations lined up. When she looked back at the page, the dots were glowing. Aleja smiled, watching the bright pinpricks.

She heard footsteps and Griete peered down at her. 'Aleja? What are you doing down there?'

Aleja looked up nervously but Griete didn't seem angry.

'Just figuring something out,' she said, glancing up to see the same constellations shining fiercely. She was in the right place. Hopefully Frances would appear soon and help her figure out what to do next.

A click sounded beneath Aleja. As she twisted round to see what the noise was, a patch of deck vanished and she fell through with a shriek.

'Aleja!' Griete yelled in alarm.

Aleja landed hard and all the air whooshed out of her lungs. A cloud of dust puffed out and she blinked it out of her eyes. The deck sealed itself back up above, leaving her lying in a dark room.

'I'm fine!' she shouted up.

Tinta melted through the planks and perched next to Aleja as an owl, looking around with huge dark eyes. Aleja sat up. Above her she could hear Griete calling for help. Suddenly there was a flare of light nearby. Flames had shot up in what appeared to be giant basins filled with a buttery substance. She was surrounded by golden walls that billowed with smoke like they were breathing and a ceiling that danced with glowing stars. Flagstones paved the floor and cracked mosaics were painted with murals of snow-capped mountains, lakes and endless sky.

This wasn't a room, it was a *temple*. Looking around, her heart skipping, Aleja spotted a small circle cut out of the side of a wall, big enough to crawl through. It led into a short tunnel that spiralled straight up, towards a trapdoor that Aleja shoved open. It thudded into the passageway to reveal Griete, who was now standing with the captain and Frances. They turned to stare at her.

'I told you to wait for me!' Frances said, holding a plate heaped with cake, her hair still glittering, Claws squirming in her other arm.

'What happened?' Captain Quint asked.

Aleja brushed some of the dust off her, coughing. Puffs of glitter fell to the deck. She couldn't stop grinning. 'Stars,' she said, waving the coded book. 'The dots in the book were *stars*. Come and see.'

Captain Quint, Griete and Frances followed her back into the tunnel – Frances still balancing her kitten and cake.

Captain Quint stood in the centre of the temple and pivoted on the spot with a look of wonder. 'Amazing.'

'It's beautiful. What does it all mean?' Griete asked.

Aleja ran her fingers over a cluster of gold statuettes. 'I'm not sure yet. But I'll figure it out.' She glanced at Tinta; maybe her shadow and its visions would be able to help.

Frances sniffed loudly. 'What's that smell?'

Aleja pointed at the basins. 'Those, I think.' They smelled strong, cloying and salty. 'Maybe it's a clue.' As soon as she'd spoken she felt another glimmer of excitement – there were probably all kinds of clues to discover in this room.

'What does this say?' Captain Quint had marched over to the other end of the little star temple and blown a layer of dust off the wall, revealing words carved into it. Aleja read them out.

'*On the roof of the world travel south from the place of gods until the golden wing awakens.*'

She thought furiously. What could it mean?

Captain Quint clapped her on the back. 'Looks like you've got another puzzle to solve.'

'And I've been teaching Claws how to do tricks, and I think something's going on between Farren and Velka, and do you think Griete's balloon will really *fly*? I hope Quint lets us try after we find the map piece. Though she's *very* stressed about how fast that owl clock is running down . . .'

Aleja was standing in line for griddle cakes in the galley, listening to Frances catch her up on every single thought she'd missed while they'd been fighting – without pausing for breath. She spotted Griete in front. 'Wait a minute,' she said to Frances, who saw who she was looking at and nodded.

Aleja sidled up next to Griete and handed her a fork. 'I'm so sorry about Raven,' she said quietly.

Griete gave her a small smile. 'Thanks,' she said. Her eyes were still haunted but she was dressed extra brightly in periwinkle blue, and diamonds sparkled in her ears.

Aleja wanted to ask her how she was but she didn't know how to find the right words.

'I'll be all right,' Griete told her anyway. 'The not knowing what had happened to her was the worst. I couldn't stop thinking about where she might be or what she was doing or if she'd betrayed us. This is horrible but I won't let François get away with it.' She clenched her fork, her eyes blazing. 'Frances told me you solved Raven's message,' she added. 'I'm sorry for snapping at you.'

'I understand,' Aleja said. 'I should have asked before going in her cabin.'

Ermtgen piled both their plates up with hot griddle cakes. She sneaked Griete a pot of whipped cream to have with hers.

'Frances also told me what you'd been thinking the last week,' Griete said.

Aleja cringed. 'I'm sorry.'

'Don't be,' Griete said. 'Death affects everyone it touches in different ways. But don't avoid us again – we're a team; we're stronger together. Your shadow's always got your back, remember?'

Aleja nodded. They were on their way to China and, though sadness still lingered around the ship like a threatening storm, the mood was slowly shifting, churning into something new, something stronger. Determination.

\*

Sitting in the tiny secret room at the rear of the ship, Aleja watched the South China Sea stream past through the submerged glass wall. She'd taken her stack of books to the Golden Lantern first but she'd accidentally stumbled on Farren and Velka stealing a secret kiss there. Smiling to herself at the unexpected turn of events, she had crept back and squirrelled herself away here instead. Spreading her books over the floor, she was attempting to solve the new puzzle from the star temple.

*On the roof of the world travel south from the place of gods until the golden wing awakens.*

She knew it by heart now. It must refer to Shanghai, to the piece of the map they were chasing . . . but the more Aleja thought about it, the more it seemed odd to call Shanghai 'the roof of the world'. She knew the Himalayas were the highest mountain range in the world – could they be the roof of the world?

She tucked her hair behind her ears and tried to ignore Tinta, who was flitting between forms. First it plodded round her lantern as a tortoise, before wisping down into a seahorse that swam over the pages of Aleja's books. Aleja batted it away impatiently, trying to read *Where the Gods Live: Temples around the World*, and the little shadow puffed out in response, growing and growing until it became a porpoise that danced up and down the glass wall.

Aleja turned back to her books. There was a mention of the Jokhang Temple built in the place of gods, but it was in a city, not the mountains, and the temple wasn't anything like the star temple. Just in case, she flicked through descriptions of temples in China but couldn't find any that matched. She closed her eyes, picturing the paintings in the star temple. *Where in the world is it?*

She held out her hand to Tinta. 'Can you show me?' But Tinta ignored her in favour of the bright school of fish darting past the window. Aleja sighed and opened another book.

Frances burst into the room. 'Claws has learned a new trick!' she said excitedly. She paused and bit her lip. 'If we're not interrupting?' Her amber eyes were wide.

'Of course not.' Aleja tore her gaze away from the page to watch, her head crammed with ancient temples and lakes and vast sweeps of treacherous land.

Frances tossed a ball across the room. 'Fetch, Claws,' she said. The kitten ran across the room and brought the ball back. 'Who's a good kitten?' Frances crooned, stroking him and letting him gobble up the treats stashed in her pocket.

Aleja smiled and reached out to stroke his soft fur. 'Very clever,' she said, crossing her legs and resting the book on her lap. Ever since their argument, she didn't mind Frances interrupting her reading, especially since she seemed much more interested now in Aleja's books and Tinta's visions.

Claws resurfaced from Frances's pocket to bat at the tropical fish swimming by and Tinta shifted into a little octopus that drifted around the room, snatching up Claws's attention. Claws chased and pounced on Tinta's shadow-tentacles while Frances chattered away.

All of a sudden, the room grew darker.

Aleja looked up. 'Tinta?' she asked uncertainly.

Claws hissed and Frances pulled him back on to her lap. 'It can't be. Tinta's next to you.'

Aleja looked down, squinting in the dim lantern light to find Tinta had melted down into a seashell resting on her page, nudging her hand with its invisible touch.

'Maybe it's a kraken?'

Aleja shook her head. 'We'd hear the kraken bells.'

Frances chewed her lip. 'Some other sea beast then.'

'*Dios*, I hope not.' Aleja stared through the glass, waiting and watching, every muscle in her body tense. 'We should warn the others.'

As soon as she'd voiced the thought, a colossal wall of grey came into view.

Frances gasped and Aleja leaped up.

A gigantic eye was staring through the glass.

'What is that?' Frances's voice shook.

Aleja gulped. The eye blinked. Then a low-pitched sound curled around the room. Deep and sonorous and wild. 'Whale song,' Aleja realized as the creature swam past, huge and sleek. 'A blue whale!'

They watched until its colossal tail swished out of view, the timeworn creature retreating back to the depths.

## CHAPTER TWENTY-NINE

### Shanghai

'I feel like we're never going to see land again,' Aleja moaned to Frances in the galley as they watched Claws drink a saucer of milk the next day. Tinta was perched next to the kitten as a hedgehog and Aleja had been trying to show Frances how the visions worked, but Tinta seemed too focused on Claws to demonstrate.

Frances nodded knowledgeably. 'Oceans always feel endless,' she said as Aada entered the galley. 'Especially with that clock staring at us every time we go into the library.'

'I am most pleased to announce we'll be reaching China within the next few days,' Aada said.

Farren whooped and cheered, Velka smiled, and Frances and Aleja grinned at each other.

Aleja – who was frustratingly no closer to solving the new puzzle – took to spending hours up in the crow's nest with Frances, Tinta and Claws, and a great stack of sandwiches, hoping to catch the first sighting of China.

It came in the shape of islands. 'Land ho!' Aleja called down, almost falling out of the crow's nest. Frances laughed and held on to her. On the horizon were several squat green islands. Tinta flapped round the basket in a seagull shape.

'Conceal us behind one of those, Olitiana,' Captain Quint ordered when Aleja climbed back down the rigging with Frances. 'I want us out of sight.' She shot a grim look at the water. 'If François is out there, he's not getting any more of my crew.'

'How are we getting into Shanghai?' Aleja asked.

'We'll row in. Shanghai's surrounded by a wall – the entire city's a fortress with a moat round it. We'll row round the island, across the river and through one of the water gates. Anyone who doesn't accompany me will be guarding the ship. There'll be no nasty surprises this time.' Penumbra hooted softly on her shoulder and Captain Quint petted him, strolling off across the deck before Aleja could ask if she'd be allowed to go along.

'Cheer up,' Frances said, noticing her expression. 'I'm sure Quint'll want us both.'

*

She did. 'Aleja, your Mandarin will come in handy, and, since you and Frances make a good team, both of you will be coming in the boat with me and Malika,' Captain Quint said. She'd called a meeting in the library after they'd dropped anchor in a deserted spot, the trees on the island shrouding their mast from view. 'Farren, you'll keep watch from the crow's nest. Shoot a warning at the first sign of trouble. Aada, you'll maintain a second watch from your cabin. Velka, supply yourself and Ermtgen with your explosives and stay stationed at the bow and stern. Olitiana and Griete, I want you to patrol the deck, cutlasses in hand.'

Come sunset, Malika handed Aleja and Frances a dark hooded cloak each. 'Tie your hair back and wear these,' she instructed, lifting her own hood over her headscarf and vanishing over the side of the ship.

In the distance a couple of fireworks shot up into the sky. Velka gazed up at them with Frances and Aleja, who would have believed anyone if they'd told her the fizzing fiery colours were magic. 'I bet I could make those,' Velka said, the sparkling display reflected in her irises. 'The green will be copper acetate and I bet if you added magnesium, you'd get white sparks . . .'

Captain Quint rolled her sleeves down over her owl tattoo and nodded at Olitiana before following Malika. 'Into the boat, girls,' she called over her shoulder, and

Aleja and Frances hurried after her as Olitiana winked and lowered the rowing boat into the water. Tinta watched them from the deck and Aleja waved back.

When they crossed the river and the first red-sailed junk ships and slanted roofs peeking above the city walls appeared, Aleja could hardly sit still.

'I haven't been in this part of the world in quite some time.' A wide smile spread across the captain's face. 'Just look at those sails.' She rowed faster and Aleja and Frances huffed harder at their oars to keep up. Malika sat like a sentry at the end of the boat, watching the fortified city come into view.

They drew closer and Malika whispered, 'Keep your hoods low. Aleja – you'll be our ears and voice. Frances –'

'Yes?' Frances asked eagerly.

'Keep your hands to yourself,' Malika said with narrowed eyes. 'We're not here to cause any trouble; this is strictly a fact-finding mission.'

Frances sulked and the captain chuckled. They rowed into a narrow moat, thick stone walls towering above them like a castle as they approached the eastern water gate. Captain Quint nodded at the wall, her eyes flashing with enthusiasm. 'These were built by the Ming dynasty to keep out the *wō kòu*, the ferocious Japanese pirates who sailed these waters hundreds of years ago.'

The water gate was manned by the local garrison and, as they neared, Aleja couldn't help holding on to her coin for reassurance. Her Mandarin hadn't been tested yet. But the soldiers on guard were too deep into a bottle of rice wine to notice them and they rowed smoothly past and into the city.

Though it was dark, Shanghai hummed with energy. Frances and the captain tied up the boat as Aleja tried to look everywhere at once. There were ancient temples with roofs that curved into the sky, pavilions and teahouses and large ponds dappled with moonlight. The streets were lined with carts that hissed with hot oil as vendors fried food and people strolled by in *qín páos*, long tunics in rich patterns.

'Malika and I shall locate and scout the collector's mansion,' Captain Quint said. 'You two stick close together and listen out for any mention of François or any other useful information. And stay out of trouble.' She gave them a warning look. 'Meet us back at the boat in an hour.'

Aleja and Frances practically skipped off, their freedom to explore unexpected and sweet.

'Let's try the teahouse,' Frances said, pushing up her glasses and looking at a steaming bamboo vat of rice. 'I'll bet there's all kinds of interesting information we could pick up there.'

They wandered over to the biggest teahouse they could find, which was buzzing with people and beaming with red lanterns. Its windows were lace-like and its crimson slanted roof looked like it could have been tiled with dragon scales. The air was perfumed with tea and flowers, and Aleja ordered a pot of jasmine tea with her tentative Mandarin and a wide smile.

'Look over there,' Frances said in an undertone. 'Sailors.'

Aleja glanced a few tables over to where a huddle of five men sat smoking pipes and drinking tea in salt-stained trousers and battered boots.

'Can you hear them?' Frances asked, her eyes wide.

Aleja listened. They were speaking French.

'– the night for it.'

'Captain wants to head there tomorrow, before those infernal women no doubt turn up again. He's still sore about that fiasco in Morocco . . .'

Aleja's blood ran cold. Could they be talking about –

'No wonder they call him the Fury!'

She met Frances's eyes and whispered, 'François's crew.'

'Time to leave,' Frances whispered back.

The instant they'd paid and strolled outside, Frances erupted. Her eyes stormed with rage and she balled her hands into fists. 'I can't believe they're here before us again. I should go back in there and pay them back for what they did to Raven –'

'No,' Aleja said firmly. 'There are five of them and they don't know we're here. Besides, they'll never find our ship now we've hidden it. We just need to get the map piece first. We can pay them back for Raven by *beating* them.'

Frances stared back at the teahouse, breathing heavily. 'OK,' she said at last, following Aleja deeper into the city.

They wandered over a crooked bridge, past a few pagodas and stopped to gobble down some dumplings. They were ambling back towards the boat when Aleja nudged Frances and raised her eyebrows at a couple of soldiers patrolling in their direction. They flattened their backs against a temple wall, blending into the shadows.

'Jì Chéng returned from the emperor's court at once,' the first soldier was saying in Mandarin. Aleja nodded at Frances – they needed to hear this.

'It's not the first time burglars have targeted his mansion,' the second soldier replied. 'Makes you wonder what he's got in there.'

The first soldier laughed. 'I don't doubt it will be the last time. Have you heard about the new guards he's had brought in?'

'I have. Apparently they're extremely ferocious – likely to rip your throat out if they stumble across you!'

The first soldier groaned. 'He's paying me a little something on the side to keep a lookout when he returns to Peking, but I don't think I want to risk bumping into his guards.'

There was a jangling noise and Aleja quickly peeked round the side of the temple. One of the soldiers briefly showed the other a set of keys.

Aleja looked at Frances. 'Jì Chéng's got some horrible new guards,' she whispered. 'The soldier's got keys to his mansion but even he doesn't want to meet them.'

Frances looked interested. Before Aleja could stop her, she popped round the wall of the temple and trudged over to the soldiers. Aleja's heart skipped a beat. She froze, watching Frances approach the soldiers, hunched over as if she was an old woman, her hood low over her face.

She accidentally bumped into one of them, mumbled something that could have been an apology in any language and carried on her way, towards where they'd tied their boat. Aleja hurried after her, keeping to the shadows.

'What were you thinking?' she cried out, racing up to where Frances stood beside the boat.

Frances whipped out a set of keys from her pocket and jangled them.

## CHAPTER THIRTY

*The Collector's Mansion*

'I didn't keep my hands to myself.' Frances grinned cheekily at Malika, waving the keys as soon as she and the captain returned to the boat.

Malika shot Frances a lethal look but Captain Quint was thrilled. 'Excellent work,' she said, taking the keys and picking up her oar. 'We've located Jì Chéng's mansion, too. We'll have half the map before we know it!'

Aleja felt bad spoiling the captain's good mood, but she couldn't put off telling them about François's arrival.

Malika nodded at Quint. 'You were right to hide the ship.'

'Aye, and we'll keep her hidden.' Captain Quint's mouth thinned. 'So he thinks he can get the map piece first, does he?' Her hands shook a little on the oar. 'Not on my watch,' she growled. 'We'll let the others know and go back tonight.'

'Are you sure it's the right place?' Aleja began, thinking of the star temple and how it hadn't seemed to point to a mansion. But Captain Quint shot her a look and she fell silent.

A couple of hours later, Aleja and Frances were perched on the emerald-tiled slanted roof of the collector's mansion, waiting for the plan to spark into action. The mansion was a huge compound of gates, courtyards and long buildings that sat low and squat in a square. Frances's stolen keys had unlocked the series of gates but gone no further. It seemed even the soldier wasn't to be trusted with Jì Chéng's mansion. The courtyard was peppered with stone statues of elephants and monkeys, willow trees and a pagoda glazed in red so deep it looked black. An owl's low hoot winged through the air. The captain's signal. Aleja looked across the courtyard in time to see Malika slip down from the slanted roof she was on and through a window, a silky whisper against the midnight sky in onyx trousers, tunic and headscarf. Also dressed in black, Captain Quint descended another wall and disappeared through a different window, heading east. Aleja nodded at Frances – it was their turn.

Frances nodded back and made to move, but a flicker caught Aleja's eye and she held Frances back.

'What?' Frances hissed under her breath.

Aleja jerked her head towards the southern wing of the mansion, where a hooded figure had appeared, crouching low on the roof. 'We're being watched,' she whispered, panic crawling over her skin.

'Do you think it's a trap?' Frances asked quickly, her amber eyes glowing in alarm.

The figure sprang up and disappeared over the wall edging the compound.

'I don't know,' Aleja said, 'but, even if it is, we still need to get inside and find the map piece; we can't let anyone get it first. Come on.'

They clambered down over the tiles and through a low window. Paintings hung from the walls, with characters inked in beautiful calligraphy against water-colours of streams and bamboo groves.

Aleja's nerves bit at her and she kept glancing back to check the mysterious figure hadn't materialized behind them.

Frances recovered fast. 'Don't worry, I've never been caught yet,' she whispered as they padded down a long corridor that gleamed in crimson and black.

Aleja shot her an incredulous look. 'Are you forgetting about the time I rescued you in Marrakesh?'

Frances flapped a hand dismissively.

'Or when you got caught in the consul's house and he locked both of us *and* the captain in that cell?'

'I've never *stayed* caught,' Frances said brightly.

That didn't inspire much confidence and Aleja's worries swelled as they crept round corners and peered into room after room after room. Tiny courtyards were hidden behind sliding doors that suddenly revealed tinkling water features and lotus blossoms. She didn't see a glimpse of any guards but the soldiers' voices kept rattling around her head. *Ferocious . . . rip your throat out . . .*

With daintily thin Ming vases, calligraphy paintings and jade carvings the collector's mansion was like a museum. But where was the map piece? All the antiques Jì Chéng had acquired around the world seemed to have been scattered across his mansion. There were no handy placards to look for, no clues left by Thomas James. Someone had reached in and plucked this map piece from where it had originally rested, leaving it without a trail. Aleja's hopes sank. Thoughts of the star temple kept niggling at her. Nothing about the puzzle fitted this place. She wondered if Tinta would have been able to show her where it was if it was here. But she'd asked Tinta about the map countless times and had only been met with the shadow's blank stare. 'We're running out of time,' she said, glancing out of a window. The sky had shifted from deepest black to velvet indigo.

'Maybe the captain or Malika has found it –' Frances swallowed her words.

Something was tapping along the corridor outside. Like a heavy-footed person or two were wandering towards them.

Aleja froze. The tapping grew louder and louder and she twisted round, looking for a place to hide, but there was none. Then the tapping passed by, continuing down the corridor and away.

'The guards,' Aleja whispered.

'We need to hurry before they come back.' Frances looked around. 'But where could it be?'

Aleja started to dig through pearl necklaces and incense burners and polished chunks of jade. When she discovered a golden compass, she clicked it open without thinking. And there, inside, was a curl of parchment – a scrap of a map. Aleja gasped. 'It's here,' she said disbelievingly.

'Finally!' Frances said, rushing over to look. 'So what do you think the puzzle in the star temple leads to then?' she asked.

Aleja shrugged, more confused than ever. She grabbed the map, along with a few jewels for good measure, and stuffed them all into her trouser pockets.

Frances grinned at her.

'What?'

'Nothing. Nothing at all,' Frances replied mischievously. 'Just that you're getting more piratey than ever.' She liberated a golden crown and sat it on her head. 'And I approve.'

Aleja giggled. 'Come on, let's get out of here.'

But Frances didn't move. All the colour had drained from her face until she looked as ghostly as Geoffrey. 'Don't . . . move,' she whispered out of the corner of her mouth, her eyes locked on the doorway. Her glasses slid down her nose but she didn't move to push them up.

Aleja couldn't have moved if she'd wanted to. She was rooted to the spot. Through the reflection in Frances's glasses she'd spotted what had terrified Frances. And she had no idea how they would fight their way out of this one.

A tiger was prowling towards them.

## CHAPTER THIRTY-ONE

### *The Decoy*

'The window,' Frances whispered.

'I've got an idea,' Aleja whispered back, slowly turning round.

The tiger tracked her every movement. It was huge. Bright stripes rippled along its sleek fur and it was as tall as Aleja's chest. She swallowed. Then a second tiger prowled in. Frances stifled a gasp. The first one growled, baring dagger-sharp teeth. Aleja reached an arm back behind her. She grasped a china handle and flung a vase across the room, over the tigers' heads and out into the corridor, where it smashed.

Both tigers jerked their heads round and Aleja jumped on to the table and out of the window, Frances at her heels, adrenalin screaming through her veins. They landed in a jasmine-scented bush, all elbows and knees. 'Quick!' Aleja could already see the tigers running towards the window. She bolted back to it and slammed it shut. Frances rushed to help hold it, giving a low owl's hoot.

'We won't be able to hold it!' Aleja whisper-shouted as the huge animals raced towards the glass.

A third pair of hands and then a fourth joined theirs. 'So that's why the guards are so ferocious,' Captain Quint mused, eerily calm.

One of the tigers pounced. The glass shuddered under Aleja's hands, threatening to shatter beneath the weight of the tiger's muscled body and gigantic, scrabbling paws.

Frances yelped and Aleja swallowed back a scream.

'Er, where did the other one go?' Frances asked.

Aleja gave her a horrified look.

'Frances, Aleja, get up on the roof. Now,' Captain Quint said.

Aleja scrambled up the side of the mansion and swung herself on to the roof. Frances joined her, her face reflecting Aleja's fear, when a low guttural growl sounded.

The second tiger was prowling towards the captain and Malika on the ground below.

'I've never seen Malika fight a tiger before,' Frances

whispered, though her face was still white. 'I wonder who will win.'

Aleja felt sick at the thought. But then the captain and Malika joined them on the roof, leaving the tiger pacing beneath them. It bunched up its hind legs and leaped towards them. Aleja scrabbled backwards in a hurry but the tiger couldn't reach the sharp slant of the roof and she let out her breath. They were safe. For now.

'Shame. It would have made a nice rug for my quarters,' the captain said. 'Kidding,' she added hastily when Malika shot her a look.

Aleja handed over the scrap of the map.

'Thank you.' Captain Quint tucked it away in the vial round her neck, next to the first piece. Inside the glass a tiny puff of smoke curled up and the first piece curled its edges away from the second. Aleja stared at it, wondering why, but the captain gave it an adoring look. 'Halfway there,' she said, stroking the glass with a fingertip.

'Let's go,' Malika said impatiently, striding off along the rooftops, away from the tiger, and leading the way back to the ship.

They returned to the ship, where Farren and Velka were left guarding the deck while the rest of the crew gathered in the library, altogether more wary now than after the disastrous heist in Ragusa, when they had been greeted by a party and cake. Tinta rushed over in its fox shape and frolicked round Aleja's legs.

Olitiana looked between them. 'Well?'

'We have retrieved the second piece,' Captain Quint announced, striding over to the table and unlacing the vial from her neck. 'And now we have half the map,' she said, her fingers trembling as she laid the pieces next to each other.

The room fizzed with excitement and everybody craned for a look at the two pieces.

They didn't match.

In fact, the new piece didn't look anything like the first piece. The parchments were different colours – one cream, one brownish – and though they both looked like the bottom edge of a map, the land and sea didn't meet. The pirates' excitement soured.

Though all along Aleja had had a feeling of uncertainty about the map piece in Shanghai, she'd never expected to find a fake. Aleja looked from one to the other. Tinta shrank down into the shadow of a tiny mouse and scurried inside Aleja's boot.

'It's not real,' Captain Quint said flatly. She flipped the parchment over. There was a small scrawl on the bottom of it. Aleja recognized it as Thomas James's handwriting from the key to the ship.

*Stop looking.*

'It's a decoy,' Captain Quint said. 'My great-grandfather must have left decoys scattered around the world to send map-seekers off on a wild goose chase. And he's certainly succeeded. Two *months* we've been sailing.' She stormed to the other side of the library, pulled a massive tome off a shelf and opened it to a hollowed centre that held a dusty bottle. She took a swig and came back to sit at the table, slamming her boots on top of the engraved map of the world. She glared at the owl clock. 'Just under eight months left. We're over halfway through the countdown and we still don't have the second piece yet. The odds are against us now.'

The crew took one look at her storm-faced expression and silently filtered out. Even the shadows glided out through the walls and floor.

Aleja slunk back to her cabin with Tinta hiding in her boot. Her eyes burned with tears – they'd wasted so much time. And every day the time on the owl clock ran lower, like sand trickling through their fingers. She curled up under her blankets and stared at the dark night through the porthole. 'I don't see how we're going to find the map now, Tinta,' she whispered. The little shadow-mouse crept closer on her pillow. Aleja squeezed her eyes shut. 'I – I suppose this is the end of my big adventure.'

## CHAPTER THIRTY-TWO

*The Hooded Figure*

Aleja tossed and turned until her blankets fell off her bunk and she gave up on sleep. 'At least I got to see China,' she said and sighed. Tinta's mouse whiskers twitched. 'I don't feel ready to go back to Sevilla yet!'

She wandered through her cabin, looking at the memories of her adventure – the golden telescope and black pearl Captain Quint had gifted her, the carpet she and Frances had carried through the streets of Tangier, even one of the counterfeit coins she had discovered last summer that led to her hiding out on the *Ship of Shadows* . . .

'That's it!' She pulled her boots back on. They *could* still buy themselves some time. She raced along the passageway and down to the library, Tinta scampering at her heels.

'Stop!' Aleja rushed over to where Captain Quint was holding the fake map piece out to the fire. She snatched it out of her hand before the flames licked it.

Captain Quint raised an eyebrow at her. Penumbra clicked his beak from Quint's shoulder.

'We know there's another map piece hidden somewhere in Asia,' Aleja said slowly, looking from the captain's bright blue eyes to Penumbra's luminous orange ones, both equally fierce and pinned on her.

'Asia's a big place, Aleja,' Captain Quint said. 'I don't have the years it would take to scour all of it and I don't know what will happen when that –' she gestured at the clock – 'ends its countdown. Not unless you've solved the clues in that secret room you discovered? Or had another of those visions?'

'Not yet,' Aleja said, ignoring a pinch of guilt that maybe Raven would have had the answers by now. She jutted her chin out, forcing confidence into her voice. 'But I will. And when I do, we'll find where in Asia we have to go. In the meantime François and his crew don't know we have this map piece.' She waved it.

The captain shrugged. 'It isn't the right one –'

'Exactly.' Aleja beamed. 'But *they* don't know that. And they don't have an original piece to compare it to . . .'

She thought of the counterfeit coins. If she'd never held a real coin, she wouldn't have known the difference.

A spark of light danced in Quint's eyes. 'So if we erase the writing and replace it –'

'Then they'll steal it for themselves and run off with it, thinking it's real and giving us a chance to find the real piece instead,' Aleja finished triumphantly.

'Excellent thinking.' Captain Quint reached out and pressed a small button hidden in the fireplace. Aleja looked at it with interest. A bell rang somewhere in the depths of the ship. A beat later, Olitiana and Malika entered the library and Captain Quint relayed the plan to them.

'I like it,' Olitiana said, nodding to herself. 'I like it a lot.'

'Keep the ship hidden,' Captain Quint instructed. 'I want *La Promesse Lumineuse* to sail straight off when they retrieve the fake map. Until then, maintain a strict guard on deck.'

'Aye, Captain,' Olitiana said, and strode out of the library.

'There's just one little thing,' Malika said silkily. Aleja and the captain turned to her. 'How do you intend on replacing the map piece without getting mauled to death?'

Aleja scrunched up her nose, deep in thought.

Captain Quint sighed, her enthusiasm waning. 'We got out of there; I suppose we can get back in.'

'Velka!' Aleja exclaimed.

Malika frowned. 'What about her?'

'She must have something we can use to immobilize the tigers. Or put them to sleep?'

Aleja was dispatched to Velka's cabin. A living canvas of butterflies and plants, it was like stepping into a jungle, steamy and lush. Peridot lounged on Velka's bunk, and Farren and Velka were sitting next to an abandoned game of chess when Aleja burst in. Their laughing stopped and Velka's full cheeks pinkened.

'Do you know how to put a tiger to sleep?' she asked, her thoughts a jumble of ideas and schemes.

Farren rested her boots against Velka's wall. 'I feel like I'm missing something.'

Aleja explained her idea as Velka began sorting through the glass bottles and vials on her desk. The colours were as vibrant as the butterflies that flitted around the glass enclosure at the foot of her bunk. Cerulean, lime green, fizzing tangerine.

'A sedative will work,' Velka said, selecting one. 'Henbane.' She measured it out into a set of curious little darts.

'Don't get eaten,' Farren warned as Aleja and Velka hurried out of the cabin.

They rushed back to the library, picked up the captain, Malika and Frances, and hiked back to the mansion.

Sitting on the emerald rooftop for the second time that night, Aleja suddenly remembered the hooded figure who had been watching them and whipped round, sure she'd see eyes staring at her through the dawn. But there was no one there. Malika tossed chunks of raw meat down on to the grass and they waited for the tigers to appear.

'There!' Aleja whispered, spotting the first sleek animal padding outside to investigate.

Velka sucked in a breath and Aleja turned to reassure her that the tigers couldn't reach them – but Velka gushed, 'They're *gorgeous*.'

Frances snorted. 'The more dangerous the animal, the more Velka loves them,' she said into Aleja's ear.

'Peridot's not dangerous,' Velka said mildly, watching the second tiger slink over. Unable to keep her eyes off the animals, she drew out a hollow tube and the first dart.

'Yeah, luckily, or the captain would've tossed him overboard,' Frances said. 'Remember the king cobra you wanted to keep?'

Velka smiled to herself. 'He was cute.'

Aleja caught Captain Quint's grimace out of the corner of her eye. She watched Velka fit a dart into the hollow tube and lie across the tiles, leaning closer to the tigers. The captain grabbed her ankles but Velka didn't seem concerned and instead murmured, 'Sorry about this,' to the nearest tiger before blowing sharply into the tube. The dart flew out of the other side and into the tiger's hindquarters. It gave a little yelp that sounded more like Claws than a tiger and Velka winced, getting a second dart ready. It landed in the other tiger's shoulder when it came over and a few minutes later they both had fallen asleep.

'We'll wait here in case they wake up,' the captain said. 'Frances and Aleja, put this back.' She handed them the map piece from her pocket.

They retrod their footsteps from earlier, Aleja unable to stop yawning as the sky pinkened with the promise of morning. Just as Frances had replaced the map, she turned to Aleja with a frown. 'Did you hear that?'

'Is it the tigers?' Aleja spun round in case a secret third tiger was sneaking up behind them, but the room was empty. She exhaled. And then she heard it. This time it wasn't the tapping of tiger claws along the corridor. It was the sound of bootsteps. And a voice she recognized. *François*.

'*Allons voir ici*,' he said in a low voice that curdled Aleja's thoughts with fear. *Let's look in here*. It sounded like an entire group of men were walking towards them.

She clutched at Frances. 'It's him!'

'Come on,' Frances whispered, leading the way out of the window and on to the roof, where Captain Quint and Velka were waiting.

Aleja caught sight of Malika creeping along another slanted roof, her onyx headscarf gently waving in the jasmine-perfumed breeze, the first peep of the sun glinting off the hilt of her scimitar at her hip. 'François is already here,' Aleja said urgently.

Captain Quint laced her hands together, brought them to her mouth and blew through them in a soft hooting sound that echoed Penumbra's.

A beat later, Malika responded in the same fashion, her hoot travelling across the rooftops. There was a shuffle in a nearby treetop and a monkey poked its head out to look at them all warily. When Aleja looked back at Malika, she was mid-air, leaping back across to their rooftop. 'It's him,' Malika hissed, her expression darkening like a storm. 'He's got his urn with him. He must be expecting us.' She spoke fiercely but her voice wobbled on the word 'urn'.

Aleja couldn't help glancing at the spot where Malika's missing shadow should have rested on the emerald tiles behind her. That shadow-stripping urn scared her more than the tigers. She hoped François would take it and the fake map piece and sail far, far away from them.

'Back to the ship,' Captain Quint ordered.

While they'd been replacing the map piece, Olitiana and Farren had sailed the ship a little further along the island. It was still hidden out of sight, except for the top half of the mast, which now was a vantage point for spying on the harbour. Aleja and Frances took to the netting, ready to scramble up to the crow's nest and fix their spyglasses on *La Promesse Lumineuse*, when a sudden rainfall poured from the sky, thick and heavy. It came with creeping tendrils of sea mist, obscuring the harbour as if a pack of ghosts were feasting on it.

'Aleja, Frances, in here,' Aada called, peering out from her trapdoor.

They ran and skidded across the deck to her ladder and climbed up into her cabin, high above the ship.

'I believe my telescope has the best view of *La Promesse Lumineuse*,' Aada said, repositioning it to look across the coast through another large window. Frances wiped her glasses and looked through it.

The rain thudded down on to the glass ceiling above and Aleja shivered as she dripped on to Aada's floor.

Aada handed her a thick fur to wrap round her shoulders. The navigator's cabin glowed with lanterns and a fire was crackling in the grate. Shadows swirled round the stone in one of her cubbyholes like the steam rising from her coffeepot. Rain sheeted down the huge windows like curtains.

Aada sat down on one of her soft purple armchairs with a fur draped across it and offered Aleja a cup of coffee. Aleja shook her head and Aada sipped one, staring out through the rain with a faraway expression.

'I think they've just come back,' Frances said, offering the telescope to Aleja.

Aleja looked through and gasped at the perfect view as the pirate hunters suddenly came into focus. She spotted François straight away and could even pick out the marbled veins across the urn he was still carrying. Aleja couldn't help glancing down at Tinta – who cocked its seagull head back at her – just to check her second shadow was still there. 'I see him,' she said grimly.

Frances took back the telescope. 'The crew are assembling on deck; they're all looking at something . . . They've got the fake map piece! Now François is talking . . . and talking . . . Wow, he really loves the sound of his own voice, doesn't he? He's talking some more and, oh, they're weighing the anchor!'

Aleja exchanged relieved grins with Frances.

'You did it, Aleja!' Frances said, her glasses smeared. 'This was all your idea! I'm going to report to the captain,' she announced, and scurried out of the trapdoor and down the ladder.

But Aleja's happiness trickled away at once. They'd managed to trick François but they were still no closer to finding the real map piece.

When Aleja looked through the telescope again, she saw a dark hooded figure step off *La Promesse Lumineuse* just before the pirate hunters' ship sailed away.

The same person who had been watching them last night.

## CHAPTER THIRTY-THREE

### *The Shadow Balloon*

Aleja rushed to train the telescope on the figure but she was too slow – the mysterious person had vanished into the rain.

Captain Quint chose that moment to pop her head up through the trapdoor. 'All this gloomy weather has given me a hankering for a hot drink. I rather fancy a cup of coffee,' she said cheerfully, her chestnut hair dripping everywhere. 'And I suspect Aleja has something to tell me,' she added, shutting the trapdoor and eyeing Aleja, who was shifting from one foot to the other.

'Sit yourselves down,' Aada said, pouring two large cupfuls of coffee and handing one patterned with stars to the captain, who immediately added several ginormous spoonfuls of sugar to it. She passed Aleja a sky-blue cup of spiced warm milk. Aleja wrapped her chilled fingers round it and told them both all about the hooded figure and being watched. She glanced at Tinta, who was sneaking over to the stone as a hedgehog. She wondered whether Tinta would be able to show her who the figure was – could the shadow be capable of showing her things happening both in other places *and* other times?

When she'd finished her coffee, Captain Quint sighed and put her soggy hat back on. 'I'll go and assign extra guards around the deck, but it would be best if we weighed anchor. It seems François's games with us haven't ended yet. Aleja, how close are you to figuring out our puzzle? None of the other crew have any leads.'

Aleja grimaced.

'Any more visions? Perhaps Tinta could help you with this one?' The captain looked at Tinta sitting on top of the stone.

'Not yet,' Aleja said, staring into her milk. 'I don't know why they happen when they do but I can't seem to make them happen.'

'Ah,' said Captain Quint, 'another mystery.' And she disappeared down the ladder.

The rain was still lashing down but Aada's cabin was so toasty that Aleja didn't want to move. She sipped her spiced milk slowly.

Aada turned her silvery gaze on Aleja. 'Remind me what the puzzle says?'

'*On the roof of the world travel south from the place of gods until the golden wing awakens,*' Aleja recited dully.

'*The roof of the world.*' Aada pursed her lips and looked up at the water splattering on the glass ceiling.

'I think it means the Himalayas,' Aleja said, 'but an entire mountain range is too big to search, so I've been trying to work out the rest of the clue.'

'It could mean the Himalayas,' Aada said, pulling out a map from the cubbyholes round her table where Tinta and other shadows were jostling for space round the stone, 'but I've also heard the Tibetan Plateau being called the roof of the world.' She unrolled the map and pointed at the raised sweep of land that was bordered by the highest, deadliest mountains in the world.

Aleja leaped to her feet. 'I've got to get my book!' she called as she half slid down the ladder and raced to the library. Tinta galloped after her as a shadow-horse. Aleja rifled through the pages of *Where the Gods Live: Temples around the World*. Then she ran up one of the rolling ladders and snatched up an atlas. 'Aha!' she exclaimed.

She took both books back to Aada. 'See here? This book mentions the Jokhang Temple that's in a city called the place of gods. I didn't think about it as I was looking for temples that matched in the Himalayas – or Shanghai – but the place of gods is a city in Tibet!'

Aada stretched a humongous map of Tibet out on the table.

Aleja pointed to Lhasa. 'There it is. According to this –' she set the atlas down – 'its name translates as *place of gods* in Tibetan. *Travel south from the place of gods until the golden wing awakens.*'

Aada traced her finger south from Lhasa.

'But what does the last part mean?' Aleja asked.

Aada's finger came to a stop on a little lake. 'Look at this,' she said, tapping it. 'What does this lake look like to you?'

Aleja looked at it. 'It's shaped like wings,' she realized a little breathlessly.

Aleja flew back down the ladder and raced across the sodden deck into the captain's quarters. 'We know the answer to the puzzle!'

Olitiana was in there with Quint and the two of them listened with increasing interest as Aleja relayed her and Aada's discovery.

When Aleja had finished, Captain Quint's face was glowing. 'It looks like we're going on another overland expedition,' she said, and Aleja lit up with excitement.

The next day passed in a whirlwind of packing and organizing.

Captain Quint had called a meeting in the library where she announced where they were heading next and assigned duties to everyone, as well as deciding who would accompany her. Aleja was told last year that Malika, Aada and Frances always went with Quint on her explorations. Velka and Griete sometimes came, and the rest stayed with the ship, guarding and maintaining it.

'We have a long expedition ahead of us,' Quint said, glancing at the clock. 'With that in mind I've decided we'll be flying over China in Griete's shadow balloon.'

'Yes!' Frances nudged Aleja enthusiastically.

Aleja sucked in a breath, hoping.

'Aleja, I want you and Tinta to come. See if you can extract any more information from your shadow as we journey to Tibet.'

Aleja grinned at Frances, who'd already been selected, along with Velka and the rest of the usual crew.

They sailed further up the coast, dropping anchor by an abandoned jetty on the mainland, far from any towns or villages. There Griete instructed Quint on how to fly the balloon while Velka readied enough fuel. Though the balloon was Griete's invention, Aleja suspected Quint had wanted Griete to stay and rest after the loss of Raven. Ermtgen packaged up food supplies, Farren organized warm travelling clothes, and Frances and

Aleja were in charge of digging up camping supplies from the hold and cleaning them up. A couple of mice scurried out from a tent and Claws ignored them, instead prowling after Penumbra, who was basking in the sunlight on the taffrail. The crew all watched the balloon being carried off the ship. Shadows trailed after it like mist. Tinta remained by Aleja's side.

Velka and Griete hooked up a canister of gas to the burner and slowly, slowly the giant balloon began to inflate. There was a buzz in the air as the pirates all watched; they were about to make history.

Aleja sneaked away as Frances thrust Claws in the captain's face, trying to convince her to let the kitten come too.

A few minutes later Aleja sat on the fluffy carpet in the middle of her cabin and tried to pack. Into her bag went the warm travelling clothes Farren had handed her, a couple of books on Mandarin and Tibetan, one she'd dug up from the library called *Tibetan Travels with Thomas*, which she'd never read before, and *The Travels of Marco Polo* for bedtime reading. If she had time. Soon she'd be in the sky and she couldn't keep still at the thought of it. After casting a final look around her cabin, she added a storm-jar.

Tinta shrank down to an inky blob that sat on top of her bag and refused to budge. Aleja crouched down next to it. 'You're coming with me this time,' she told it, smiling, and it perked up. She dipped her fingers in the shadow. 'Can you tell me who the hooded figure is?' Tinta shifted into a badger and tipped its misty head up at her. Aleja almost imagined it looked at her enquiringly but Tinta was all shadow and she never saw an expression wisp across its many faces. 'Show me something,' Aleja said. '*Anything.*' She concentrated as hard as she could. But Tinta just stared at her.

For their last breakfast Ermtgen served helpings of eggs, sausages and hot buttered toast until the captain joked that the balloon wouldn't be able to lift them. She wore a light shirt and Aleja suddenly noticed the map piece was missing from her neck. Captain Quint winked at her. 'I stashed it in the hiding place you and Frances found,' she told her in an undertone. 'Olitiana's guarding it for me.'

Then it was time to say goodbye.

Velka launched herself at Farren, who looked surprised but quickly hugged her back. 'Don't say goodbye,' Farren said, grinning. 'It's bad luck.'

'– and you'll be sure to feed him three times a day and make sure he gets enough water and brush his fur and play with him and –' Frances was rattling off instructions to Griete, Claws meowing and trying to escape as Frances held on to him.

'Look after my ship for me,' Captain Quint told Olitiana, setting her hat down on the wheel and stroking

Penumbra, who gave a mournful hoot and nipped her fingers.

Ermtgen sneaked slices of cake into Frances's and Aleja's pockets and Aleja felt a ripple of sadness as she realized how much she would miss everyone and the ship over the next few weeks.

Farren had built a thin wooden ramp lined with bits of stone that now formed a walkway between the ship's taffrail and the balloon's basket, allowing shadows to travel between the vessels. Aleja took a deep breath and stepped up on to the taffrail, Tinta leaping up as a shadow-fox. 'Are you ready?' she asked her shadow before walking along it. She scrunched up her eyes and jumped into the basket with her fingers crossed. When she opened them, Tinta was still at her side. 'Yes!' she cried. 'It worked!' she shouted to Frances and the rest of the pirates, who cheered.

Frances strode along after, dropping hers and Aleja's bags into the basket and sitting next to her and Tinta on the little built-in bench round the sides. Velka sat with them, a leather satchel slung over her shoulder.

'Er, Velka?' Frances said. 'Your bag's moving.'

Velka lifted the flap. 'Oh, not again.' Inside were a set of vials secured by padded straps, a pistol and her hollow tube with a set of darts. And Peridot. Velka scooped the iguana out. 'You're supposed to be staying with Farren!' She jogged back to the ship to hand a disgruntled Peridot back as Malika and Aada leaped into the basket.

Griete rushed over and handed a small stone pot with a lid to Aleja. 'This is made of the same stone,' she told her seriously. 'If anything happens to the balloon, keep the shadows safe in this.'

Aleja alternated between staring up at the colossal balloon suspended above them, the wooden basket straining at the ropes securing it to the jetty, and Tinta, who was curled up at her side. Captain Quint vaulted over the side of the basket. 'All ready?' she called out cheerfully. 'Then off we go!'

Olitiana and Farren cut the ropes. Aleja squeezed Frances's hand as they watched the shadows ripple darkly around the balloon. With a swoop and a lurch the balloon began to rise. The pirates on the jetty whooped and clapped, and Aleja couldn't stop grinning as they soared up into the sky.

## CHAPTER THIRTY-FOUR

*Crossing China*

Up, up and up they rose until the other pirates were pinpricks below and China sprawled out ahead of them. China was vast. Aleja knew this from the books she'd devoured in the library and from Aada's maps. But knowing it and seeing it were two very different things. It felt dizzying.

They travelled further into China, flying along on the wind currents, assisted by the shadows that swirled around the balloon like smoke and guided their course. Aleja and Frances wore thick knitted jumpers and coats against the chill of the sky and watched the scenery grow lusher beneath them. Emerald rivers, little waterfalls and vibrant greenery tumbled down stony hills. Their supplies for venturing into the Himalayas were bundled up round the basket, and a little while later Aleja and Frances built themselves a nest out of canvas tents and sacks. They sat inside it, chatting and munching on cake. Tinta hopped around as a bird after a flock flew past the basket and Aleja laughed delightedly. She longed to reach out and touch the clouds that popped up alongside, which were as fluffy and wispy as the shadows. Captain Quint and Velka flew the balloon between them with Aada navigating and Malika keeping a wary eye on everything.

It wasn't until days later that Aleja felt it. A prickling uneasiness. She was sure that something wasn't right.

The Yangtze snaked below them like a jade ribbon and, as Aleja gazed down, Tinta hopped on to her hand. Then Aleja's stomach lurched. She blinked and found herself standing on a large sampan – a flat boat – travelling along the river. And the hooded figure from the collector's mansion was standing before her. Aleja's breath caught. She tried to see the person's face, but they were facing away from her and looking up at the sky. When Aleja glanced up, she saw the shadow balloon floating above. Then the vision melted away.

She stared down. Mountains rose on either side of the river like slumbering dragons, towering over it and blotting out the sun, making it difficult to see the water. Dark greenery spilled down the mountains, with giant creepers trailing along the top of the gorge, and now and then she spotted a golden monkey leaping across. Aleja frowned as she noticed they were about to fly into a patch of mist.

'What is it?' Malika said.

'I had another vision,' Aleja said.

Everyone's attention snapped on to her. 'What did you see?' the captain asked immediately.

'It was the hooded figure again. They're following us . . .' She trailed off, looking down at the impossibly steep gorges below.

'Through this terrain?' The captain frowned.

Malika and Aleja both peered closely at the view below. Aleja picked out a flight of narrow stairs that teetered up the side of a mountain. It led to a tiny town perched at the top like it was floating in the clouds. It glowed with oil lamps through the thin mist that snaked along the gorges. It suddenly felt eerie and Aleja shivered in the chilly wind, tugging her sleeves down over her fingers.

'We'll keep a watch out,' Malika said eventually and resumed sharpening her throwing knives.

Aleja cracked open *The Travels of Marco Polo* to distract herself, dipping back into the thirteenth-century Italian merchant and explorer's travels in the Mongol empire and China. Tinta poked its fox nose on to the page and Aleja couldn't focus – her thoughts whirled, wondering who was under the hood and why Tinta showed her some things but not others. She didn't like not knowing when a vision was coming.

She swapped books and plunged back into a tale of Thomas James witnessing the ritual of creating a *ro-lang* – a risen corpse – in Tibet. Aleja shuddered, which Frances immediately noticed. She moved next to her, reading over her shoulder and saying, 'I told you my story of *ro-langs* was real!' as she sprayed cake crumbs over the page.

A few nights later, the cold and cramped conditions inside the basket had them all longing to stretch their legs. Captain Quint conceded and opened a valve to begin their descent. Air hissed out and the balloon began to sink lower in the sky. 'We need to drop some of the ballasts,' she shouted out, and Velka and Aada immediately set to untying the weighted sacks that hung round the edges of the basket. When they dropped, so did the balloon. The shadows rippled darkly, keeping them on a steady course down. Tinta pressed into Aleja's side as a shadow-cat and Frances sighed. 'I hope Claws is OK,' she said. 'You don't think Tinta could give me visions of him, do you?'

Aleja shrugged. 'I don't know. Try it.'

She watched Frances reach her hand out to Tinta, but when she neared enough to touch, Tinta shrank away from her.

'Worth a try,' Frances said, turning her attention back to the balloon.

Aleja didn't have time to wonder at this – the ground rushed up at them all of a sudden and they hit it with a bone-shaking jolt.

Aleja still hadn't lost the feeling that they were being followed. Hooded figures stalked her dreams and her worries bit at her. But there wasn't anyone to be seen after they'd landed, so they pitched their tents beside a bamboo grove and made camp. They'd tied the balloon down and were to guard it in shifts throughout the night, taking care to keep it inflated. Tinta remained on the balloon and Aleja kept wandering over to the basket to check on it.

That night Aleja pulled out her storm-jar to read by, but it looked like it was filled with ash.

'It won't work away from the shadow magic,' Velka said, amused, as she peered through the tent flap. 'Leave it on the balloon with Tinta. Come on, the captain and Aada are back from the village with dinner.'

They ate *chāo shòu* – crescent-shaped dumplings in chilli oil that were sweet and spicy and garlicky all at once – and *suān là miàn* – sweet-and-sour noodles – by the campfire. They followed them up with *dòu shāo bāo*, which were a kind of fluffy bun, like biting into bits of cloud filled with sticky, sweet lotus-bean paste. These were Frances's and Aleja's favourite and they gobbled up half the plate before the captain noticed and slid it away from them.

'I love spicy food,' Velka said, scooping up another dumpling and biting into it.

'I read that some people say Marco Polo brought home tales of noodles in China and that's how Europeans came to make pasta,' Aleja said eagerly, chomping down on another sweet bun that Frances had sneaked to her. One glance down revealed Frances's bulging pockets.

'Is that true?' the captain asked, leaning back on her elbows and watching the fire contentedly. She was wearing a *qí páo* and her own trousers and battered boots. Aada was dressed the same but the rest of the pirates wore the trousers, boots and thick knits they'd worn in the balloon – even Malika, who had abandoned her usual glamorous dresses. Aleja couldn't get used to the change, though Malika still wore a headscarf and had lined her eyes in turquoise.

Aleja shrugged. 'I'm not sure. When I read about history it's just stories from people who lived in the past. If they believed it, then it was true for them, but it doesn't mean it's actually what happened.'

Aada raised her eyebrows. 'Very astute,' she murmured into the fire.

'So does that mean *we* could make it into history books?' Frances asked, spraying mulched bits of bun as she spoke.

Aleja tried not to giggle at Malika's look of distaste.

'We're pirates – we don't want our identities revealed,' Velka pointed out. 'Piracy still carries the death sentence.' She absent-mindedly patted the silk scarf concealing her crop of emerald hair.

'We live on a legendary ship; taverns around the world whisper tales about us – you can't get better than that,' Captain Quint said, reaching for a sweet bun only to find the plate empty.

Frances suddenly found the fire very interesting.

'It's burning low. I'll fetch some more firewood,' Velka said and got up.

'I'll join you,' Frances said, hurrying after her to avoid the captain's narrowed eyes.

Smiling, Aleja pulled out *Tibetan Travels with Thomas* and opened it to where she'd left off. She squinted to read it by the dying fire.

'I'll get some water,' Aada said.

'I'll make another round of the perimeter,' Malika said, and the captain added, 'I'll take this side; we'll meet in the middle.'

When Aleja looked up from her book, she realized she was alone in the campsite. She lay on her stomach and turned the page. She'd just got to the part where Thomas James was crossing a crevasse on a glacier when she heard a great rustling in the bamboo behind her.

'Very funny, Frances,' she called out.

When Frances didn't answer or jump out, Aleja frowned and shut her book. 'Frances?' A chill ran down her back. Was it the hooded figure? She glanced at the balloon. It glowed softly with the storm-jar she'd hung in it and the silk was mottled with dancing shadows. Tinta was perched on the basket rim as a shadowy owl, watching.

A loud, high-pitched bark sounded nearby and she jumped and dropped her book. *Not the hooded figure, then.* The trees shook.

Before Aleja could reach for her dagger, a beast came lumbering out of the bamboo. Aleja stared at it in disbelief. Then she laughed; it was a panda.

It ambled towards Aleja and she reached out a hand. Gently she stroked the panda. 'I'm just visiting,' she murmured. 'We'll be on our way soon, don't worry.' Its fur was thick and wiry and its liquid eyes peered at her with interest before it huffed and went on its way.

'Why didn't you come and get me?' Velka exclaimed when she and Frances returned with armfuls of branches.

'It'll make a brilliant story,' Frances said, dumping her firewood. 'You can tell the others you survived a panda attack!'

## CHAPTER THIRTY-FIVE

### *The Roof of the World*

The next afternoon, they were back in the balloon and it wasn't long until they were soaring across plains and earthy brown hills with snow-capped mountains looming in the distance. Aleja abandoned her books in favour of watching the world glide by with Frances, Tinta forever by her side.

'Wake up, Aleja,' a low voice said, shaking her awake some hours later.

Aleja rubbed her eyes. She was curled up in a pile of furs with Frances while Aada flew the balloon through a velvet starred night. The storm-jar lit the basket with crackling light, revealing everyone else to be still asleep. Tinta was resting as a badger by Aleja's feet.

'I thought you'd want to see this,' Captain Quint said, smiling at her.

Aleja scrambled to look out and her mouth fell open.

The Himalayas rose before them. Great jagged peaks cut into the sky, glistening with ice and moonlight.

Later that day, they ascended on to the Tibetan Plateau. It was coated in thick snow and silence. Every now and then they passed circling vultures. The air thinned and the temperature plummeted.

'We're on the roof of the world now,' Captain Quint said, her blue eyes as bright as the sky around them.

But as they passed over mountains, the balloon seemed to sink lower and lower in the sky. It wasn't long until they'd dipped beneath the clouds and could see the endless mountains stretching out in all directions around them.

'We're losing altitude,' Aada said, casting a worried look at Captain Quint.

Velka frowned and fiddled with the burner.

'What's happening?' Aleja asked, looking down. She couldn't stop picturing a pair of eyes boring into her. Had they managed to lose the hooded figure or were they still being followed?

'It's easy to imagine things up here,' the captain said to her when she voiced her suspicions. 'The remoteness does things to a person.'

Malika's eyes flitted between them but she said nothing.

'Death surrounds us in these mountains,' Aada said, her voice rougher than usual. When Aleja followed her gaze down, she saw bones crumpled in a pile on a mountaintop.

'Probably a lost climber,' Frances said, eyeing the rusted ice pick beside it. Aleja shivered, her hand finding her coin beneath the layers she was wrapped up in, and Tinta crept closer.

The balloon seemed to slip in the sky and the mountains suddenly lurched closer. Aleja eyed the nearest snow-coated one in alarm. Any lower and they'd fly straight into it . . .

She exchanged a nervous look with Frances. 'That peak looks a bit high.' Aleja pointed it out to the captain.

The captain and Velka leaped into action, cutting ballasts free and wrenching the burner. A huge jet of flame licked the inside of the balloon and the shadows rustled around it, jerking the balloon up. The basket rocked. Then the balloon slumped lower again.

'Take us higher,' Quint ordered. 'At once.'

'I can't!' Velka said, tugging the burner, which sputtered and sparked. 'I don't know what's happening and I can't fix it in the air!'

The peak drifted closer. Aleja reached out for Tinta.

'We're going to hit it,' the captain said. 'Hold on, everybody!'

Aleja grabbed the leather handholds inside the basket. Tinta fled into her boot.

The balloon bumped into the peak and with a loud screeching noise the basket scraped over the mountain-top and hurtled on, rocking dangerously fast.

'We need to land,' Velka said.

Frances gulped. 'Here?'

Aleja looked at the sea of mountains surrounding them like blades. As the others argued on the best course of action, holding on around the basket as it steadied its path, Aleja heard the rasp of something against the snow and stone just below. She leaned further out of the basket to see. There were more crunching, rasping sounds and this time she identified them – slow, strange footsteps.

Frances and Velka fell silent too. It sounded like an entire army was trudging through the mountains. A low moan sliced through the too-thin air and Aleja swallowed and rummaged for her dagger. Nothing human could have made that sound.

Frances pulled out her knife too. 'What was that?' She was wearing a furry hat and her glasses were crooked on her nose.

'There's something out there,' Aleja said. Her stomach pitched like a ship caught in a storm.

Quint pulled out her pistol and she and Malika walked round the basket, looking down. Velka and Aada fought with the burner and the shadows crept round the basket, just keeping it afloat. They scraped against another mountaintop as the balloon sank even lower.

A hand shot up and closed round the basket rim.

Aleja jumped and Velka shrieked. The hand was withered and stiff and scrabbled at Aleja's clothes, trying to pull her out.

Frances and Velka grabbed her in a hurry. Captain Quint fired her pistol at it and it disappeared.

Aleja swallowed and clutched her dagger. 'Maybe it was just the one –'

Another low moan rippled through the mountains. Captain Quint cursed. Malika unsheathed her blade with a zing. Two more hands appeared and clutched at Aleja like claws. She screamed and whacked at them with her dagger while Tinta puffed out like smoke, becoming a shadow-panther that growled and snapped its shadow-jaw at the hands.

'Hang on, Aleja,' Quint said, aiming her pistol.

But the hands were too strong, and the balloon and its passengers rocked under the attack. When they bounced off yet another mountaintop, Aleja fell out of the basket.

## CHAPTER THIRTY-SIX

*Army of the Undead*

Aleja screamed as she plummeted straight down on to the nearest mountain. She skidded down a patch of ice and fell into a snowdrift.

When she could breathe again, she climbed out.

Her blood froze in her veins.

An army of the undead was crawling over the shadow balloon. They lurched stiffly, their arms held out in front of them. The whites of their eyes were blue, their tongues were black and poked out of their mouths, and their skin was rotting.

The shadows flickered inside the silk and Aleja could tell from its sudden jolts upward that they were trying to lift the balloon back into the sky. Her heart stuttered.

Would they leave her behind? Then she saw Tinta roaming frantically back and forth on the edge of the basket, searching for her. 'Tinta!' she cried out, racing towards the balloon and slipping on the ice. 'I'm down here!' She waved her arms at it.

The undead turned and fixed their cold stares on her.

Aleja's breath died in her throat. She pointed her dagger out in front of her.

Tinta suddenly spotted her and froze. It collapsed out into a ream of silken shadow, flowing up and around the balloon, trying to fly back to her.

The nearest undead were now marching on Aleja.

A hissing echoed around the peaks and the balloon began to deflate with the force of Tinta's panic, sliding out of the sky and thudding into the mountain.

'Frances!' Aleja shouted as the balloon and all its passengers fell out of sight. 'Tinta!'

She started running.

As she rounded the mountain, gasping to fill her lungs with the weak air, she saw the pirates fighting off the advance of the undead. They poured over the mountain in a never-ending wave.

The balloon had collapsed; the basket was just shattered remains. And there was not a flicker nor glimpse of the shadows. 'Tinta,' Aleja whispered, and ran into the thick of it.

Captain Quint and Velka were shooting their pistols, Aada was swinging her battleaxe, Frances had her knife and Malika was a whirling, attacking force.

'Aleja!' Frances shouted, relief flitting over her face. 'Over here.' She yanked Aleja through into their defensive core.

'They're *ro-langs*,' Aleja said, remembering them from *Tibetan Travels with Thomas*. 'Corpses raised by a necromancer.'

'There's too many of them,' Velka said. 'We're outnumbered.'

Aleja tried hard to recall everything she knew about *ro-langs*. The doorways in Tibet had been built lower than usual because *ro-langs* had stiff limbs . . . and couldn't bend at the waist. 'We need to hide somewhere low,' she said, looking at the mountain surrounding them. 'There must be a cave somewhere nearby.' She squinted at a dark, gaping mouth in the side of a snowy rockface. 'What about there?'

Velka shot at the *ro-langs* blocking the way and began hurrying Aleja and Frances towards the cave.

Frances cupped her hands to her mouth. 'We've found cover!' she shouted across at the captain, who was trying to slash her way through the undead.

One of the *ro-langs* slowly turned to face them.

Aleja felt fingers of fear stroke her spine at its ice-blue blank eyes. It moaned and staggered in their direction. The rest of the *ro-langs* started to turn too.

'Well, that's distracted them,' Frances said bleakly.

Aleja grabbed Frances and ran after Velka, glancing back to see Aada plunging through the *ro-langs*, the captain and Malika at her heels.

A dead hand grabbed Aleja's shoulder. She screamed and fumbled with her dagger but her hands were cold and it slipped out of her grasp. Frances quickly whipped out a second knife and launched it into the air. It whistled past Aleja's nose and into the *ro-lang* attacking her. Its hand snapped off her shoulder, leaving its fingers behind. Aleja yelped and slapped them off.

As Frances tugged her into the cave Aleja shot her an admiring look. 'You can be a little bit vicious sometimes,' she said when Frances handed her dagger back.

Aada, Captain Quint and Malika hurtled into the cave. It was a tight squeeze with all six of them. But the *ro-langs* couldn't enter.

Captain Quint slid her pistol back into its holder. 'Everything is in that balloon. Our food and water. Our shadows.' Her chestnut hair was escaping around her face and she looked frazzled under her layers of fur.

'We have to rescue Tinta,' Aleja said at once. Her chest felt tight as she thought of the collapsed balloon. The balloon that Tinta had brought down in a panic before it left Aleja behind. Now she had to save her shadow in return.

'Death is everywhere,' Aada said ominously. Her tunic had been ripped, baring her shoulder and displaying the constellations that were tattooed on her back in midnight ink.

'That's stating the obvious,' Frances muttered to Aleja.

'There are too many to fight,' Malika admitted, though her eyes sparked with fury and she hadn't yet sheathed her knives. 'But we have to retrieve our shadows. Time is not our friend here.'

The *ro-langs* prowled outside, their bony feet scraping against the snow, their voices harsh and guttural.

Aleja wondered who had made them and if they'd been sent after the pirates intentionally. An idea dawned on her. 'What if we lured them into a trap?'

'What are you thinking?' Captain Quint asked.

Aleja pointed at the captain's pistol. 'Gunpowder.'

Velka hurtled out of the cave, running straight for the closest overhang. Aleja and Frances crouched down in the cave to watch her. The *ro-langs* had spotted her as soon as she'd emerged from the cave and were barrelling after her in their horrible lurching run.

Aleja crossed her fingers. When Velka neared the overhang, heavy with the weight of snow, icicles dangling down like daggers, she waited for the *ro-langs* to reach her. She disappeared from view, swarmed with hordes of the undead.

Captain Quint cursed and Aleja held her breath.

The sound of an explosion echoed into the mountains and the smell of gunpowder billowed out.

Like a gunshot, Velka flew out of the crowd of *ro-langs*. Frances cheered.

There was a deep rumbling and then everything turned white. For a moment, Aleja felt as though the sky had fallen down.

'It worked,' Åada said as they watched snow pour down the mountain. The avalanche flooded the overhang and crashed down on to the *ro-langs*, burying them.

Aleja rushed out of the cave, running and sliding on the steep mountainside until she reached where she'd last seen the balloon.

She stopped dead. There was nothing but snow as far as her eye could see. Tinta had been buried under the avalanche too.

## CHAPTER THIRTY-SEVEN

### *Tashi and Norbu*

'¿*Qué? No*,' Aleja whispered in horror, staring at the spot she'd last seen Tinta. 'No!'

Captain Quint appeared behind her. She laid a hand on Aleja's shoulder. 'Get digging, pirates,' she said, her face pinched with concern. 'Those are our shadows buried under there.'

They dug at the snow, heaving armfuls of the stuff aside until they couldn't feel their fingers through their gloves. Aleja's heart sank lower and lower the deeper they got. And then there was a flash of purple silk. 'I found the balloon!' She scrabbled faster. The others joined her and they unearthed the balloon together.

When they'd cleared most of the snow, Aleja looked eagerly for Tinta. 'Where are the shadows?' she asked.

Frances clambered into the wreckage of the balloon. 'I don't know but . . .' She looked at Aleja, aghast. 'Look at the basket – all the stone bits have been smashed in the crash-landing.'

Aleja gaped at her.

'Does that mean we've lost the shadows?' Velka asked quietly.

Captain Quint cursed.

Malika turned her gaze down the mountain. 'We have far to descend, Captain,' she said. 'We need to salvage what we can and start walking. If the shadows are lost . . .'

'If the shadows are lost, we have to find them!' Aleja said.

Captain Quint sighed. 'The stone smashed when the balloon came down, Aleja. I don't want to lose our shadows any more than you do – with François and that clock we need every speck of magic we can get.' She rubbed her forehead. 'Our shadows are a part of us,' she said, her voice ragged. 'But I don't believe there's anything we can do and we're running out of time. I'm sorry.'

Aleja stared at her in horror.

'Malika and Aada, retrieve our camping supplies,' the captain continued. 'Velka, collect as much of the food and water store as you can. Frances and Aleja, you can divide the supplies out into six packs for us to carry.'

Aleja ignored her. With shaking hands she reached into the bundle of furs where she'd stashed the pot Griete had given her. 'Please don't be broken,' she whispered, and Frances looked over. She pulled it out. 'It didn't break,' she said unbelievingly.

'Ah, I had forgotten about that,' Captain Quint said, rushing over. 'Is there anything inside?'

Aleja pulled off the lid and looked inside. She felt Frances's hair tickle her cheek as the other pirates all craned for a look, too. Inside the pot was a dark swirling mass. Like bottled smoke. The shadows had survived.

Aleja heard someone puff out a sigh of relief but she didn't feel it herself – not yet. 'Tinta?' she said.

A shadow-squirrel popped its head out of the top of the pot.

Aleja felt tears prick her eyes. 'I thought I'd lost you,' she said hoarsely.

'How do you know that's Tinta?' Frances asked. Velka shushed her.

Aleja smiled through her tears. 'I just know.'

They trekked down the mountain and through a perilous path. When they emerged, there was a valley before them and there, nestled in the centre, next to a winding river, was Lhasa. 'We'll camp here,' the captain announced. 'No one's to enter Lhasa – we'd stick out a mile and I'd rather not attract any more attention right now. It seems

Aleja's vision was right – someone's been following us.' She gave Aleja a grim nod. 'And I'd wager a doubloon they were the one to send those corpses after us.'

There was a small village nearby and Captain Quint took Aleja there while the others set up camp a short distance away. There they exchanged gold for *chubas* – long sheepskin coats – thicker woollen trousers and underlayers, and huge fur hats. When they returned to the others, Aleja took back the stone pot from Frances straight away and checked on Tinta. Her shadow seemed thinner and more transparent than usual and she worried that it had been weakened by bringing the balloon down.

She sat with the pot beside the fire, chatting to Frances and Velka while Malika heated stones in the fire and boiled water. A sudden crunch of snow signalled company. The pirates looked up, instantly on edge.

A Tibetan woman and man were approaching their camp, accompanied by a pair of yaks pulling a wagon.

Malika stood at once, but the captain murmured something to her and she sat back down, her hand vanishing into a fold of her *chuba* where Aleja was sure she had a dagger stashed. Everyone else watched the pair trudging through the snow towards them. They were dressed in thick colourful layers and the woman carried a small pot. *Probably traders*, Aleja thought, wondering if they'd come from nearby Lhasa. She hopped up, eager to try out the Tibetan she'd learned.

'*Ta-shi de-lek!*' she said enthusiastically, making Frances jump and choke on a biscuit.

The man's face cracked into a smile. '*Ta-shi de-lek.*' He reeled off a long strand of Tibetan and Aleja's smile faded. The woman noticed and gestured at her pot, then the yaks, smiling at the pirates.

'I think she wants to share her food with us,' Aleja said to the others. 'And something about the yaks.'

Captain Quint sprang up and ushered them to sit down round the campfire, offering round a slightly battered tin of Ermtgen's biscuits. They pulled off their mittens and warmed their hands on the fire, eating the biscuits with nods of approval. Then the woman pointed at the pirates' cups and ladled out the contents of her pot.

'*Tu-jay-chay,*' Aleja said. *Thank you.* She took a sip of the hot drink but it was very salty and she struggled to swallow it. Frances took one look at her expression and politely declined.

'Ah, yak butter tea,' Captain Quint said jovially. 'Lovely!' And to Aleja's and Frances's amazement she went for seconds.

The woman beamed at her, her eyes enveloped in a sea of crinkles.

The man took out a carved wind instrument and began to play, filling the mountains with a haunting melody.

Aleja listened and breathed deeply. Her lungs felt like she was submerged in water and her head was pulsing.

'I hate this altitude,' Frances moaned beside her. 'Did you know that altitude sickness can make your brain explode?' she added, a little brighter.

'I don't think that's true,' Velka said quickly.

Frances ignored her. 'Your lungs have already filled with puddles of blood, though, so you're as good as dead by the time it happens. You're just alive enough to see chunks of your brain dribbling out of your nose and –' She stopped suddenly.

'Are you all right?' Aleja asked, noticing she'd turned a funny shade of green.

Frances vomited into the campfire.

Captain Quint snorted then covered it up with a cough when Malika raised an eyebrow at her.

'She's got mountain sickness,' Aada said as Aleja handed Frances a cup of water.

The Tibetan man suddenly broke out into guffaws of laughter. Frances stared at him and then started to laugh. The captain joined in and Aleja shook her head, giggling, and said, 'I can't believe your *own story* made you sick.'

After the last of the butter tea and biscuits were gone and Aleja had exhausted her basic Tibetan, Malika and Quint haggled over the price of the yaks and the wagon, then the couple smiled and ambled off on their way, their pockets jingling with gold.

The pair of yaks were huge and shaggy.

Frances wrinkled her nose. 'I can smell them all the way over here!' She looked at Aleja. 'Why don't we name them?'

Aleja looked at her doubtfully. 'I've only learned a little Tibetan . . .'

'Doesn't matter,' Frances said confidently. 'We'll just call them something you do know.'

Aleja looked at the hairy, hulking animals and thought. 'How about Tashi – that means lucky – and . . . Norbu? That means jewel.'

Captain Quint barked out a laugh.

'Very nice,' Velka said, the corners of her mouth twitching.

Night was descending upon them and Aleja wandered over to the tent, intending to check on Tinta. On her way she paused. Snow crunched under her boots. She smiled happily and jumped to see what would happen, excited now that the danger appeared to be over. She'd never seen snow before and had no idea it would make that sound – she'd imagined it would be soft and fluffy, like walking on clouds. Just as she was marvelling at the way it glittered like a sugared meringue, something cold and wet hit the side of her face and slid down her *chuba*.

'Ugh!' she shrieked, scooping snow out of her neck and turning to see Frances duck out of sight behind Tashi. Aleja snatched up a handful of snow and raced over to Norbu. The next time Frances peered up over

Tashi's hairy back, she was ready. This time Frances got a faceful of snow. Aleja laughed so hard she wheezed and Frances looked alarmed.

'That'll be the altitude,' Malika said. 'Drink plenty of water and get an early night.'

The stars that night were huge and hungry. Aleja wished she could sleep under them but the temperature was falling and her head was pounding. She collected her stone from the fire and crawled inside the tent. The canvas had been coated in linseed oil so it was dry even though it had been pitched on snow. Aleja curled up with the shadows and warmed her fur-wrapped feet on the hot stone inside her bundle of blankets. She closed her eyes. The world felt still and silent and she couldn't believe she was sleeping on top of it all. She was exhausted and freezing and aching. But her thoughts refused to sleep.

Lhasa was tantalizingly close. *What will it look like?*

She shook Frances awake.

'Go away,' Frances mumbled from within a sea of furs.

'Let's sneak into the city,' Aleja whispered, careful not to wake Velka, who was sharing their tent.

Frances shot up. 'I'm in.'

Lhasa, quite literally, took Aleja's breath away. Partly because she was still suffering from the altitude. But mostly because the city looked as if it had been *dreamed* into being. Spread across the plateau, locked in by a ring of snow-capped peaks, the streets smelled of incense and were filled with wonder. She wished she could explore them, snatch a closer look at the Potala Palace, the grand red-and-white structure perched regally atop a mountain in the middle of the valley. But they were already breaking Quint's rules by gazing at it from a distance.

'It's beautiful,' Aleja said, drinking it all in. She noticed Frances watching her with a peculiar expression. 'What?'

Frances shrugged. 'I never got to see your face when you saw the Sahara Desert for the first time,' she said a little sheepishly. 'This feels . . . right.'

Aleja beamed at her. 'I'm glad you didn't get left behind this time,' she said, nudging Frances. Down in the city she spotted the Jokhang Temple gleaming in the moonlight and smoky with incense from its huge burners. Golden prayer wheels were mounted into walls and colourful Buddhist flags were draped along the flat roofs. 'I feel like I'm creating my own map of the world in my head and each city I travel to fills it in a bit more.'

'I'm mostly in it for the cake,' Frances said, rummaging around in her *chuba*. 'Ah, I knew I had some left.' She divided a smushed slice of Chinese sponge cake in half.

Aleja nibbled at the cake, watching a huddle of early risers walk round the prayer wheels, setting them spinning. 'It's so peaceful.' A couple of black-necked cranes flew overhead and she heard faint chanting in the distance.

It was immediately ruined by Frances being loudly sick. Aleja patted her back and when she'd finished Frances wiped her mouth with her sleeve and grimaced. 'We really should sleep – the sun'll come up soon and Quint will have us poking around the entire lake before I'm properly awake.'

Aleja stared at her.

'What?' Frances dabbed delicately at her mouth. 'Did I miss some?'

'You're a genius,' Aleja said, glancing up at the still-dark sky and sprinting back to the camp. 'Come on!'

## Chapter Thirty-Eight

*The Temple of Sacrifices*

'*Until the golden wing awakens,*' Aleja quoted, marching towards the wing-shaped lake beside Aada, who was holding a compass and a map. The pot of shadows rested in Aleja's arms. The rest of the pirates stumbled along, half asleep, in their wake. 'The entrance to the temple must only appear before sunrise! I don't know why I didn't realize before.'

The lake was a pool of silken moonlight. It looked as if it could soar off over the mountains.

Malika narrowed her eyes at it. 'I can't see a temple.'

'If the entrance is only visible before sunrise then we've got just an hour left. Let's start searching,' Captain Quint said and strode off to the left wing. Aleja watched her pace round the edge of the gently lapping lake, occasionally stopping to peer in.

'I'll take this side,' Velka said, muffling a yawn and heading right. Malika followed her and Aada went off after the captain.

Frances looked at Aleja. 'Where d'you reckon we should look?'

Aleja squinted to see further round the lake. They were in the centre of the wings, the water arcing away from them to either side. The riddle had led them south, to this exact point. 'I think we should look here,' she said.

'Are you sure?' Frances asked dubiously.

'Maybe it's a concealed entrance?' Aleja murmured to herself, walking up a short stretch and looking into the water. One step further and a shaft of golden light shone up at her. 'This must be it!' Aleja said. She put an arm in, rippling the mirror-smooth surface.

'Careful,' Frances said. 'You never know what could be in a strange lake. This one time in the jungle I went swimming and, just as I'd struck out from the riverbank, there was this monstrous piranha . . .'

Aleja's fingers touched stone. 'Oh!' she exclaimed. 'There are steps going down into the lake.'

Frances raced to fetch the others. Aleja couldn't touch the bottom of the steps and itched to swim down to investigate, but she couldn't plunge in and leave Tinta on its own.

Captain Quint reappeared and clapped her on the back so enthusiastically, Aleja almost fell into the water. 'Excellent work, Aleja.'

'Who's going in?' Velka asked.

Captain Quint gleefully tossed her boots aside. 'Whoever feels like a swim!' And with that she took off her outer layers and jumped in.

'Someone ought to keep watch,' Malika said seriously.

'And someone needs to look after Tinta and the other shadows,' Aleja added.

'I will,' Aada said, taking the pot and sitting down beside it.

Aleja walked down the huge stone steps and gasped – the water was icy. It nibbled at her like freezing teeth. Feeling with her feet for the next step, she strode deeper and deeper into the water. Until it was time to take a huge breath and dip into an underwater world, as black as the spaces between stars. Swimming in the direction of the steps that led deeper into the lake, she found a stone path along the lakebed. It was glowing.

She swam along it, after the captain. It ended in a luminous pillar. Captain Quint gestured at it and Aleja nodded, guessing there was something else they needed to find. Her lungs ached to be filled, and an altitude-headache gnawed at her skull, as she looked for clues. Just as she was about to paddle back up to the surface, she noticed the outline of a door. She waved to get

Captain Quint's attention before trying to open it. It wouldn't budge. She pushed harder – surely there was an air-filled cavity inside? Captain Quint swam towards her. Then Malika materialized out of the thick gloom. They all pushed together. The door flew open with a dull thud and silt billowed out.

Inside, more steps spiralled down into darkness. Trying not to panic, Aleja climbed into the narrow chamber, curious at what was inside. Water rushed around her, turning the stairs into a gushing waterfall, but there was air inside and she took deep, grateful gasps of it. After Velka and Frances had clambered in, Captain Quint and Malika shut the door, struggling against the force of the lake. The walls suddenly glowed in a blue as deep as the ocean. Anticipation rippled through Aleja.

'On we go.' Captain Quint began walking down the steep coil of stairs. Her steps were cautious at first and Aleja shivered, hoping there weren't any traps. After a few minutes, the captain called out an all-clear.

Water continued to run down the steps, rushing over Aleja's feet and numbing her toes. Shivering, she followed the tight spiral down and down, deeper into the blackness that awaited them beneath the bottom of the lake.

Through another ancient stone door was the temple.

In a flicker of light and rush of warmth, great vats of buttery candles lit up. Aleja's heart beat faster. The temple was wide and low and its gilded walls twinkled in the candlelight. Rippling smoke wandered out from the walls. When Aleja looked down at the flagstone floor, smoke swirled round her ankles. *It looks exactly like the star temple on the ship*, she thought. The ceiling was a flickering canopy of stars that danced in and out of constellations. Occasionally a star slid down the smoking walls, leaving a sparkling trail behind. In the centre was a gold podium. On top of it sat a smoking basin. And mounted above that was a stone hand, its fingers clenched tightly round a few chunks of turquoise. A curl of parchment was nestled between them. Aleja peered closer at it. She could just work out the jagged edge – it was the bottom right quarter of the world.

She sighed happily. They'd made it. François was nowhere in sight and the map piece was almost in their hands.

Captain Quint appeared behind her. 'There it is,' she breathed. She eyed the smoking basin. 'I'm betting that's a trap.'

'The star temple on board was a perfect recreation of this temple,' Velka said as the rest of the pirates filtered through the door. 'Which means there could be more clues hidden here.'

Aleja went to explore. She wandered over to where the puzzle had been inscribed in the *Ship of Shadows* version of the temple. Here there was no puzzle. Instead, rudimentary pictures were carved into the wall like cave paintings. 'Instructions,' she whispered, tracing her fingers over them.

Frances joined her and squinted at the stick figures. 'Are they chucking things into the basin?'

'Not just any old things,' Aleja said, studying the images. 'Look, here's some writing.' She wiped a smear of algae off the Tibetan letters that scrolled along the wall. '*Temple of sacrifices*,' she read aloud, and Frances looked at her with wide eyes.

'We have to kill someone?' she asked, her gaze shifting between the other pirates as if she might offer one up.

'Not a human one,' Aleja said, squinting at the carvings. One of the stick figures carried a necklace, another, a bowl. They wore comically sad expressions. 'More like something that's personal to us. It has to be a sacrifice. Something we don't want to lose.' She felt a flash of relief that she'd left Tinta outside. That was one sacrifice she couldn't have made.

'How does it work?' Velka asked, looking reluctant.

'I can't read it all,' Aleja said, 'but there's a warning of some kind here.' She pointed at the final carving where all but one stick figure held offerings. All were struck down. 'We all have to share the cost or . . . death will follow?'

There was a chilled silence. Captain Quint broke it by strolling over to the podium, pulling a glimmering stone out of her pocket and tossing it into the basin. The smoke danced around it, shrouding it from view, but not before Aleja had glimpsed the yellow diamond. 'The Light of a Thousand Stars,' Aleja whispered to Frances, remembering the Pirate Lord's story – Quint really would do anything to get the map.

Next, Malika gently dropped a creased letter in. Aleja guessed it had been from Habiba. She bit her lip, knowing what she needed to sacrifice but finding it impossible to force her feet forward. Frances stepped up and let a golden pearl fall from her fingers and into the basin, which was now smoking steadily. She shot the captain a rueful grin. Captain Quint gave a short laugh. 'I can't believe you kept that all these years,' she said, and Aleja knew then what Frances had pickpocketed from the captain many years ago when she had been a street urchin. She almost missed Velka rushing up to the podium and hastily dropping in a miniature that had been strung round her neck, her cheeks flaming.

'Did you see that?' Frances hissed to Aleja.

'Shh,' Aleja whispered back. She had seen it – it was a tiny painting of Farren.

Frances looked delighted. 'I knew it!' she crowed quietly to Aleja, who would have shared in Frances's excitement if it hadn't been her turn next.

Aleja trudged up to the podium and untied the coin round her neck. It was her only reminder of home. She wondered how her family were and when she'd see them again. It would be her birthday soon, the first one away from them, and she thought with a pang of the special cake Miguel would bake for her and the stories her abuela would tell her of when Aleja's mother was Aleja's age.

But the second piece of the map was *right there*. It marked her quest with the *Ship of Shadows* as halfway finished. The pirates were her second family now. She closed her eyes and dropped it in.

'Thank you, Aleja,' Captain Quint said quietly. 'I know how much that meant to you.'

Aleja's throat felt tight. She watched the smoke bloom around her coin as it vanished from sight.

'Why isn't it working?' Captain Quint asked impatiently, staring at the map piece.

'Patience, Elizabeth,' Malika cautioned.

Aleja watched blue sparks pop and fizz in the rippling smoke. 'I don't know; that should have worked.'

The stone fingers snapped open.

Captain Quint reached through the sparking smoke for the map piece. But, before she touched it, the stone hand started to close again. The captain grabbed the map piece in a hurry. 'It's the same,' she whispered, stroking it with a finger. 'We have half of the map.' Her eyes gleamed.

They all crowded round to see. It was an identical match to the first piece, down to the magic that whispered through it and the edges that curled away from Captain Quint's finger as if she were tickling it. The captain tucked it safely away in an empty vial and strung it round her neck.

Then, as if they'd been blown out like a candle, the stars went out.

Before anyone could speak, a dark-blue glow illuminated the smoking walls and a deep rumbling echoed through the room. More smoke flowed on to the flagstones and the temple shook angrily. All the candles flickered.

Aleja's fingers crept to her throat but it was bare. She clutched the hilt of her dagger instead.

Water began gushing out of the cracks between stones above them, splattering on to the shaking floor like they were on treacherous seas.

'Something's gone wrong – it must have closed again for a reason,' Malika told the captain, who shouted, 'Everybody out – now!'

Aleja gulped. They'd all offered something from their lives to the temple for the map; why had it gone so horribly wrong? She turned to race back up the stairs. But, before anyone reached them, a hooded figure stepped out into the centre of the temple.

## CHAPTER THIRTY-NINE

### *The Assassin*

It was the same figure Aleja had seen on Jì Chéng's roof. And stepping off François's ship. The one Tinta had given her a warning vision of. 'You've been following us since we left Shanghai,' she said. Thinking hard, she turned back to look at the stone hand. 'That's what made the hand close again,' she realized out loud. 'When you entered the temple without making a sacrifice!'

'Who are you?' Malika demanded.

Captain Quint, Velka and Frances all looked at them warily, hands on hilts and pistols.

The figure lowered their hood. A silken wave of chin-length black hair spilled around her face, framing hard brown eyes. She was lithe and muscular and carrying a heavy sword. Still watching them, she raised it.

'You?' Malika spat.

Aleja glanced at her, surprised.

'How do you two know each other?' Captain Quint asked.

Malika's smile was slow and venomous. 'We trained together. We're old rivals.'

Frances whipped round to Aleja. 'She must be an assassin!' she said loudly.

The temple creaked and groaned like it might topple down any second. 'It's falling apart,' Velka said, gesturing at the stones crumbling under the pressure of the lake above.

'The carving on the wall said we had to share the cost or death would follow,' Aleja said worriedly. 'Even if she made a sacrifice now, it's too late. The balance is already upset.'

Malika fell into a fighting pose. 'I'll get rid of her.' She unsheathed her scimitar, the wicked blade gleaming in the pulsing blue glow.

The other woman adopted a similar position as Malika blazed towards her. The woman swirled away, deflecting Malika's attack in a shattering clash of metal and Aleja's heart sank. It seemed Malika had an equal. This woman was a formidable foe.

'Whoa,' Frances said quietly.

With a resounding crash a chunk of stone fell from the top of the temple, smashing down to the floor. Cracks cobwebbed out from it. Water foamed round the edges of the temple, cascading through fissures and pouring down. Before she knew it, Aleja was standing ankle-deep in freezing lake water.

'We need to intervene,' Velka said, eyeing the ferocious battle unfolding before them.

Captain Quint plucked a large rock from the sloshing water. She raised her arm, her muscles flexing, but lowered it again. 'They're moving too fast.'

The two women spun and twirled, their blades a blur as they whirled round the temple, striking out and parrying, their weapons hurtling against each other with incredible force. Malika ducked a swipe that would have beheaded her and lashed out a side kick into the woman's stomach. She flew back and landed in the now knee-deep water. But, as soon as she fell, she leaped back up, her reflexes fast and dagger-sharp, and launched herself at Malika, slashing her sword everywhere at once. Malika's hand moved faster than Aleja had ever seen, blocking every blow, but Aleja knew the fight couldn't last forever. As soon as one of them slipped or grew tired it would be over for good.

'Can we distract her?' Frances asked.

'And risk distracting Malika instead?' The captain watched the sparring women grimly. 'I fear this is one battle Malika cannot win.'

Still watching the sword-fighting women, Aleja asked, 'Why not?'

Quint's sigh was heavy. 'Though she would rather perish than admit it, when faced with a fighter of equal strength, without her shadow Malika will be first to tire.'

The temple heaved and a large section of the floor cracked apart. Aleja was left standing on an island of stone surrounded by flood water. It tilted and she lost her balance, scraping her leg on the sharp edge. The last of the butter candles flickered out, leaving the temple bathed in the eerie blue glow.

'Jump, Aleja!' Velka shouted and Aleja scrambled to her feet and leaped across the water. Frances and Velka grabbed her as she landed on the edge of the main floor.

'I wonder if all assassins fight like that,' Frances said a beat later somewhat admiringly. Captain Quint shot her a look.

'François hired her,' Aleja said, wiping her stinging leg with her sleeve. '*Ouch*. And I'm sure she's behind the necromancer creating those *ro-langs*.' She shivered at the memory of the risen corpses but she'd given herself an idea. '*Tíng zhǐ*,' she shouted out. *Stop*. The assassin and Malika didn't stop but the woman's gaze flitted over to Aleja for a sliver of a second and she knew she had to speak quickly. Before the entire temple came raining down on them. 'We know François hired you,'

Aleja continued in Mandarin. 'Why are you working for him?'

Malika slowed her attack and the woman glanced at Aleja. 'I need the money,' she said, switching to English.

Aleja pulled a fistful of doubloons from her pocket. 'We have money.'

The assassin looked at them hungrily. She was silent but her sword had paused mid-air.

'If François hired you, then you already know we're pirates,' Aleja said. She tried on one of Malika's smiles, slow and sliding. 'And the thing about pirates is, we like treasure. We're *much* richer than François. We can pay you a lot more if you work for us instead.' She wasn't actually sure that they were richer than François – his resources and funding were a mystery. But he was also a nasty person and Aleja doubted he'd paid the assassin well.

The woman tilted her head, considering. She glanced at Malika.

'Whatever I have done, I have done with honour,' Malika said. 'You know this to be true. François isn't honourable.' She gestured at her missing hand, her scars. Her absent shadow.

An ominous loud creak bellowed around the temple. 'We aren't your enemies,' Aleja said, determined to make her case before they ran out of time. She thought about what Captain Quint had told her. 'There are too few women fighting for a place in the world to fight against each other.'

The woman jerked as if she'd been shot. She stared at Aleja. 'Very well,' she said, sheathing her sword and speaking in English. She inclined her head. 'I pledge my services to you, pirate girl, in exchange for double the sum Captain Levasseur offered me.'

'Done,' Aleja said, a little stunned.

Frances slid her an admiring look. 'You just hired an assassin!'

Captain Quint looked taken aback.

With a gigantic crash the temple collapsed.

## CHAPTER FORTY

### Yù Lán

Aleja let out a strained whimper. Thousands of years' worth of history was crashing down around them. She stared at the toppling temple in horror.

'Move!' Frances shouted, shoving her out of the way as half the ceiling hit the floor. The candles suddenly flared back to life in great bonfires that raged in phosphorescent green, resistant to the surging water. A fireball shot out of the nearest one and Aleja ducked, plunging into the water as its heat blazed over her.

She surfaced, the water rushing up to her chest, trying to find her balance on the tilting flagstones. She peered through the haze of smoke and water and fire. Frances and Velka dived into the water just before what was left of the ceiling bowed and caved in. Aleja inhaled and dived back into the water to avoid the stones falling her way, then swam up through the fractured temple ceiling and into the lake, fighting against the current. Kicking hard, she broke the surface of the lake with a lung-aching gasp. Frances and Velka were treading water nearby, waiting for her, and the three of them struck out for shore, the temple hurling fireballs after them.

The sun had risen over the horizon and the lake was a dazzling bright turquoise.

Aada never looked surprised. Not even when they emerged from the lake with an assassin holding a great big sword. She passed them their *chubas* and Captain Quint whispered to her – Aleja doubted she wanted the assassin to know where the map piece was – and they returned to their campsite, starving, soaked and shivering. Aleja held on to Tinta and the rest of the shadows the whole way.

The assassin turned her gaze to the snowy peaks around them, keeping guard after they'd all changed and eaten. '*Nǐ jiào shén mē?*' Aleja asked her a little shyly. *What's your name?*

'*Wǒ jiào* Yù Lán,' the assassin replied.

Aleja smiled, remembering seeing the pretty white flowers Yù Lán was named after in Shanghai.

Yù Lán paced off to survey the perimeter.

'I didn't trust her then and I don't trust her now,' Malika said at once. 'She jumped sides far too quickly for my liking.'

Captain Quint sighed. 'You don't trust anyone.'

But after Malika had struck up a conversation with Aada, while Frances was helping Velka ready the yaks, the captain took Aleja aside. 'Since you hired the assassin, she's your responsibility now.'

Aleja reached for the coin she no longer wore. 'Am I in trouble again?' She worried that Yù Lán switching sides might be a trap – what if Malika was right and she was just pretending to be on their side so she could lead them straight into François's hands?

Captain Quint's eyes twinkled. 'You have good instincts, Aleja. Trust them.'

As they trekked back to the snowy peaks of the Himalayas, Aleja kept an eye on Yù Lán just in case. It seemed Malika wasn't the only pirate to entertain doubts about her. Aada was quieter than usual and now and then muttered the odd superstition about invading wolves and lurking enemies that gave Aleja an avalanche of fresh concerns. Even Velka threw the assassin the odd calculating look. Captain Quint didn't seem concerned with anything other than the map piece and Aleja often caught her murmuring soothing words to it like it was a timid pet when she thought no one was watching. Frances was enthralled. During their trek she pelted Yù Lán with questions ranging from 'How many people have you killed?' to 'What's the most gruesome way you've done away with someone?' After the last one, Aleja hastily tugged Frances away. She had a thousand and one questions to ask the assassin herself – starting with how François managed to get to China ahead of them and where he was now. But she had put them aside for the time being, until she could be sure that Yù Lán would tell her the truth.

Soon they had reached the mountains. They looked impossibly high from below and Aleja suddenly realized how much longer they'd take to cross on foot than by magic balloon. 'How are we going to cross these?' she managed to ask.

'Like anything else,' Captain Quint said rather cheerfully. 'One step at a time.'

Malika glanced across at her. 'Elizabeth, the clock. It was more than halfway through its countdown when we left. If we are to proceed on foot . . .'

Captain Quint's lips thinned.

Aleja noticed Yù Lán looking curiously between them. 'If you are in a hurry, then there is another option,' she said.

Malika arched an eyebrow at her. 'I'm listening,' she said coolly.

'Do you remember our time in the Zagros Mountains?'

Malika stopped walking. 'Are you referring to that . . . pulley system?'

Yù Lán inclined her head. 'It is much faster. How else do you think I caught up with you?'

Aleja looked at Frances, raising her eyebrows. Frances shrugged and grinned.

Yù Lán pored over Aada's geographical maps and directed Captain Quint, who was steering the yak-pulled wagon. They twined through narrow passes between sheer mountains. The temperature dipped. The pathways grew rockier and rockier still, until the wagon couldn't be tugged along any more. They wrapped it in waterproof canvas and left it for someone else to claim, then bundled up their supplies on to the yaks' backs instead.

Yù Lán preferred to sleep beneath the stars outside Aleja's tent, and that night Aleja had just dozed off when she heard the assassin leave her bed. Aleja grabbed her dagger and followed.

Aleja was crunching along the snow when a hand reached down from a nearby rock and lifted her on top of it. Yù Lán held a finger to her lips. 'I heard a noise,' she whispered, pointing at a sweep of stone coasting down a nearby mountain. Aleja couldn't make out what she was looking at. Then a pair of green eyes, bright as fireflies, came into view and she stifled her surprise.

'Snow leopards prowl this territory,' Yù Lán said, watching it. 'We are in their land now.' She glanced up at Aleja. 'The pirate with the green hair – Velka – she has been feeding them. She is a friend to the animals.' Aleja wasn't surprised but she did feel a pinch of guilt for suspecting Yù Lán and began to doubt her fears over the woman's loyalty. Maybe Yù Lán would be able to tell them some information about François . . . and the mysterious enemy behind him.

The next morning, Aleja was strapped to a pulley that was fastened on to a long stretch of rope suspended through the mountains.

'That does not look safe,' Frances said, passing the stone pot to Aleja and tying it tightly to her waist.

'Nonsense – it'll be great fun,' Captain Quint said. 'Malika and Yù Lán are waiting for you on the other side. Do hurry before one of them starts brandishing their sword at the other.'

'I'm ready,' Aleja said, swallowing her nerves.

'Excellent,' Quint said, giving her a shove.

Aleja shot through the mountains, her feet lifting up from the ice and dangling over sheer rock faces. It was faster than standing on the prow of the *Ship of Shadows*, faster than soaring through the sky on the shadow balloon. 'I'm flying, Tinta!' she shouted as she zoomed between the highest mountaintops. The air whipping by her face was freezing and her eyes streamed, her lungs too tight in the thin air, but she whooped and laughed. Suddenly Malika swung into view and Aleja felt the pulley-and-rope system begin to slow as she braced her feet out, ready to hit the snow like Yù Lán had instructed them. She slammed into the mountain and Malika's outstretched arms all at once, laughing madly. 'I want to do that again,' she told Yù Lán.

Yù Lán looked amused. 'There are a few more before we reach passable land.'

Aleja settled herself on the furs beside a fire with the stone pot to wait for the others. She took off the lid and Tinta appeared at once, a shadow-fox that perched atop the pot, its inky tail dipped inside, rooting the shadow to the stone.

'Show me something, Tinta,' Aleja murmured to it. 'What's François doing now? What happened when you came aboard the ship?'

Yù Lán wandered over, looking at Tinta. 'What are you doing?'

Aleja resisted the temptation to slam the lid shut on her secrets. 'This is my shadow. My second shadow. I call it Tinta.'

'How curious.'

Aleja looked at her. 'You don't seem surprised.'

'I have seen many strange and wonderful things in my travels. And Tinta shows you things? How?'

Aleja shrugged, reluctant to tell her everything. 'I don't know how it happens and I can't seem to control them.'

'Hmm.' Yù Lán looked hard at Aleja. 'And what do you do to bring these visions about?'

Aleja frowned. 'I ask Tinta.'

'Perhaps you might benefit from a little meditation,' Yù Lán said.

Aleja glanced at Tinta, whose black eyes were fixed on her. 'What do I have to do?'

'Try closing your eyes. Empty your mind in preparation to receive the vision.'

'But before my mind was the opposite of empty!' Aleja said, thinking of the horrible storm.

Yù Lán was patient. 'If you want to achieve greater control, you must work at it.'

'OK, I'll try.' Aleja closed her eyes.

'Good. Focus on your breathing. Feel your bond with Tinta.'

Aleja breathed deeply and relaxed, feeling everything else fall away. She reached out a hand to Tinta. When she opened her eyes, she was standing on board the *Ship of Shadows*, watching herself listen to Frances's first ghost story in the cave of shadows last summer. Aleja gasped and looked at herself. Then she noticed something that past-Aleja hadn't yet. Tinta. It was huddled close to her back, peeking up at her. Aleja flooded with happiness.

The ship faded to snow and Aleja beamed at Yù Lán. 'It worked!' She tickled Tinta's nose. 'And, better than before, this time I could actually feel what Tinta was feeling, too.'

'Good.' Yù Lán suddenly stood up.

Aleja clambered to her feet, too. Something huge and hairy was flying towards them. It bellowed loudly. 'It's Norbu,' Aleja said, laughing as she ran to help unstrap the yak from the pulley.

The next week whooshed past in endless snowy days and thrilling dashes on the pulley system across the mountaintops. With Captain Quint waking them early each morning for another day of intense hiking, Aleja's feet and legs ached. Just when she was beginning to think she couldn't walk another step, they traded the yaks for horses and carts, waving goodbye to Tashi and Norbu as they rode the clacking wagons deep into China. Although it hadn't felt like it in the Himalayas, it was well into spring now and Aleja, Frances and Velka picked apricots off the wild trees and munched them as they rode on the back of the wagons, the juice dribbling down their chins, making them as sticky-sweet as the fruit. Frances told stories and Aleja practised opening herself up to Tinta, thrilled each time the visions came, clear and bright with emotion.

When they first caught sight of the *Ship of Shadows*, sitting happily anchored where they'd left it, Aleja's nerves jangled – were they walking into a trap? But then she spotted Penumbra perched on the mast and Farren waving both her arms at them from the crow's nest and her spirits soared. They'd made it.

## CHAPTER FORTY-ONE

*Home at Last*

Aleja raced up the gangplank first, eager to see the ship and the rest of the crew. She unstoppered the pot and, after a pause, the shadows drifted out and twined back round the ship. 'Tinta?' Aleja asked and her shadow hopped out as a squirrel, its form slowly darkening once more. Olitiana, Farren, Griete and Ermtgen all looked at Yù Lán, who had just stepped on to the ship. Shadows hissed and reared up around the deck and Yù Lán glanced at them warily.

'I knew this would not be a normal ship after seeing your shadow,' she said. 'How curious.'

Aleja beamed with pride. Tinta grew into a little pony that refused to leave her side as the rest of the pirates bounded on to the ship and everyone began talking and laughing all at once.

Farren whooped and grabbed Velka in a hug that lifted her off her feet. When they'd disentangled, Velka's cheeks were pink and Frances was beaming again.

'Stop staring,' Aleja told Frances, smiling.

'I can't help it,' she said. 'They're just too adorable.'

'Not. A. Word,' Velka said in an aside, teeth gritted under her smile.

Frances grinned. 'Pirate's honour.'

Aleja noticed her fingers were crossed behind her back and groaned. 'You really shouldn't interfere.'

Frances looked offended. 'I'm not going to interfere! Just sort of . . . help them along a little bit.'

Aleja opened her mouth to protest that they didn't need helping along but Griete chose that moment to reappear with a noticeably larger kitten and Frances's attention was lost.

Griete was smiling widely again and she hugged Aleja with a 'welcome back', as Ermtgen produced a freshly baked cake that was frosted like a snowy mountaintop.

When Aleja realized Yù Lán was standing to one side with the captain, she went over with a slice of cake.

'Are you sure?' Captain Quint was asking. 'We can always use good fighters.'

Aleja passed Yù Lán the cake. 'Are you leaving?'

'I have heard tales of an all-female assassins' guild in Peking. I think I would like to see if they are real. Life at sea isn't for me.' She pulled a face. 'I get terribly seasick.'

Captain Quint let out a booming laugh and wandered off.

'A likely story,' Malika said, appearing behind Aleja.

Yù Lán narrowed her eyes at her.

Malika rested her hand on her hilt. 'We both know why you're leaving,' she said.

'Do inform me then,' Yù Lán said icily.

Aleja hesitated, wondering if she was about to be caught in the middle of another fight.

Malika's smile was chilling. 'You're running away before I have a chance to defeat you.'

Yù Lán laughed. 'Oh, Malika, you've had plenty of chances and you haven't yet won once.'

'And neither have you.'

'Then I look forward to our next encounter,' Yù Lán replied. 'I fear this ship isn't big enough for the two of us.'

Malika's smile cut wider.

Aleja excused herself to dig beneath the floorboards in her cabin for her jewels. Enough to secure Yù Lán's silence and hopefully encourage her to share what she knew of François. She looked around her cabin, patted her stack of books with a happy sigh, and dashed back up on deck.

'*Xiè xiè*,' Yù Lán said, stashing the bag of jewels in her *qí páo*. *Thank you.*

'You must not speak of this ship to anyone,' Aleja cautioned her.

She hesitated, her eyes locking on to Aleja's. 'I shall not. Though you should know that Captain Levasseur has declared this ship his mortal enemy. He is prepared to hunt you down to the ends of the earth to destroy you. Do not underestimate him.'

'I know,' Aleja said quietly, glancing over her shoulder at the rest of the pirates eating cake and swapping stories of the past month. 'He killed one of our own this year.' The words were thick in her throat. 'Before she died, she left us a message; she said that François was working for someone else. Did you see who?'

Yù Lán shook her head thoughtfully. 'I only saw his crew of pirate hunters. But I did overhear a conversation that the Duke is not pleased with his failure to find a map.'

Aleja seized the nugget of information like a jewel. 'The *Duke*?'

'I am afraid I know nothing more,' Yù Lán said. 'I wish you luck, pirate girl.' And with that she slipped off the ship as if she were a shadow herself.

When the cake had all been eaten and the excitement had faded to contentment, Captain Quint donned her massive tri-cornered hat and wrist guard and whistled to Penumbra. He came shrieking down from the puffy clouds and settled himself on her forearm. Captain Quint grinned. 'What say you we set sail for a lovely little spot while we plan our next adventure?'

'Aye, Captain,' Aleja said with the others, putting her own hat on.

'Then hoist the mainsail, weigh the anchor and sail me into that horizon.'

As they sailed away from their hidden spot, leaving the castle-like fortifications of Shanghai in their wake, a cluster of shadows hiding behind a barrel of grog rose up and formed the likeness of Yù Lán.

Aleja pointed it out to Olitiana. 'What does that mean?'

Olitiana smiled. 'It means she's loyal to us now. Well done, Aleja – you found your first shadow for us.'

Being back at sea felt strange. The ship rocked beneath Aleja's feet, and dim lanterns swung below decks and shadows scurried past, making her feel as if the entire world was dark and moving. She and Frances were having a feast of sponge cake and goblets of starshine in the Golden Lantern with Griete, Farren and Velka when she suddenly remembered she'd forgotten to tell Quint something important. She rushed to the library, Tinta racing along in wolf form at her heels.

When she burst through the door, Captain Quint, Olitiana and Malika all looked up, mid-discussion.

Geoffrey was skulking in a shelf of ancient books. 'Still alive, I see.' He sniffed dourly, returning to his globe.

'Half the world,' Aleja said, gazing at the two matching pieces of the map on the table. 'But Yù Lán warned me about François before she left – he's working for a duke.'

'We shall investigate further when we weigh anchor.' A dreamy expression wandered across Captain Quint's face. 'We're heading to a particular favourite destination of mine and there we shall figure out where we need to sail next and how to beat that infernal clock.' She glowered at the owl clock, which was more than halfway through its countdown. Just seven months left now.

Aleja winced. Then she perked up as Quint's words registered. 'Where are we going?'

'All in due course,' Captain Quint said, stroking Penumbra and kicking her boots up on to the table. 'Ah, it's good to be home. Is there any rum?'

Olitiana laid a hand on Aleja's arm. 'Why don't you go and get some sleep? It's past midnight and you must be exhausted.'

Aleja suddenly found she couldn't stop yawning. She plodded back to her cabin, Tinta slouching along, girl-shaped beside her, then kicked her boots off and fell into her bunk, too tired to bother with undressing, let alone unpacking. Her bunk was soft and warm and the best feeling in the world after camping. 'We did it, Tinta,' she mumbled, her eyes already closing against the moonlight pouring in through her porthole and storm-jars crackling in violet hues. 'We found the map . . .'

When she opened her eyes the next morning, she lay there all snuggled up, not wanting to move.

Until a massive boom exploded through the ship.

Aleja sat bolt upright in her bunk. What was *that*? A wave of dread hit her; had François found their ship?

Tinta wisped down to a baby bunny that hopped on to her lap, its shadow-whiskers twitching anxiously.

Aleja stood up and peeked down the passageway. Emerald owl eyes gleamed back at her but it was far too quiet. There were no distant clangs from the weapons room, no clatter of pots and pans from the galley, no chatter and laughter ringing out from the other cabins. The bustling pirate ship was still. Eerily so.

Her heart bouncing in her chest, Aleja pulled on her boots in a hurry, sliding her dagger into one, and crept down the passageway into the galley.

Another gigantic bang erupted.

'Oops, sorry about that,' said Velka, looking chagrined. 'That was meant to be much smaller.'

'It was smaller than the last one,' Frances said brightly.

Aleja's mouth fell open.

The firework had raged through the galley in a dazzle of blues and greens, singeing one of the benches, with little silvery stars whizzing everywhere. All the crew were gathered round the table, on which rested a large cake with sky-blue frosting and sweets spelling out *Happy Birthday, Aleja!*

Griete beamed at her. 'You didn't think we'd forget, did you?'

Aleja didn't know how to answer. She hadn't even realized it was the first of May today. Tinta zoomed happily around the galley as a rabbit, chasing a cluster of shadow-mice with Claws. Penumbra perched above the fireplace that filled the space with a glowing warmth and clicked his beak at them.

'Happy birthday, Aleja.' Frances rushed over to thrust something into her arms. It was a gigantic jar filled with a rainbow of sweets. 'Now we're both thirteen!'

The captain occupied herself with divvying up the cake – with a dagger – and Aleja sat down and looked at the pile of presents in front of her. 'I hadn't expected this,' she whispered. Tiny fireworks sparkled and fizzed around the galley in a glittering kaleidoscope of colours as Aleja dived into her presents.

Farren had built her a beautiful bookcase, Velka gave her a potted fern for her cabin and Griete a copy of *Storming the High Seas*. 'I made Raven read it; now it's your turn,' she said with a smile, twizzling one of her diamond earrings.

Aada had gifted her a painting of her favourite constellations in a swirl of blues and blacks and silvers, and Ermtgen had baked her a box of her favourite spiced and sugared biscuits. Malika suddenly whipped out a cutlass, making everyone start, and presented it to Aleja. 'To match your dagger,' she said, and Aleja noticed it also had owls engraved round the hilt. 'And to practise with,' she added seriously, prompting Captain Quint to give her gift in a hurry, before Malika started talking about their next weapons-training class.

'I chose this especially for you,' the captain said as Aleja opened the small box she'd presented her with. Inside was a creamy-green pearl strung on a chain.

'Ooh, green pearls are rare,' Velka said, admiring it.

'It'll match your eyes, too,' Griete said.

But it wasn't just a pearl. 'It's a tiny globe!' Aleja realized, spotting the outlines of land and sea marked on it in miniature. Then it spun on the chain and she saw it was backed with shadow stone. She sucked in a breath. 'Is this –'

'It goes with these,' Griete said, and she and Farren held out a bracelet each. They were silver with carved stone owls embedded in them. 'I hammered the metal and Farren engraved them.'

'Now when you step off the ship, Tinta should have its proper form with you. You won't need to carry your shadow in a pot,' Farren said.

'Thank you,' Aleja said, choking the words out. She slid them on her wrists and Tinta hopped over at once, nuzzling her hand.

The captain fastened the pearl round her neck. 'To replace your coin,' she said. 'Because you are every bit one of us.'

Aleja looked up at them all, happy enough to burst. The *Ship of Shadows* was so much more than a legend to her now.

It was her home.

## ACKNOWLEDGEMENTS

Writing a book is much like sailing a ship. Luckily for me, I have the most fantastic crew.

To my utterly wonderful agent, Captain Thérèse Coen, I owe a treasure chest of thanks. For your constant support, wisdom, kindness and cat pics.

To Captain Emma Jones, editor extraordinaire, I've had the best time working on this book with you at the helm. I can't thank you enough for all your enthusiasm, encouragement and brilliance.

I owe a barrel of gratitude to the Puffin team for making debuting in a pandemic the smoothest it could be. My publicist, Phoebe Williams, and marketer, Michelle Nathan, deserve an entire cupboard of cake for all their incredible work in a stormy year. Huge thanks and appreciation to Shreeta Shah and Wendy Shakespeare for their valuable input. Thank you to Toni Budden, Kat Baker, Ashleigh James and Katy Finch for everything. To my copy-editors and proofreaders, Jennie Roman, Claire Davis, Petra Bryce and Leena Lane, I really appreciate your keen Penumbra-like attention to detail!

A kraken-sized thanks to Karl James Mountford for your magical illustrations, including this cover of dreams.

Thank you to Maya Saroya for doing such a brilliant job reading *The Ship of Shadows* audiobook.

With thanks to Inclusive Minds for connecting us with their Inclusion Ambassador network, in particular Monica Yu for her input on the cover.

A big thank you to Sissi Zhang for your help with my Mandarin. (Though any mistakes are my own.)

For all the bookshops and booksellers that put *The Ship of Shadows* in windows, on tables and into readers' hands, I can't thank you enough – you're all magic. Special thanks and a bottle of rum to Blackwell's for making me their CBOTM, all the lovely people at Waterstones Nottingham, and Helen at The Barrister in Wonderland.

For all the wonderful bloggers, bookstagrammers, book tweeters and booktubers who took the time to shout about my pirates, you're all honorary shadows,

# Acknowledgements

particularly Gavin Hetherington, Scott Evans and Eddy Hope.

My friends deserve the sparkliest pirate bounty for being there for me throughout this voyage, especially Christine Spoors, Alex McGahan, Sarah Hackmann, my Shakespearean Sisters, (who always assemble when I need you), the Swaggers (you keep me afloat!), Vic James, Lee Newbery and L. D. Lapinski.

To all my family for listening to me talk about my writing and celebrating my books with me – I love and appreciate you all.

For my husband, Michael Brothwood, I would sail to the ends of the earth with you – you're my home.

And for anyone who's holding this book in their hands right now, thank you for coming on this voyage with Aleja and me. I hope you feel at home on board the *Ship of Shadows*.